Also by Lily Everett

Sanctuary Island

Available from St. Martin's Paperbacks

The Firefly Café

The Summer Cottage

Island Road

The Fireside Inn

Bonfire Beach

Lantern Lake

E-books available from St. Martin's Press

Shoreline Drive

LILY EVERETT

St. Martin's Paperbacks

This is a work of fiction. All of the characters, organizations, and events portrayed in this novel are either products of the author's imagination or are used fictitiously.

SHORELINE DRIVE

Copyright © 2014 by Lily Everett.

For information address St. Martin's Press, 175 Fifth Avenue, New York, NY 10010.

ISBN: 978-1-250-01839-7

Printed in the United States of America

St. Martin's Paperbacks edition / February 2014

St. Martin's Paperbacks are published by St. Martin's Press, 175 Fifth Avenue, New York, NY 10010.

10 9 8 7 6 5 4 3 2 1

For Mama
You are the smartest, strongest, most engaged
and loving woman I know. Every single day,
I'm grateful for you.

Acknowledgments

Writing a book seems like a solitary effort, but it definitely is not! I couldn't do it without my fabulous team of some of the most amazing women in publishing: my insightful editor, Rose Hilliard and her crack assistant, Lizzie Poteet; the talented Elsie Lyons, who designs my lovely covers; the SMP marketing gurus led by Anne Marie Tallberg and Eileen Rothschild; and my soul sister/agent, Deidre Knight. My thanks go out to all the people I haven't named, behind the scenes at St. Martin's—I feel lucky to be in such good hands!

And then there are my writing friends, the other writers in the trenches with me day to day, brainstorming and encouraging and supporting and just generally being indispensable. All the gratitude in my heart goes to Kristen Painter, Roxanne St. Claire, Tracie Stewart, Ana Farish, Sarah MacLean, Amanda Carlson, Kresley Cole, Gena Showalter, Kate Pearce, and so many more. Romance writers know how to do friendship!

Special thanks to my beta reader, Bria Quinlan, who has her fingerprints all over Dr. Ben Fairfax. Sorry, ladies, she claimed him first!

I couldn't write a single romantic word without the love and support of my parents, my sister, my in-laws, and most of all, my handsome, charming, wonderful husband. Always ready to talk through a sticky plot or deconstruct a story, perfectly happy to eat out or order in every night I'm on deadline, and the first person to celebrate every milestone with me—Nick, I love you to pieces. I'll never be able to name one of my heroes Nicholas, because no fictional character I create could ever live up to the reality of you.

Shoreline Drive

Prologue

May 2013

Rain lashed across the cracked windshield of Dr. Ben Fairfax's ancient pickup truck as it roared over the pitted inland roads, churning up mud and gravel as he raced across Sanctuary Island.

Ben raked wet hair out of his eyes and tightened his grip on the steering wheel. A single thought repeated itself over and over in his head.

Get to her. Get to her. Get to her.

He bared his teeth at the clash of thunder that rocked his truck, rattling the state-of-the-art large animal trailer hooked to his trailer hitch.

Go ahead and do your worst. Nothing's going to stop me from getting to Merry's house in time.

The same cold wash of fear he felt when he got the call froze his belly again, but there was no time to fool around with doubts and worries.

Meredith Preston was in labor. At least three weeks early, in the middle of the worst spring storm he'd ever seen roll in off the Atlantic Ocean. And according to her mother's phone call, Merry's contractions were approximately three minutes apart and lasted a full minute each.

No time to get Merry to the ferry that would shuttle her the hour from Sanctuary Island to the big hospital in Winter Harbor, Virginia. No telling if the ferry was even running in this weather.

No choice but to step up and do what he could to make sure both mother and new baby made it out of this alive.

Which wasn't all that different from Ben's normal practice—he'd helped countless mothers deliver healthy newborns over the course of his seven years on Sanctuary.

Of course, most of those newborn babies had been foals or calves. There was the occasional lamb or goat kid.

Animals were easy. Even when things went wrong, they knew what to do—lie there and let Ben handle the situation. People were more annoying, which was why he tended to avoid them.

Not an option tonight. He had to push everything aside and focus on helping Merry.

Even though the last time Ben had been involved with a human birth was before he'd chucked it all to study veterinary medicine. He hadn't been the attending physician, he'd been the father.

Grimly beating back the dark surge of memories, Ben refocused his gaze on the road.

I was better off when all I was thinking about was getting to Merry's bedside.

With that in mind, he pushed the grumbling engine as hard as he dared, making the half hour trip from his farm on Shoreline Drive to Windy Corner, the big, dilapidated plantation house on the northeastern end of the island where Merry lived with her mother, Jo Ellen Hollister.

Hauling his canvas duffel off the truck's bench seat, Ben tore up the wooden porch steps, heedless of the rain. He swerved to avoid the ragged, gaping hole in the sagging boards and crashed through the front door just as thunder boomed overhead.

Silence.

Ben stood in the dim hallway for an instant and held his breath, listening. A soft murmur of voices from down the hall had his adrenaline pumping and instincts clamoring.

Merry.

Shoving down the terror and worry, Ben gritted his teeth. He had to get these . . . feelings under control. Merry's life, and the life of her soon-to-be-born baby depended on Ben keeping a clear, level, unemotional head.

So what if Merry was pretty, and his body reacted inconveniently to being around her. He'd been attracted to women before. Sure, maybe never one as sweet, vivacious, and universally adored as Meredith Preston, but all that meant was that she was even less likely to ever think about a man like Ben that way.

Rationally, he knew he needed to get over this ridiculous infatuation. And since Ben was a man who prized rationality, he would. End of story.

Braced and ready, he opened the door. Meredith Preston paused in her pacing of the hardwood floorboards, one hand at the small of her no doubt aching back, the other arm hooked around her mother's strong shoulders.

"Up and walking? Good," Ben said, moving to lay out his medical instruments on the dresser top.

"I didn't know what else to do." Jo sounded more afraid and uncertain than he'd ever heard her, the tremor in her voice noticeable even for a man who did his level best never to notice other people's emotions.

"I'm fine. Oh—" Merry gasped out. Her pretty, even features tightened as a spasm of pain gripped her abdomen. With a clinical eye, Ben took in the hectic flush over her high cheekbones, the rapid throb of the pulse at the hollow of her throat. The bow of her back and the whiteness of her knuckles as her bloodless lips moved silently to count out the seconds of the contraction.

Without conscious thought, Ben moved to her and nudged Jo gently out of the way just as the contraction released Merry. Exhausted, she swayed on her feet. Ben caught her as gently as he could, supporting her weight against his chest, and froze.

He had his arms around Merry Preston.

Shaking his head to rid it of the frustratingly persistent thoughts, Ben slanted a glance at Jo, wringing her hands a few feet away. "Can you boil some water for me? And we'll need clean towels or sheets, a big stack."

Looking grateful to have a task, Jo straightened and leaped for the door. "Yes! Sure, only . . . Merry, honey, I hate to leave you."

Merry lifted a shaking hand to wipe her damp, dark hair off her sweaty forehead and attempted a smile. "It's okay, Mom. Dr. Fairfax will take care of me."

But as soon as the bedroom door shut behind Jo, Merry pulled away from Ben. He tried not to notice how empty and cold his arms felt.

Irrelevant, Ben told himself firmly, appalled at his lack of focus.

"Ready to get back in bed?" he asked, hands out and ready to steady her if she wobbled. "You can walk some more, if you want."

"What I want is to get this baby out of me." She panted for a moment, then looked up at him from under her dark, sooty lashes. Ben read the fear and nerves in her gaze as clearly as if she were shouting it in his ear. "You can handle the delivery, right?"

Forgoing the usual sneer at anyone who questioned his incredibly overqualified competence, Ben still couldn't quite force the gentle, soothing bedside manner they'd talked about in his residency program.

There was more than one reason he'd dropped out of the neurosurgery program and redirected toward veterinary medicine.

"Yes," he told her, giving it to her straight, no waffling. "I've delivered healthy babies in far worse conditions than a clean, dry, warm, well-lit room."

Not human babies, but he had enough sensitivity not to remind her of that. The brief flash of humor in her blue eyes said she hadn't forgotten, but her only response was to climb up onto the high mattress and settle in the nest of downy white pillows.

"Birth is birth." Ben rolled up his shirtsleeves and went back to setting out his tools. "It's the first clue we get that life is going to be messy and painful, but the actual process of baby entering world isn't complicated."

"Unless there are complications." She sounded calm, but Ben saw the way her fingers clutched, white-knuckled, at the quilted bedspread. "I'm three weeks early."

He wanted to tell her to stop worrying, the baby was done cooking and everything was going to be fine—but he wouldn't say that until after he'd examined her.

It was weird, almost like an out-of-body experience, to stare down at Merry's pale, strained face and the taut, swollen line of her stomach. With a conscious effort, Ben made the switch in his head.

Merry wasn't a person right now. She wasn't the woman who reminded him he was human and made him want to snarl and snap and avoid her for it. She wasn't beautiful or sexy or funny or stubborn or kind.

She was his patient, and she was in pain. Nothing else mattered.

The next hour passed in a blur. Merry showed a surprising amount of backbone and determination for someone who generally faced the world with a sunny grin and a twinkle in her eye. She battled her own body and the forces of nature to bring her son into the world.

Hands moving on automatic, the dance of his fingers and muscles a response choreographed by hours of practice and an unswerving instinct, Ben was there for all of it. For Merry's heaving breaths and near-silent cries of pain to her exhausted, incandescent smile when he said, "It's a boy."

Ben stared down at the wrinkled, red-faced infant in his hands and felt his heart thrill strangely at the first thin cry from his mouth. The baby clenched his tiny fists in rage and bewilderment at being suddenly thrust into the bright cold air, and it was as if those perfect little fingers gripped Ben's heart and squeezed.

Doing a quick count, Ben said, "All ten fingers and toes." He barely recognized his own voice, it was so hoarse. Another reedy cry from the baby jerked Ben back into motion, and he dealt quickly and efficiently with the umbilical cord before laying the naked, squirming infant on Merry's quivering stomach.

No matter how many times he witnessed it, Ben knew he'd never get tired of the rush he felt at the awe-inspiring spectacle of birth. What he'd told Merry was true—it was painful and messy, for sure.

But it was also the closest a man like Ben was ever going to get to touching pure joy.

Ben kept his head down through the confusion and chaotic happiness of Jo Ellen crying and her older daughter, Ella, rushing in dripping rainwater all over the floor with Ben's best friend, Grady Wilkes. He resisted being included in the round of hugs and chatter, preferring to spend the time shoring up his defenses against Merry Preston.

It was simple relief that made him feel light-headed and raw—relief that he'd been in time, been there to help, and that his patients were doing well. It was the satisfaction of a job well done that made his hands shake as he packed up his medical kit.

Ben studiously ignored the memory of crippling fear that had gripped him when he got the call from Jo. Obviously, he would've helped any woman in Merry's situation. She wasn't special.

"What's your middle name, Doc?"

Ben frowned at Merry. His heart rate picked up— due to being startled, obviously.

"Why?" he countered.

Merry rolled her eyes. "I'm not planning to steal your identity or something. Come on, answer the question."

Ben paused, debated. Couldn't come up with a reason not to tell her. "Alexander."

Her bright, open face went thoughtful.

"Alex. Ooh, or Zander. I like it."

"Like it for what?" Ben ducked his head over his canvas satchel, staring sightlessly at the tidy array of medical instruments. He was holding his breath, and he didn't even know why.

"For Baby," Merry said, and Ben's lungs contracted as if he'd taken a punch to the solar plexus.

"Alexander Hollister Preston," Merry continued, oblivious to the fact that she'd just destroyed any hope Ben had of maintaining his emotional distance.

Rummaging unnecessarily through his kit had the dual advantage of allowing Ben to keep his expression to himself while he tuned out most of Jo Ellen and Merry's conversation.

His overactive brain couldn't help but latch on to the fact that Merry hadn't chosen to name her son after the kid's absentee father. She'd severed ties in a meaningful way by keeping Preston as the baby's surname. And giving him the middle name of Hollister meant Merry wanted him to have a connection to her mother's family.

Maybe all of that meant that Merry planned to move to Sanctuary Island permanently.

The intense flare of hope in Ben's chest resisted any attempt by his brain to question why he should care.

Merry had named her son Alexander—nicknamed "Alex" within an hour of being born—for Ben.

At some point after Grady and Ella cleared out to let Merry get some much-needed sleep, Jo excused herself to take a phone call in the front parlor, leaving Ben to watch over her daughter and new grandson.

"Thank you." Merry sighed, eyelids fluttering as she struggled to stay awake with her son lying on her chest under the sheet.

"You said that already," Ben reminded her, but his usual sharpness was blunted around the edges. He felt . . . shaken. Unsure of how he felt about any of this.

Part of it was exhaustion—now that the adrenaline was draining out of his system, he was aware of every ache and pain—but even more unsettling was the simple happiness that suffused his chest as he gazed into Merry's bright blue eyes.

Propping his hip on the edge of the bed, Ben struggled for his normal cool composure. "Besides, the hard part was all you. I was basically just here to be your catcher."

Merry gave him a slight smile. "You're not as much of a jerk as you want everyone to think you are."

"No, I really am," he told her honestly. "Doesn't mean I can't give credit where it's due."

Beneath the sheet, baby Alex snuffled against Merry's breast and made a sound that was like nothing so much as a piglet rooting for its mother's milk. Merry winced as he latched on, an odd expression on her face.

"Hurts?" Ben stood up, ready to dig through his canvas bag for . . . what? He didn't exactly keep plastic nipple guards in human sizes on hand.

"A little. It's weird." She let her head fall back against the headboard with a muted thunk. "But also of satisfying."

You're going to be a good mother, he wanted to say. Ben clamped his lips shut stubbornly. Sentimental idiocy. There was no guarantee Merry would be any better at parenting than anyone else.

The only guarantee was that she'd mess up that kid the way all parents messed up their kids, even the loving parents. Maybe especially the loving parents.

But at least she'd have the chance to try and get it right.

A familiar ache swelled and bloomed under his breastbone, like a spreader inserted between his ribs, cracking him open wide.

Dr. Ben Fairfax stared down at Merry Preston nursing her baby for the first time, and all of a sudden, he knew exactly how he felt about having that kid named after him.

He liked it.

But it wasn't enough. He wanted more.

Merry yawned, a real jaw cracker, without a trace of self-consciousness, her deep blue eyes hidden under the sweep of long lashes a shade or two darker than the spill of wavy brown hair over the pillow. Alex was an impossibly small, perfect bump under the sheets.

Ben stood there and felt all his careful walls and emotional defenses come tumbling down around him as he finally stopped lying to himself.

I want Merry and Alex to be my family.

Chapter One

Four months later . . .

When his truck rolled up to the wide-open doors of Jo Hollister's barn, Ben was conscious of a familiar lift in his spirits. It happened every time he came out to Windy Corner on a call. He didn't want to understand it at first, but by now, he'd admitted the truth to himself.

Even the possibility of running into Merry was like a pair of warm hands taking him by the shoulders and shaking him, hard.

But in a good way.

He swung down from the cab carefully, avoiding the loose runner board by habit, and hauled his battered canvas medical kit over his shoulder. Rolling his shoulders, he blinked up at the puffy clouds billowing across the fading brilliance of the sunset.

Sanctuary Island, off the coast of Virginia, had satisfyingly defined seasons—cold winters with the occasional ice storm, rainy springs leading to profusions of blooming flowers, steamy summers cut by cool ocean breezes . . . but fall was by far Ben's favorite.

The humidity of summer finally overtaken by the

oncoming chill, the turning of the leaves from green to burnished orange, red, and gold. The air was so clean and clear, it almost sparkled. Breathing it in, Ben felt his lungs open up, greedy for more. After the strenuous work of the last two hours, vaccinating Pete Cloudough's herd of weaning calves, his muscles twitched with the need to stretch.

He'd deliberately left his weekly Windy Corner visit to last on his schedule for the day, so he could take his time and maximize the chances of seeing Merry and baby Alex. The vaccinations had gone on longer than he'd planned, though, and now he was pretty sure he'd missed his window.

Jo's younger daughter was almost as invested in the scheme to turn Windy Corner from a regular boarding and training stable into a therapeutic riding center as her mother was. When Ben came by to check the horses, Merry was often working in the barn office, with her infant son in a playpen by the desk.

Since that stormy night when he'd gazed down at the new mother and baby boy and realized how much he wanted to be a part of their lives, he'd worked to establish a fairly friendly rapport with Merry. He'd asked her about the process of learning to write grant applications and how much money they could hope for from government programs to supplement the bank loan the Hollister women had fought so hard for last spring. He'd shared his management woes when yet another receptionist quit on him, and heard Merry's complaints about how hard it was to hire the perfect person to start building their therapy staff.

But that was about as far as Ben had gotten. Anything more personal, and either he froze up or said something cutting without even meaning to. It was intensely frustrating that he seemed to have no control over his demeanor when he'd always prided himself on his self-control. But then, all that so-called self-control was actually a conditioned response, a habit of behavior he'd developed at a young age to keep people at arm's length.

He locked people out, behind the impenetrable wall of his sarcasm and cynicism. Sure, it meant he spent most of his time alone . . . but at least it was by his own choice. It worked for him.

Or it used to. But ever since he'd met Merry, ever since the night when he was the first person to hold Alex . . . well. He wanted to change. But change didn't come as easily as he'd hoped. It didn't help that he knew Merry had disliked him from the minute they met.

Not unusual—he had that effect on most people. And for the most part, Ben was happy to keep the world at arm's length. A few folks made it their business to nudge in closer, like his friend and neighbor, Grady Wilkes. But when it was up to Ben to invite someone in because he wanted to be closer, he choked.

It just wasn't something he'd learned how to do while growing up in that big, cold, empty estate just outside of Richmond. Esteemed surgeons Tripp and Pamela Fairfax hadn't had a lot of time for personal relationships, including parenting.

And of course, there was Ashley.

Grimacing, Ben shook his head to dislodge the image of his pale, perfect ex-wife, and strode into the barn.

The welcoming scents of cut hay, leather, and oats enveloped Ben the moment his boots hit the rough concrete floor of the open corridor between the horse stalls.

An inquisitive, dappled gray head poked over the door of the stall closest to him. Ben took a moment to run a hand down the mare's soft, whiskered muzzle, automatically using the caress to check that her nostrils were dry. All summer, this little lady had sported a runny nose like a sniffly kid, and Jo had been in a flap, worrying about issues like tooth rot, a sinus infection, or worst, strangles. But after Ben did some blood work and an endoscopic, he'd diagnosed the mare with allergies.

"Looks like I was right, yet again. Swapping out that old, dusty straw for clean wood-pellet bedding took care of those sniffles, exactly as I predicted." There was nothing like the satisfaction of having a diagnosis proved right, and a patient on the mend. A feeling almost like happiness uncurled, warm and soft, in his chest.

The mare blinked her long-lashed eyes at him dreamily, nosing at his pockets for the peppermints he carried as treats. Ben gave her a grin as he unwrapped a piece of candy.

"You've got my number, huh? A little light flirting, some nuzzling, and I'm all yours," he said, holding the candy on the flat of his palm for the horse to lip up.

"I'll keep that in mind."

The throaty, amused voice behind him squeezed at Ben's heart, forcing it into an irregular rhythm.

Merry.

Ben froze, his ridiculous pulse racing as the mare crunched down that peppermint in half a second and went back to his empty hand for more. Finding nothing, the mare blew out a breath and removed her head from the stall opening, and Ben swallowed.

Time to face the woman who'd crashed into his well-ordered life like a comet exploding through the atmosphere.

"Or does flirting only work for your four-legged patients?" Merry asked as he turned and stuck his suddenly sweaty hands in his pockets.

"They *are* my favorites." He shrugged, pleased at the cool steadiness of his tone.

Merry tucked her wavy dark hair behind her ears and gave him a knowing look. "I don't believe that for a second."

Awkwardness stuck his tongue to the roof of his mouth as he wondered if she'd figured out how he felt about his last human patient. The silence stretched for an embarrassing moment, broken only by the shift of horses in their stalls.

Finally Merry rolled her eyes, prompting Ben to notice the deep purple smudges of exhaustion in the fragile skin under them. "I meant Alex, Doc. Don't worry, I know you don't particularly like me—but I've seen you with Alex. You can't pretend you don't like him."

Relief made Ben a little light-headed. "Don't be ridiculous. I don't like anyone," he reminded her. "But speaking of Alex, where is the little monster?"

Merry's mouth quirked up at one side. "You want to say hi to him? And kiss his chubby little cheeks and rub your face in his pudgy belly. Because you don't like him."

She paused dramatically before poking him in the arm. "You looooove my kid."

Ben stepped back hurriedly. When had he drifted close enough to touch her? "I like to see Alexander in a professional capacity. After I went to all the trouble of helping him into the world safely, it only makes sense to check periodically and make sure you're not screwing him up too badly."

He said it to tease her, trying to get into the swing of bantering. Merry made it look so easy with everyone else. But Ben proved, yet again, that what was easy for other people turned to crap in his hands.

Instead of laughing or poking him again, Merry

reared back as if he'd slapped her face. "I'm not going to screw my son up!"

Torn between the desire to apologize and the need to correct an obviously inaccurate statement, Ben pressed his lips together, then shook his head. "That's moronic. You're a parent. All parents screw up their kids in some way."

That one hit home—he saw it in the way her gaze suddenly darted to the door of her mother's office on the left side of the main barn corridor.

"Why are you bringing this up?" She narrowed her eyes. "Did Mom say something to you?"

Ben was beginning to regret getting into this conversation at all. "I didn't bring it up as a serious concern," he said, impatience at being misunderstood sharpening his voice. "And I'm hardly the person Jo Ellen would unburden herself to, if she's got an issue. What issue could she possibly have, anyway?"

Stubbornness firmed Merry's soft, dimpled chin even as her lips curved up in a bright smile. "Nothing. Everything's great." She paused, tapping her lower lip. The playful expression on her face couldn't quite mask the intensity in her voice when she said, "But you think I'm going to be a bad mother. Admit it."

"Oh, for the love of—" Ben planted his hands on his hips. "Yes, studies show that single mothers are prone to using male children to replace the absent adult partner, attempting to tie the child so closely to them that bonds of codependence are often the result."

Merry's pretty cupid's bow of a mouth lost its curve, going flat and thin. Ben didn't like it.

Working to soften his voice, he tilted his head to study her. "Look. Statistically, yes, it's likely you'll smother Alex with attention and affection, and turn him into a classic mama's boy. But I promise you, there are worse fates. Better too much love than too little. Everything else will work itself out."

He wasn't sure he believed his own words, but he could see from the struggle on Merry's expressive face that she wanted to.

Rubbing her hands over her flushed cheeks, she pulled an embarrassed face. "Too much love—is that really possible? If so, well . . . too bad, because there's not much I can do about it." She lifted her eyes to his, glittering fiercely. "Alex is my whole life."

Ben tried to swallow, startled at the tightness of his own throat. She was so passionate, intense in her devotion and open about showing it. Before he could think better of it, he said the words beating in his brain, barely managing to hold back the deeper truth of his heart.

"Alex is lucky to have you."

He clenched his teeth around the rest. *Anyone would be lucky to have you in his life.*

The line of her shoulders loosened even as her eyes widened a bit. He'd surprised her. "Thanks. I really needed to hear that today. And I'm sorry I jumped all over you. I know you're not exactly Mr. Warm and Fuzzy—it's dumb for me to expect that from you. I don't know what's wrong with me—I would've thought the pregnancy hormones would be out of my system by now!"

Ben, who'd recently hauled out his old medical school textbooks and done some brushing up on human pregnancy, childbirth, and the aftermath, shook his head. "The pregnancy hormones are long gone, along with any potential postpartum shifts in mood. Whatever you're feeling now is all you, and the effects of your current life choices."

Merry tossed her hair over her shoulder and gave him another of those gleaming smiles that somehow didn't reach her eyes. "My life choices. Is this your version of the you-made-your-bed-now-suck-it-the-hell-up speech? Because not everyone in the world has unlimited options, Doc."

Dismay clutched at Ben's gut. This interaction wasn't going well at all. Why this should be so hard for a person of his intelligence and education, he could never figure out. Frustration tightened his chest, and for one scorching moment, he hated himself.

Retreat was the only option he could see. Turning abruptly, he muttered, "No. Sorry. I should get to work."

The sad part was, he acknowledged silently as he slipped into the dappled mare's stall, he knew he'd be back again next week. Hope was an irritatingly resilient emotion, especially considering that the definition of insanity was running the same experiment over and over, and expecting a new result.

Insane. Because unless Ben somehow achieved a personality transplant, every conversation he ever had with the woman of his dreams was going to turn out exactly this way—crossed wires, misunderstandings, and distance.

Merry watched him go with a funny sinking sensation around her heart. It almost felt like disappointment—an emotion she ought to recognize instantly, after the trail of loser boyfriends stretching behind her, all the way back to Shawn, who'd written her a heartfelt love letter in second grade, then torn it to shreds when his friends laughed at him—but it made no sense.

She barely knew Ben Fairfax, except as the taciturn, abrasive large-animal vet who took care of her mother's horses, as well as most of the animals of all sizes on Sanctuary Island. And she had no intention of getting to know him better. Considering the sizzle of attraction she felt every time she saw his perfectly sculpted jaw, his tousled dark hair, his broad, muscled back hunched over as he inspected a horse's hoof . . . that way lay danger.

If Merry's heart beat faster at every glimpse into Ben Fairfax's intense gray eyes, it was a sure bet he was no good. Her track record with men didn't lie.

And, oh yeah—Dr. Ben Fairfax also happened to be the man who had gotten more than an eyeful of Merry's goodies when he braved a storm to deliver her baby.

And wasn't that just about the most awkward thing ever? This man who clearly hated every moment of making conversation with her, impatience and annoyance all over his stern, sculpted countenance, had seen her red-faced and screaming, heaving and crying and sweating and *gross*.

Meanwhile, he'd had his hands up her skirt and all over her ladybits, and not in the fun way.

Even for a seasoned expert in repression like Merry, that was pretty hard to sweep under the rug and roll past. She had to give him credit, though—he didn't look at her any differently now than he had before she spent two hours grunting in his ear.

Of course, that was partly because, since the moment Jo introduced them five months ago, he'd watched her with the same intent glare. A dark, searching glare that seemed to imply Dr. Ben Fairfax could see right through her veneer to what was underneath . . . and boy, was he unimpressed.

Clearly she was a glutton for punishment, because she couldn't quite make herself leave the handsome, taciturn vet alone, the way he so obviously wanted.

Wandering over to prop her arms on the stall's crossbeam, Merry watched attentively as Ben stooped and ran his strong, square hands down Oddity's back leg.

He was checking for any swelling or hot spots, she knew from pestering him with questions on previous visits. Apparently he didn't find any because he got to the bottom of her leg and leaned his shoulder into Oddity's side. With a gentle cluck, he said, "Come on, sugar. I know you're tired, but I need to check your feet."

Merry shivered again, but this time, she couldn't fool herself that it was the evening breeze.

Ben turned into another person when he was around animals. All his rough edges sanded down to a smooth, comforting voice that tickled over her nerves like a feather. Merry knew she should go back to the office—nothing good could come from feeding her unwanted attraction with images of Ben's big, careful hands sweeping gently up the mare's sensitive legs—but she didn't move.

With a sigh, Oddity picked up her back left hoof and allowed Ben to scrape away the accumulated dirt of the day with the pick he tugged from the back pocket of his jeans. Merry had to fight not to echo the horse with an appreciative sigh of her own at the way Ben's jeans molded to his lean hips and cupped his rear.

The silence in the barn was oddly intimate, like a warm blanket cocooning the two of them away from the rest of the world. With a rising sense of the trouble she was courting, Merry broke the silence. "You're later than usual today. Did you have a lot of calls?"

Ben didn't jump—as usual when he was around the horses, all his moves were slow and deliberate, with the easy grace of a man accustomed to spending time around animals much larger and stronger than himself. But from the way he glanced over his shoulder at her, a wave of black hair tumbling over his forehead, she could tell she'd startled him.

The moment spun out, strangely charged and fragile as a Tiffany glass lamp.

Ben dropped their locked stare first, going back to his exam of Oddity's hooves. "A few. Semi-interesting case of bloat out at Miss Ruth's farm. But then Mr. Leeds called with a Pippin emergency."

He straightened up and sent her a wry look over Oddity's back, and Merry bit her lips over a smile. Percy was a fifty-two-pound bulldog who was the light of elderly Mr. Dabney Leeds's existence—especially since his scheme to get his hands on her family's ancestral home was foiled last spring.

Percy the bulldog was arguably the most spoiled, cossetted animal in the history of the world, living a pampered life of luxurious cashmere doggie beds, gourmet canned food, and designer outfits. Crotchety old Mr. Leeds adored him unreservedly—but his love was mostly unrequited.

The poor dog was frequently sick—at least, according to his worried owner, who had a subscription to WebMD and wasn't afraid to use it. Ben had been called out for varying complaints ranging from canine restless leg syndrome to hiccups.

To top it off, Percy appeared to find the dainty costumes he was forced into to be the worst sort of torture imaginable. He was often seen around town wearing his tweed coat and miniature lace-up booties, straining at the end of his custom-tooled leather leash, a wild look in his bulging eyes.

"Oh no. What did Mr. Leeds think Percy had this time?"

"According to Mr. Leeds, he was concerned that after my last visit when I told him Percy needed to lose weight, the dog had become bulimic. Evidently, he'd been exhibiting binge-and-purge behavior."

Merry grimaced in sympathy. "Lots of puppy puke, huh?"

"Oceans of it," Ben agreed. "Of course, what Mr. Leeds failed to take into account was the fact that Percy's so-called binging occurred when Mr. Leeds fed him foie gras as a special treat."

Suppressing laughter, Merry cocked her head. "Well. I guess . . . it looks like dog food?"

"That was exactly his justification when I yelled at him for giving brandy-laced, fattened goose liver paste to a dog. This is why I hate the small-animal calls! Only in a backwater town like this would a large-animal vet get called in to tell a moron to stop giving his dog a fifty-dollar-a-pound purgative stuffed with black truffles."

The aggrieved, long-suffering tone of Ben's voice made Merry grin. "You know you love it here, Dr. Crankypants."

He shot her an unconvincing scowl and she couldn't help but smile.

He shook his head, loose wavy curls slipping into his eyes as he bent back to his task.

"Merry! Sweetie! Can you come here a sec?"

Jo's voice echoed authoritatively through the quiet barn, and Merry couldn't help it. She winced.

She'd wanted a closer relationship with the mother she'd been estranged from for most of her life—but maybe living together and raising baby Alex with Jo Ellen Hollister constantly looking over her shoulder and offering advice on everything from how long between feedings to when he should start crawling wasn't the best way to go about learning to love her mother.

Checking on Ben, who appeared very absorbed in his examination of the sores she'd noticed earlier behind Oddity's front legs, Merry blew out a steadying breath.

"Sure," she called back, once she had her voice under control. There was no reason for Jo, or anyone else, to know that Merry was having a tough time figuring out how to be a good daughter.

I'm lucky, she reminded herself. *I should be thanking my lucky, lucky stars with every breath. I have a home, and a family, and the most beautiful baby ever born.*

"See you next week," Ben called.

Merry glanced over her shoulder at the man in the shadows and felt another quiet shiver of warmth tingle down her spine, chasing the chill away. Nodding a hurried good-bye, she made her escape before he commented on whatever he'd seen with those laser-sharp eyes of his.

She had enough worries without falling prey to her old habit of obsessing over a guy. Especially one as harsh, sarcastic, and infuriatingly hard to figure out as Dr. Ben Fairfax.

Chapter Two

Ben laid a soothing hand on the mare's warm, strong neck and watched Merry go. The way her round little behind twitched from side to side in those jeans ought to be outlawed.

He frowned. If he were in charge of the world—and he often lamented the fact that he wasn't—he'd also make it illegal for Merry to ever exhibit that look he'd glimpsed when her mother called for her. It must be hard, trying to navigate being a new mother and having a new mother at the same time. And Jo, with years of regrets to make up for, was overloading Merry with attention and well-meaning advice. It was all there on her face.

She was so open, so expressive. Everything she felt was out there for the whole world to see, and it was a revelation for Ben. Sometimes even looking at her made him feel uncomfortably exposed. Had to be a sympathetic, mirroring emotion, because he knew for a fact that his own expression never gave anything away.

When he was a kid, he'd figured out how to turn to stone on command. It was a skill that had come in handy many times during his life. When he became Supreme Emperor of the Known Universe, he'd make sure it was taught in every elementary school.

But Merry, clearly, had learned a variation on it. She'd figured out that if she smiled big, she could fool most people into believing that everything was fine.

Ben wasn't most people. Especially not when it came to Merry.

When he'd made that conversational misstep about her life choices, he'd read the shame and disillusionment in the lines of her body as clearly as if she'd burst into tears.

His best friend, Grady Wilkes, liked to say that with the way Ben watched Merry and with Grady dating her older sister, Ella, between the two of them they were the world's foremost authorities on the Hollister women.

But as Ben let himself out of the mare's stall and peered down the hallway toward the office, he knew there were limits to his understanding of what made the Hollister women tick.

That knowledge, plus the insatiable curiosity that had driven him into medicine in the first place, propelled Ben's feet down the hallway.

Scuffing his boots in the fine red clay dust that filmed the poured concrete hall, Ben drifted close enough to the office doorway to hear the murmur of female voices inside.

Only for a second, he promised himself as his heart kicked into high gear.

He closed his eyes, listening, pretty sure he could pick Merry's happy, bubbly tones out of a crowd of gabbling, chattering voices.

Although . . . he frowned. She didn't sound all that bubbly right at the moment. She sounded uncertain and frustrated.

"I think . . . the books said this was the right way to start holding him now. We're past the four month mark, and his head isn't all wobbly anymore."

"Well, sure, that's fine." Even Ben, not the most attuned to social cues, could plainly hear the soft doubt in Jo's voice.

She tried to shake it off by being overly hearty about saying, "However you want to do it is fine! Kids are resilient—they're basically made out of rubber bands at this age. Of course, Aunt Dottie always used to . . . but that's not important."

In the short pause that followed, Ben realized that he wasn't going to be able to get his quick fix of Merry's voice to carry him through the rest of his Merry-less week, and leave. There was something going on here.

Something he might be able to turn into an opportunity.

Merry sighed almost inaudibly. But her voice was calm and reasonable when she asked, "What would Aunt Dottie say?"

"Here, pass him over to me," Jo said happily. "Oh, who's a big boy? Who's Grandma's big boy?"

Ben shifted his weight carefully to line up his eye with the crack in the door just in time to see Merry do that quick, jerky wince he'd caught before.

And the expression on her face when her mother lifted the baby out of Merry's arms and turned away slightly, cuddling him close . . . Ben narrowed his gaze in confusion as everything in his chest tightened in empathetic misery.

What did this all mean?

Fading back into the shadows of the barn, Ben felt his heart thundering in his chest the same way it had the day after the divorce, when he'd made the abrupt decision to leave his comfortable life and surgical ambitions in Richmond and move to Sanctuary Island.

A sense of possibility, exciting potential, raced over his skin and raised the fine hairs on the back of his neck.

It didn't take a degree in psychology or a high score on the emotional IQ test to see that Merry Preston was in trouble. She needed help. She needed a hero.

Which was bad luck for her, because all she had was Ben. Who was no one's idea of a hero—but for the chance to get the family he'd always wanted?

Ben could fake it.

Merry watched her mother holding her fussy baby boy the "right way," and felt something inside her chest positively shrivel up into a dried-out knot.

Part of her wanted to grab Alex and stomp out of the barn. The other part of her was terrified that Jo was right.

Merry had no idea what she was doing.

A sharp rap on the wooden door frame behind them had Merry whirling to face Ben's determinedly neutral expression.

He lifted one black brow. "Can I get a word?"

Jo gave him an easy smile, her face soft and handsome in the warm light of the barn office. "Sure, let me just—"

"Sorry," Ben interrupted, lifting his chin. "I meant with the kid."

Warmth spread through Merry's insides, banishing the bad feelings. "I knew it!" she crowed, pointing at the vet. "You can't resist snuggles with Alex."

Pulling his mouth into a disgruntled line, Ben marched into the office and held out his arms in an imperious gesture. Looking mildly confused, Jo handed Alex over with a swift glance at Merry.

But Merry didn't have time to reassure her or explain what was going on, even if she were able to puzzle it out herself, because in the next instant, Ben spun on his heel and walked out of the office.

"Well?" Ben stuck his head back through the door, impatience sharpening his already razor-edged voice. "Are you coming?"

Merry jumped and gave her mother an apologetic glance. "Sorry! This will be fast, I'm sure, and then we can go home."

Amused, Jo waved a hand and sank down into the chair behind her ancient desk. "You kids go on. It's not as if I'm running low on paperwork."

Merry hustled out into the hallway and paused, glancing up and down the wide, dark corridor. Moths banged recklessly into the floodlights set high in the rafters, and the horses they'd brought in from the paddock for the night sighed and shifted in their stalls. Other than that, the evening air was quiet.

That was when she realized that Alex had stopped making those little complaining cries that meant he was tired but would rather work himself into a full-blown screaming fit than sleep.

He'd been fussing off and on for the last hour, ever since his dinner, and no amount of holding and walking by either Merry or Jo had helped. In fact, Merry had needed to give herself a stern talking-to about the glimmer of gladness she'd felt when being picked up by Jo hadn't immediately fixed Alex's bad mood.

Now, as she spotted Ben down at the end of the hallway just inside the open double doors to the outside, Merry smiled. Looked like where she and Jo had failed, Ben had effortlessly succeeded.

Alex was completely silent in Ben's arms, staring up at the man's face with wide, fascinated blue eyes. As

Merry walked up to them, Alex lifted his dimpled hand and made an uncoordinated grab for Ben's granite-hard jawline.

When Ben didn't jerk his head away, Merry noticed that he was staring down at Alex as if he'd never seen anything so miraculous. Seeing Ben's normally shuttered gaze broken open by such tenderness tugged hard at Merry's bruised heart.

The intensity of the look on Ben's face kept her from teasing him any further about his interest in Alex. This man, who professed to care for nothing and no one outside of his veterinary practice, definitely cared about her son.

"What are you showing him?" she murmured, glancing past Ben's broad shoulders to the dark night outside the circle of light spilling from the open doors. A brisk wind rustled through the evergreens that surrounded the barn, the whisper of pine needles almost drowning out the chirruping song of the frog who lived in the stable yard.

Ben hitched Alex in his arms so that the baby faced the night sky, his butt supported on Ben's muscled forearm. Merry turned to look up, too, and caught her breath at the stillness and quiet, the velvety softness of the autumn night. A harvest moon glowed golden and bright, outlining the tips of the tall pine trees against the star-studded expanse of midnight blue.

"Nothing important." Ben shrugged. When she looked up at him, his dark gray eyes were shadowed and searching. "You wanted to get out of there. So I got us out."

A lump thickened in Merry's throat, something like fear squeezing tight. This man saw too much, made her feel too much . . .

She shook her head, but she couldn't deny Ben was

right. Breathing in a gasp of chill night air, Merry felt as if she were sucking in the right amount of oxygen for the first time all day. It was enough to make her light-headed.

Ben was still watching her, studying her as if she were a specimen on a slide under his microscope. It made her want to squirm . . . but it wasn't entirely unpleasant.

She shook her head. "I don't . . . what are we doing out here?"

"You're unhappy." The blunt force of his words hit her like a hammer. "Living with Jo Ellen. You need to move out."

Winded, it took everything Merry had to force a laugh. "That's ridiculous. What gives you the right—"

"I have no right," Ben said, looking impatient. "I know that. But someone has to say it, since you won't."

"I want a relationship with my mother," Merry protested. "That's the whole reason I came to Sanctuary. It's why I decided to move here permanently."

"No," Ben corrected her. "You stayed for Alex. Because you want to raise him here, and you're smart enough to take help when it's offered."

Merry had the feeling that this entire conversation was happening on multiple levels—but she could only follow one. "I guess that's partly true, but—"

"And you didn't expect help from Alex's father." Ben pronounced it like it wasn't a question, but the way his searching gaze bored into her soul told Merry her answer mattered, for some reason she couldn't fathom.

Still completely at sea, and definitely not wanting to get into the whole Ivan mess, Merry looked up and connected the dots of Orion's belt to give her time to steady her voice. "Alex's father is out of the picture."

The words sent the familiar sharp stab of regret

lancing through her. She knew what it was like to grow up missing a parent, and she hated the idea of Alex wondering what he'd done to make his father abandon him.

Giving a short, satisfied nod, Ben muttered, "Thought so. Good."

"Good?" A roil of emotion choked her for a blinding instant. "You don't think my kid deserves to know his father?"

Ben's jaw tensed above Alex's downy head. "Not if that father is a worthless loser."

Merry's mouth dropped open at the sheer, galling presumption. But before she could hiss that Ben didn't know what the hell he was talking about, he sighed hugely and lifted Alex in his arms. Staring up into the baby's cooing face, Ben muttered, "I'm saying this all wrong, aren't I?"

Crossing her arms across her chest, Merry demanded, "What *are* you saying, exactly?"

Visibly gathering himself, Ben folded Alex in close to his chest, where her baby pressed his little face and rubbed a wet spot on the shoulder of Ben's hunter-green thermal knit shirt. Merry struggled to hold on to her indignation while her heart melted into a puddle of goo.

Ben took a deep breath and met her gaze directly. "I'm saying, Alex does deserve a father. And you deserve the chance to build a relationship with your mother that isn't mired down in feeling smothered by her constant attempts to help you. That's just going to give you a case of the belated adolescent angst you missed out on during your teenage years."

Merry sucked in a breath—this conversation passed inappropriately intimate about ten exits back—but Ben wasn't finished.

"I'm saying I can help, with both of those things," he

said clearly, his deep, resonant voice rumbling out of his chest. Ensnared by the intensity of his tone, by the magnetic pull of his steely eyes, Merry held her breath.

"I'm saying . . ." Ben paused for a heartbeat, long enough that Merry had to gasp in air that seemed too thin to fill her lungs.

"What?"

Ben squared his shoulders and firmed his mouth, his stare never wavering. "Marry me, Meredith Preston."

Chapter Three

Merry swayed on her feet, her face as pale as the sand on Sunrise Beach. Cursing inwardly, Ben juggled baby Alex onto one shoulder to try and get a hand free to catch her, if she was planning to topple.

But he should have known better. After one sharp, wheezing breath, Merry got her balance back, along with her voice.

"Is that a command or a question?"

"It's a solution to your problems. It would get you out of Jo's house, give you some distance so you and she can interact in a healthier way. Plus you won't have to feel dependent on her good will, which will free you up to be the parent you want to be—and maybe the daughter you want to be, too."

Her gaze sharpened on his, glittering in the moonlight. "So I should be dependent on you, instead. A man I hardly know, who barely seems able to tolerate me for the length of a normal conversation, much less love me enough to marry me. What's wrong with this picture?"

Maybe he'd made his move too quickly—it might have been smart to take the time to consider the best way to convince Merry. But Ben preferred not to wait for the iron to get hot when he could make it hot by striking. He saw his chance, and he was taking it.

So here they were, standing in the darkness of her mother's empty barn. Hardly the romantic proposal women dreamed about.

Of course, he could fix that by telling her the truth— that she and Alex had unearthed something inside him that he'd buried years ago, that when she smiled it made Ben want to smile back, that all he wanted in the world was to keep Merry and Alex safe and try to make them happy.

The words clogged in his throat, choking off his air. He couldn't do it. He couldn't open himself up that way, knowing Merry didn't feel the same.

But this doesn't have to be about romance, he reminded himself firmly. *As far as Merry is concerned, it's about practicality.* And there was his angle, right there.

"Look, don't get bent out of shape and emotional about this. I'm proposing a simple transaction, one that has occurred over and over between men and women since the dawn of time." Ben kept his voice even and calm, rational. "You want independence from your mother and sister; I can give you that."

She narrowed her eyes. "And what do you get in return?"

You and Alex.

The words lodged in his chest, a truth so deep he couldn't force it to the surface. Clearing his throat, he said, "I'm from Richmond, originally. Have you ever lived there?"

Confusion dragged out her response. "Nooo. What does that have to do with anything?"

Come on, Ben, you've got to give a little to get a little.

Every word like pulling splinters out of a snarling dog's paw, Ben opened up. Just a crack, but enough to make him feel uncomfortably exposed.

"The Fairfaxes of Richmond have been leaders in the FFV for generations. First Families of Virginia," he clarified when she still looked confused. "It's an exclusive set of Virginia society made up of folks who can trace their ancestry back to the original settlers of the colony. There's a lot of prestige, a lot of tradition. A lot of ridiculous, meaningless, shallow posturing and backbiting and maneuvering for status."

"Sounds like a blast." Merry shook her head, a frown creasing her pale brow. "I'm still not seeing the connection."

"I'm an only child," Ben told her, thinking quickly. "And my parents are getting on in years. They've been after me to settle down, and I know the one thing that would please them more than anything would be if I were to provide them with an heir. I don't see why that heir can't be Alex."

"But," Merry stammered, eyes wide and bewildered. "He's not yours."

The words seared through Ben in an unexpected rush of bitter pain, but other than firming his hold on the wriggling baby in his arms, he didn't react. "I know that. But I could make him my legal heir, all the same."

Not that adopting Alex and giving him the Fairfax name would actually please Ben's parents. *Blood will tell,* he'd heard them say to each other with significant eyebrow arches over the morning paper, whenever some family outside their set did something of which they didn't approve.

But a legal heir was better than nothing, Ben reasoned. It was the best they could hope for from Ben, so surely he'd be able to convince them to play along.

Merry shook her head, and when she reached out her arms for her son, Ben handed the kid over. Reluctantly, and with a pang for how empty his arms felt without Alex's soft weight, but he said nothing.

"No. I can't believe we're even having this conversation. No! I'm sorry, I'm not marrying you just to give your parents a grandkid."

"To be clear," Ben said, "there's an inheritance involved."

And that was a miscalculation. Ben realized it the instant the words left his lips and Merry stiffened as if he'd shoved a speculum somewhere uncomfortable.

"I don't need your money," Merry snapped. "Alex and I are doing just fine, thank you very much."

Cursing himself silently, Ben stepped back. But he wasn't ready to admit defeat yet. "This could be the answer to both our problems. People have gotten married for far stupider reasons. Love, for example."

He held his breath, counting off the solid thuds of his heartbeat. Was that the right tactic? To leave emotion out of the equation? It certainly felt safer to Ben— and since he knew Merry barely liked him, let alone loved him, it felt smart. If she said yes, it wouldn't be because she expected hearts and flowers and candlelight.

Please say yes.

Down the hall, the light in Jo's office clicked off, casting Merry's face into further shadow. He couldn't read her expression anymore, although he caught the slight tension in her shoulders when Jo called her name.

"Coming, Mom," she called back, her opaque gaze never leaving Ben's.

He swallowed down a plea and forced his tone to a firm command. "Tell me you'll at least think about it. Alex deserves the best. Between the two of us, we can give him everything—two parents, a stable home, the best schools and opportunities in life."

Merry curled her arms tight around her son. "I'm sorry, but it's too crazy, even for me. And I've practically made a career out of leaping before I look when it comes to men. I promised myself I was done with that part of my life."

She took off down the hall toward her mother, whose pickup truck was parked out back behind the barn. Ben watched her go, his heart aching in his chest. When she paused, that stupid heart leaped—until she said over her shoulder, "But thanks for the offer, Doc. It means a lot to me, for Alex's sake."

Ben's heart dropped back into his rib cage where it belonged, beating a steady rhythm of hope.

For Alex's sake.

That's what it came down to, Ben knew. And that was his ace in the hole. This was a chance to ensure Alex's future. Merry wasn't going to pass that up.

He hoped.

Merry blanked all thoughts of Dr. Ben Fairfax out of her brain. She was good at that—selective memory loss was one of her special talents, and it had gotten her through a lot of tough times. She wasn't about to abandon it now, when even a stray, curious question from Jo wanting to know what she and Ben had been talking about in the barn could cause a hot flush to flood Merry's body.

She'd deflected Jo's questions and focused on Alex during the car ride home—which was easy, since he remembered his earlier determination to have a bad night the instant Merry walked him away from Ben. Alex sobbed the entire way back to Jo's house as if his little heart were breaking.

Hoisting her precious bundle of blanket-wrapped baby higher on her shoulder, Merry skirted the hole in the porch—they had to get that fixed before Alex learned to crawl—and struggled to open the front door with the two free fingers from her left hand.

The rest of that hand was lugging the unwieldy diaper bag that was her only accessory these days, and she clenched her jaw against a curse when the process of turning the brass knob had her nearly dropping the heavy bag. She managed to get it under control and keep her balance without jostling Alex too badly, and breathed out a long sigh of relief as she stepped into the foyer.

The house settled around her, creaky and old and welcoming. After only five months, Merry already felt more at home here at Windy Corner than she had anywhere since she was a kid.

What was wrong with her that she couldn't be content with that?

"Honey! You should let me get the door for you," Jo chided her, the screen door banging shut behind her. "I'm here to help."

Merry actually felt her shoulders hitch up, tension pulling her spine straight. "I was fine. Thank you, though."

Jo paused and uncomfortable silence descended for a moment. It lasted long enough for Merry to wish her sister, Ella, were on the island instead of back in D.C. with her new boyfriend, local handyman and noted hottie Grady Wilkes, packing up her apartment and dealing with the ramifications of taking a leave of absence from her high-powered real estate firm.

Ella was a pretty good buffer, and she had the added bonus of always being completely on Merry's side, ever since they were little. Merry was as well adjusted as she was because of her older sister.

Not that Merry was going to win any medals in the Life Skills Olympics, but she'd be willing to bet she'd be a lot bigger mess if the only mother figure she'd had while growing up had been her actual mother.

She pursed her lips against the surge of resentment. Thoughts like that had been creeping in ever since she woke up the morning after Alex's birth and realized that this tiny, helpless scrap of humanity was entirely dependent on her. Hers to love, hers to protect . . . hers to screw up.

From that vantage point, it was suddenly a lot harder to look back at the choices Jo had made throughout her daughters' early lives and feel quite so forgiving.

But you forgave her months ago, Merry reminded herself firmly. *You were the one who wanted to end the estrangement, you were the one who wanted to get to know our mother. You were the one who decided to move to Sanctuary for good.*

So suck it up, buttercup. This is the bed you made, and if it's not quite the soft, easy rest you thought it would be, you have no one to blame but yourself.

Which, of course, reminded her of that insane conversation with Dr. Ben Fairfax back at the barn. What an impossible man he was. For the life of her, Merry couldn't get a handle on what made him tick. Any man who would propose marriage, out of the blue, to a woman he didn't even like was an enigma.

Not that Merry had ever been great at understanding men. At least, not at understanding more than the fact that they seemed to like her brightly dyed, punky hair and tendency to wear skintight leather pants.

Considering how long it had been since she'd felt

sexy enough to pour herself into those leather pants, or to bother to do more to her hair than give it a whack with a hairbrush, maybe it wasn't such a surprise that Ben didn't like her very much.

Not that he seemed to like anyone at all, other than Alex. Which was another crazy thing, but one that gave Merry a warm glow deep in her chest.

Of course it was nuts, in this day and age, to even consider marrying someone to secure an heir—what was he, the king of England?—but Merry couldn't fault Ben's taste.

"What are you smiling about?" Jo asked, an eager answering smile tugging at the corners of her mouth. Hope shone clear as day in her blue eyes—the same blue eyes Merry saw every morning in the mirror—and Merry felt a pang of guilt.

None of Merry's newly discovered angst was Jo's fault. Except in the sense that Jo was the one who'd been a raging alcoholic when Ella and Merry were little, who'd chosen whiskey over her family and allowed her husband to move across the state and take their children with him.

But that was nearly two decades ago, and Jo had gotten clean. She'd reached out, she'd apologized—she'd done everything right. Back when Merry and Ella first arrived on Sanctuary Island last spring, Ella had been the one who struggled to find a way to forgive.

Merry had done what she always did. She put on a happy face, ignored the past, and shoved determinedly forward into the future.

The fact that she was having second thoughts now was seriously unfair, to everyone involved. Because since Alex's birth, Jo had been nothing but supportive and helpful.

It wasn't Jo's fault that every time she tried to help these days, Merry had to bite back a protest.

In her arms, Alex squawled fretfully and made a snuffling push against her shoulder. He was ready for his bedtime snack, and Merry said a silent prayer that tonight would be one of the nights he dropped off to sleep immediately afterward.

She was lucky. For the most part, Alex slept straight through from feeding to five-thirty or six the next morning—but there were a few nights here and there that made Merry worry he'd inherited her lifelong insomnia.

And of course, after a full day of mucking out stalls, helping tack horses for the riding lessons Jo gave to local kids, revising the cover letter for her latest attempt at a grant application, and that shocking conversation with Ben, tonight was one of Alex's bad nights.

He cried. And cried. And screamed, and then cried some more until Merry was on the point of bursting into tears herself. If she walked him up and down the stairs, he'd calm down for a few minutes, but if she tried to lay him down in his crib . . .

After the fourth unsuccessful repetition of this maneuver, Jo said from the doorway of the nursery, "I know it's hard. But when you pick him up, you're just teaching him that if he cries, you'll magically appear and make everything better."

Merry stared down at her son, on his back in the white crib Grady had built for him. Alex's tiny face was screwed up tight, angry squawks issuing from his rosebud mouth as he waved his legs and fists in furious demand.

"I want him to know that I'm here for him," Merry said through the numb daze of exhaustion.

"But he has no incentive to stop crying," Jo said with maddening calmness. "You need to let him cry it out. He'll go to sleep eventually."

Merry reached down to touch the fleecy square of blanket Alex had managed to twist around himself like a pretzel. "He's so little. The world must seem like a huge, cold, terrifying place to him. I can't leave him all alone in it. I won't."

The harsh intake of breath behind her made Merry replay what she'd said. Turning suddenly, she surprised a look of pain on her mother's face.

"I didn't mean—" Merry broke off uncertainly. Because maybe she did mean it.

After all, Jo Ellen had abandoned her daughters in every way that mattered before they even learned to walk.

"It's fine," Jo said at once, brushing it away with a graceful sweep of her hand and a determined smile. "And of course, Alex is your son, you raise him the way you think best. I know parenting styles have changed a lot in the last twenty-five years."

Alex let loose with a particularly piercing shriek, and Merry, pushed beyond all resistance, leaned back over the crib and swooped him up into her arms. When he clutched at the cotton of her T-shirt with both sticky hands and mouthed wetly at her neck, Merry's heart throbbed and expanded until it pressed painfully at her rib cage.

"It's late," she said, giving Jo a tight, apologetic smile. "And tomorrow's coming fast. Why don't you go to bed, I've got this."

"No, I'm not tired at all!" Jo's protest was somewhat undercut by the fact that she yawned hugely in the middle of it. Making a face at herself, she said, "Really. I can stay up and keep you company."

The need to be outside, out of this house and away from Jo, seized Merry by the throat. "That's okay—I'm going to try the car."

Sometimes Alex could be soothed by being strapped into his car seat and driven slowly around the island. Something about the vibration of the engine beneath him or the sound of the ocean waves through the open car windows—Merry didn't know, but it was like magic.

"Our little future Nascar champ." Jo smiled faintly. Backlit by the gentle glow of the hall light, she looked more than tired—she looked old, her face lined with the cares and regrets of more than fifty years.

Jo felt the strain and distance that had been growing between them, too—Merry knew she did.

Feeling guilty, ashamed, exhausted, and annoyed at herself, Merry attempted to put some real warmth in the smile she gave her mother. "More like Formula One. Aren't they the guys who just go around and around the track? That's what Alex likes best—driving in circles."

One hour and three full circles around the island's paved roads later, Alex was asleep.

But Merry was wide awake, her thoughts as circular as the route she'd taken to lull her son into slumber.

Tell me you'll at least think about it.

In the still darkness of the deserted country roads, cutting through pine woods and over salt marshes, Merry was at the mercy of her thoughts.

And all of them centered on Dr. Ben Fairfax and his proposal. Which might be the craziest thing she'd ever heard . . . but somehow, she couldn't get it out of her mind.

Sighing, Merry turned down the road that would lead her back through the center of town to Windy Corner and all the problems she'd left behind when she escaped from the house tonight.

It was so late, the gas street lamps that lined Main Street were dimmed to dark blue flames. No one in this little early-to-bed-early-to-rise island town was up and about this late except desperate single moms.

But as she drove slowly past the grassy town square, Merry caught movement in the shadows of the white-latticed bandstand in the middle of the park.

Her heart clutched into a fist in her chest.

What on earth was that?

Chapter Four

Taylor wandered across the dewy grass of the town square toward the dark bandstand in the center.

It was weird how creepy everything looked at night. She stuck her hands deeper into the pockets of her jeans and hunched her shoulders against a shiver.

That pack of cigarettes better still be there, or this whole curfew-breaking escapade was a pointless waste of time and energy. Either way, though, she'd needed to get out of the house after that fight with Dad about restoring her computer privileges.

Hack one little school-system Web site, and get banned from the Internet for life? Unfair. It had been literally years since she'd used her techie powers for evil. But did Dad give her any credit?

No, it was all, "I see you pulling away again, pulling into yourself, just like after Mom died, and it scares me."

Please. Sure, Taylor wasn't ecstatic about life right now, but that didn't mean she was about to do a swan dive off the deep end into juvenile delinquency.

Her father's paranoia had the opposite effect he was

probably hoping for, anyway. As soon as the light winked out under his bedroom door, Taylor had her window open and was shimmying down the old magnolia tree to retrieve her long-lost pack of cigarettes from the park.

At the edge of the gazebo, Taylor crouched down and wiggled the loose board at the back of the steps up to the stage, feeling around in the dirt.

Completely focused on the search for a nicotine fix she hadn't craved in months, Taylor didn't hear the steps behind her until a guy's voice said, "Hey there. Did you lose something?"

Taylor would deny it with her last breath, but she let out a frightened squeak and whipped upright, whirling to face the tall boy staring down at her.

Silhouetted against the flickering light of the old-timey street lamp behind him, his face was cast in shadow. Taylor's heart raced out of control as she realized she didn't recognize him.

On an island so small that the entire high school only had two hundred students, that was a big deal. Taylor had been in classes with basically the same sixty-two kids since kindergarten. By the start of junior year, you'd think she'd know every single one of them well enough to recognize them even in the pitch-black dark.

Not so much.

Feeling like she'd swallowed a clutch of tadpoles and they were all swimming around in her belly, Taylor tossed her blond hair over her shoulders and lifted her chin. "Who wants to know?"

The guy put his hands on his lean hips. Big hands, she noticed with a nervous thrill. Broad palms, long fingers, bony at the knuckles like he was still growing into them. But at five foot nine, Taylor was one of the tallest girls in school—and this guy already towered over her by at least four inches.

She racked her brain for which guys from school were taller than her when they finished sophomore year last spring. But lots could happen over the summer—nobody understood that better than Taylor.

"You really don't recognize me." The guy ran his fingers through the short spikes of his buzz-cut hair. "Who would've thought getting contacts and a haircut would make that big a difference."

Instantly more at ease, Taylor shivered in delight at the mystery. When the glow of the street lamp caught the edge of his sharp jaw, Taylor leaned back against the white bandstand railing and let a smile curl her lips.

"No more hints," she told him, blood sparking with the thrill of something new, something different, something exciting.

"What, you don't want to know who I am?" He sounded surprised, his deep voice cracking a little on the word "know." Taylor breathed in and let the night air fill her lungs. An enigmatic pseudostranger was better than a smoke, any day of the week.

"Nope. But you know who I am, don't you?"

"Taylor McNamara," he answered promptly. She couldn't see his smile, but she could hear it in his voice. "Sanctuary High's resident bad girl."

"Not anymore," she protested, feeling the burn of shame across her cheekbones. Hopefully it was too dark out here for him to see it. "I turned over a new leaf last year. Not that anyone noticed."

"Sorry if I touched a nerve." He held up both hands in a placating gesture. "At least I recognize you. Whereas I'm clearly so forgettable that I'm invisible in a class of less than seventy. Besides—"

He pushed past her before Taylor knew what was happening, bending down to swipe his fingers through the dirt. When he straightened up, there was a crumpled pack of cigarettes in his hand, and even in the shadows, Taylor could see the lift of his dark brows.

"About that new leaf," he started dryly.

"Okay!" Taylor lifted her chin. "The new leaf is . . . a work in progress. I have the occasional backslide. But whatever, I only do it out here, at night. Nobody else gets my secondhand smoke, my dad never has to know—it doesn't even count, really."

"I've got a new name for you: Sanctuary High's resident rationalizer."

"Shut up!" Taylor's mouth twisted to hide a smile. "Seriously, I'm not, like, a smoker or something. I'm not addicted. But sometimes . . ."

She hesitated, but the darkness, the chilly air, and the anonymity of the quiet boy in front of her made it easier to talk. "Have you ever felt like the walls of your room are closing in? Like the whole house is heavy and pushing down, trying to smother you, and you just have to get out and away?"

The boy cocked his head to one side, and the angle of it tugged at Taylor's memory. "Yeah," he said softly. "I know what you mean."

They shared a silent moment of understanding that warmed Taylor more than her hands jammed in her pockets. "Anyway," she said, tossing her hair back. "You don't get to go all judgy on me—we're both lurking around the town square in the middle of the night."

"And on a school night, too," he murmured with a little laugh. "Which is why I'm out here. Couldn't sleep—first-day jitters."

"Funny. I'm actually looking forward to school

starting," Taylor confessed. "Or maybe I'm just ready to be done with my summer job."

"You work out at Windy Corner Stables, right? I would've thought that would be a cakewalk since your dad is dating Jo Ellen Hollister. Doesn't she own the barn?"

Small towns, Taylor reflected gloomily. Everyone was all up in everyone else's business . . . but still only aware of half the story.

"It's complicated," she hedged. Pulling herself up by the railing, she swung up the steps and slipped onto the bandstand stage under the friendly darkness of the gazebo roof.

The guy followed her, his long legs taking the steps two at a time and carrying him over to sit down next to where Taylor had settled on the floor with her back to the wooden railing.

"You don't like Jo," he guessed. "Worried she'll end up as your evil stepmother?"

"No, you're way off." Taylor rested her head against the wooden slats, content in the knowledge that her face was now as shadowed as his. "I love Jo. She and my dad have been together, off and on, for a long time. She's already like a mom to me, ever since my mom died."

"So what changed?"

Her real daughters showed up.

Before Taylor could swallow down the sudden lump in her throat and decide how to answer him, a pair of headlights swept through the gazebo in a glaring flash.

"Crap!" Nobody on this sleepy little island was out driving around this late except the cops. Scrambling to her knees to peek over the railing, Taylor searched for the lights. They weren't shining out of Sheriff Shepard's SUV, and she went limp with relief for about five seconds.

Until she recognized the dented rear bumper of the little gray four-door currently idling at the edge of the town square.

"Crap on a *cracker*!" Taylor squatted back down out of sight as the driver's door opened. Her heart flapped against her rib cage like a seagull's wings. Dropping her head into her hands, Taylor moaned, "Oh God, please let her get back in the car and drive away."

She so didn't want to deal with this tonight.

"Is that . . . ?" The guy's deep voice trailed off as he twisted to get a glimpse through the wooden slats.

"The reason I'm glad to go back to school? Yeah. One of my insta-sisters," Taylor confirmed with a groan. "Merry Preston."

"Taylor, is that you?" Merry called across the green.

Busted.

"You might as well come out. I know it's you." Merry was smiling like this was all a big freaking joke to her, and the indignation over that was enough to propel Taylor to her feet.

Propping her elbows casually on the gazebo railing, Taylor gave Merry her best bored stare. "What?"

Merry leaned against the car and peered over her shoulder into the darkened backseat. Swiveling her head to look at Taylor again, she said, "Come over here. If I keep shouting across the town square, I'm going to wake Alex up. Not to mention the rest of the island."

If the baby was in the car, Taylor realized, then there was no way Merry was going to catch them if they decided to run. Every muscle in her body tensed for flight, but then Merry got this look on her face.

Kind of a resigned, knowing look. As if she could tell what Taylor was thinking and had already decided how Taylor would act.

And if there was one thing Taylor hated, it was being predictable.

"You don't have to go down there if you don't want to," the guy beside her whispered. "I'll make sure you get home okay."

Taylor bristled, the warm intimacy of secret-sharing and trading confidences shattered. "I don't need any help getting home, I'm fine on my own. But if she yells, someone could wake up and call the cops on a disturbance," Taylor pointed out. "I'll go see what she wants."

"Do you want me to come with you?" He stood up, and for the first time that night, Taylor got a good look at his face.

Her jaw dropped open. "Fatty Matty?"

Ever since he and his mom moved to Sanctuary Island a few years ago, Matthew Little had been short and pudgy, round all over—from his moon-shaped face to the thick lenses of his glasses. But the guy beside her was no fatty. He'd shot up almost a foot over the summer, and his shoulders had widened while the rest of him slimmed down. Taylor could hardly believe her eyes.

Matthew froze into shocked stillness, like she'd whipped off her shirt and flashed him. His lean jaw hardened as he ground down audibly on his back teeth. "Not anymore. I've changed, and I thought you had, too . . . but obviously, I was wrong."

Without giving her a chance to apologize or even catch her breath from the shock, he marched down the gazebo steps and away across the cut grass of the town square.

Taylor felt sick to her stomach. Kids at school all made fun of Matthew Not-So-Little, just not usually to his face. But the surprise, the unexpectedness of who her midnight confidant turned out to be— Taylor swallowed.

There was no excuse. She'd have to apologize to him at school tomorrow.

Great, there were the first-day jitters she'd denied having.

Sighing, she slunk out of the gazebo and trudged over to Merry's secondhand car. Taylor prepared herself for one of those dumb grown-up questions like "What are you kids doing out here so late?" But what Merry said instead was, "Hop in. I'll give you a ride home."

"What if I'm not ready to go home?"

Merry glanced over Taylor's shoulder. Turning her head, Taylor caught a glimpse of Matthew Little from behind, head down and strides long as he walked in the opposite direction, toward the Harrington house, where he and his mom lived as caretakers.

When did I turn into such an awful person? Taylor wondered as her heart squeezed like a lemon.

"You're ready," Merry said gently. "Come on."

She'd been running on adrenaline and the thrill of breaking the rules for hours. Now, having driven away the one person she'd found who seemed to actually understand her, Taylor didn't have the energy to fight. For once.

Shoulders slumping, she slouched around the front of the car and climbed in without another word.

A car ride with one of her least favorite people in the world, who now had something to hold over Taylor's head—as if it weren't enough to swoop in and claim Taylor's family as her own. And tomorrow, on Taylor's first day as a junior, she'd have to suck it up and apologize to Matthew Little for being a total bitch.

Oh yeah. This was going to be a great year.

* * *

Merry checked on her son in the rearview mirror as she pulled smoothly away from the curb. Yep, still out like a light.

The sullen teenage girl next to her sighed loudly and made a point of staring out the passenger window for the first ten minutes of their drive. After the last few months of Jo and Harrison's rekindled romance, Merry knew the way out to the McNamaras' big white house overlooking the beach, but she almost asked for directions just to have something to say.

Merry saw a lot of herself in Taylor. They'd never made much of a connection, especially after the way Taylor had snooped around and made trouble between Ella and Grady. But there was always hope.

"So, who's the guy?" Merry tried.

"Nobody," Taylor muttered, leaning her temple against the glass of the window.

"He was pretty cute, for a nobody," Merry observed, remembering the lanky kid with shoulders that showed the promise of breadth when he grew into himself.

"Surprise, surprise." Taylor snorted. "Not like it matters, I'm sure he hates me now. Whatever."

Merry recognized the thrum of pain and regret under Taylor's attitude, and boy, did that bring back her own misspent youth. She wanted to ask why the boy would have reason to hate Taylor, but she didn't truly need to.

The feeling that no matter what, she'd always be a screwup clutched at Merry's throat, but it was only a reflection of the angry flush on Taylor's cheeks. Changing the subject, Merry said, "I guess I should probably tell your dad or Jo about this. It's the responsible thing to do . . ."

"Tell whoever you want." Defiance pulled Taylor

upright in her seat, her glare burning across the dimness of the front seat. "I don't care."

"You do care," Merry said. "You care like crazy. But maybe I'm missing the point of all this curfew-breaking and running around with boys in the middle of the night. Maybe you want your dad to find out."

"What?" Taylor scoffed as only a sixteen-year-old girl can scoff. "That's stupid. Of course I don't want him to know, I'd be grounded till prom."

Merry, who had once been a sixteen-year-old girl with massive parental issues, said, "Sure. But at least you'd have his attention. And maybe Jo's, too?"

Taylor jerked as if Merry had slapped her across the face, her pretty features tight with shock. "I'm not trying to get anybody's attention! I'm not some dumb little kid who needs her dad to watch her go down the slide at the playground or something."

"Sure you are," Merry told her. "We all are, no matter how old we get. It's one of the facts of life you learn as you go along. You never outgrow that need for your parents' approval, and that's okay. Just don't go overboard with it."

Taylor narrowed her eyes. "You mean like uprooting your whole life and moving to Sanctuary Island to live with your mom, even though you're a grown-up?"

Zing! "Okay, that's fair," Merry acknowledged. "But clearly, that makes me an expert. I know what I'm talking about here."

"So I should listen to you? Please. As if I'd want to end up like you, with a kid and no husband, no job, and no life."

"Ow," Merry said, giving Taylor two raised brows. "Words hurt, you know."

Interestingly, Merry thought she detected a slight

sheen to Taylor's brown eyes, even as the little brat sneered. "The truth hurts," Taylor said crushingly.

And it was the truth, Merry realized. The least flattering take on it possible, but still, nothing Taylor had said was a lie.

"You're right," Merry said slowly. "I can't say I regret much about my life—if I'd made other choices, maybe I wouldn't have Alex. And I'd never give him up for anything. But if I'd had him when I was your age . . . I can't imagine. I'd be even more dependent on my family for help than I already am. And maybe it's time for me to realize I *am* a grown-up. I have options; I can choose."

Taylor looked interested against her will. "What do you mean?"

"I mean, thanks for the tough talk." Merry smiled into Taylor's confused, suspicious face as a sense of possibility rushed through her like an ocean breeze. "You helped me see that it's time for a change. And in return, I'll let you decide whether I keep your secret about what you were up to tonight."

"Whatever. You're a whack job." Taylor rolled her eyes, her slim fingers fidgeting fretfully with the hem of her T-shirt.

Silence stretched through the car, broken only by the soothing sound of the tires on the road. Merry flicked off the headlights and turned in to the long, winding driveway that led up to Harrison McNamara's house on the bluff, overlooking the ocean.

Slowing the car, she looked at Taylor. "What's it going to be? I can let you out here, and chances are you'll get away with tonight scot-free."

"You really do know all the tricks," Taylor said, unwillingly impressed.

"Babe, I've forgotten more tricks than you'll ever know," Merry told her. "Really, when I look back, I'm surprised I'm still alive."

"Drama much?" Taylor rolled her eyes again, then bit her lip. "I guess I'll get out here. I don't care about getting in trouble, but my dad has a lot going on right now at work, and he's so happy to be back with Jo. I don't really want to make trouble."

"Sometimes you just can't help it though, right?" Merry held back the sympathetic smile that tugged at her lips. "I get that."

Taylor only huffed and climbed out of the car. But she didn't slam the door shut—after a swift glance at the sleeping baby in the backseat, she pressed the door closed quietly, then hesitated for a moment.

Hitting the button to roll down the passenger side window, Merry asked, "You okay?"

"Yeah." Taylor wrapped her slender bare arms around herself, and Merry fought down the urge to remind her to bring a jacket the next time she snuck out. Mother of the Year, she was going to be!

"I just wanted to say thanks." Taylor squinted into the distance as if worried that meeting Merry's gaze would reveal too much. "For the ride, and everything. And for not saying anything to my dad or Jo. I don't really care about getting in trouble for the curfew, but if my dad caught me out with a boy, even one I'm not going out with or anything . . ." She grimaced. "Bad news. Anyway, Dad and Jo are happy. They don't need to be stressing about me right now."

Merry didn't know how to explain what she'd only recently come to understand, herself—that parents always worried, but even that worry was a joy and a privilege because it went along with a love so deep and pure that it was worth any amount of stress.

"It'll be our secret," she said instead, and was rewarded with a quirked, reluctant half-smile before Taylor disappeared up the hill toward the white house.

Connection made.

As Merry backed slowly up the driveway, she felt that same flutter of possibility she'd gotten during the conversation with Taylor. The sense of the world opening up before her like an empty road unfurling into the horizon—that was something she'd felt before in her life, but only a few times.

Most recently was when she decided to keep her unborn baby and raise him without any help from his father . . . and then again when she'd made the choice to stay on Sanctuary Island, against the express wishes of the older sister who'd taken care of her since they were kids.

Cold night air blew in the open passenger window, invigorating and refreshing against her hot cheeks. She'd made a life-changing decision tonight, with no more thought and reason than that it felt right.

What the heck, she thought, checking the rearview mirror to see her baby boy, plump and flushed with sleep, drooling onto his own shoulder. *It's worked out okay for me so far.*

"What do you think, Alex?" She kept her voice soft, not wanting to wake him. But he had to be included in this momentous decision, because it was all for him. "Wish me luck, baby boy. Tomorrow, Mama's getting engaged."

Chapter Five

What was a girl supposed to wear to her own engagement?

Merry smoothed a hand down the front of her black Misfits T-shirt and wished she owned something a little more businessy. After all, this was more of a straightforward contract negotiation than a romantic love scene.

Bet Miss Manners never covered the dress code for the modern marriage of convenience.

Anyway, it doesn't matter, she decided, lifting her chin and raising a hand to knock on Ben's office door. *He can take me as I am, no illusions, no bull, or not at all.*

The idea that she might have missed her chance at this sent a weird tingle of unease to tighten the hairs at the back of her neck. She had no idea if she'd be relieved or disappointed.

This is bonkers. What am I even doing here?

Before her feet could get any colder, she swung open the door and marched into the vet clinic.

It wasn't the first time Merry had visited the office— she'd dropped off the payment for the weekly bills

Windy Corner Stables racked up a couple of times. Both times, she'd handed the check off to a sweet-faced woman wearing glasses, a messy bun, and a harried expression, and both times, Merry had considered asking the poor woman if she wanted to grab a drink after work. For sure, being Dr. Crankypants's office assistant would drive anyone to alcohol. But since she'd been pregnant at the time, she hadn't done it, and now look— the woman had quit several weeks ago, and she'd taken every last vestige of organization and efficiency with her.

Haphazard piles of paper littered the desk by the door, cascading from the overflowing black metal in-box and onto the floor. Three of the four drawers in the corner file cabinet were pulled open, with color-coded manila folders sticking out of them at random. As Merry stood in the doorway, eyes wide, the phone on the desk started a shrill pattern of ringing that clicked almost immediately over to the answering machine. Glancing down at it, she saw the red light blinking, frantically signaling that the answering machine tape was almost full.

"Whoever you are, go away! Unless you're here about the job, in which case, pick up the damn phone and get to work." Ben's shout was muffled through the door of his exam room, but Merry could clearly discern his impatience. Not a subtle guy, her future husband.

If he was in the exam room, he might be with a patient. Of course, she wouldn't put it past him to be hiding in there with a cup of coffee and his paperwork, keeping his head down and hoping the mess out here would magically disappear.

Giving him the benefit of the doubt, Merry rubbed her damp palms on her thighs and decided to wait. But the only chair in Ben's completely inhospitable waiting area was the one behind the receptionist's desk, and it was buried under a mountain of paper.

Merry sighed. It might be a long wait, and she'd been on her feet since Alex's predawn wake-up call. She marched over to the chair and started sifting through the bills, prescription pads, advertisements for new medications, and payment notifications. But once she had the chair cleaned off and ready for duty, it no longer matched the rest of the disaster area of an office. And what the heck, she already had several piles going for later filing, so she just kept adding to them and adding to them, until finally she looked up and realized that she'd tidied up the entire desk.

Rolling her shoulders to stretch out her stiff neck, Merry jumped in surprise when the exam room door opened and a retriever with a plastic cone around his fluffy neck bounded out. In the next instant, Merry had a cold, wet nose in her crotch and her hands full of soft, curly fur the burnished gold color of the leaves falling off the maple tree out front.

Crouching down to the dog's level as two people followed him out, Merry ruffled his silky ears. "Oh now, who's a good boy? I love your new collar, such a fashion statement, very avant-garde. All the lady retrievers are going to be all over you."

"That collar isn't decorative," Ben said from above her. "It's a cone of shame, to keep Bosley from licking himself raw."

"Oh, Doctor," an old lady's voice quavered. "Don't call it the cone of shame. I hate for him to feel we're laughing at him, even if he does look silly. Bosley, the girl dogs will love it!"

Ben snorted. "Trust me, Bosley doesn't care if he's a hit with the ladies—why should he? When his tongue can reach his own—"

Merry stood up so quickly, all the blood rushed from her head. "Hi, Mrs. Ellery. Great turban."

Mrs. Ellery blinked the slow, lazy blink of a woman who'd had an extra good time in the sixties. She smiled and the tiny bells sewn into her purple paisley head scarf tinkled merrily. "Meredith, honey. How's your mama? And that sweet little boy of yours. He was getting so big when I saw y'all at the playground last week."

This, right here, was why Merry was determined to bring Alex up on Sanctuary Island. The warmth and welcome she'd received was beyond anything she'd ever imagined—especially since she'd shown up in this tiny town five months ago as an unwed mother.

But no one here batted an eye. Maybe Merry was automatically accepted as one of the Hollister women, who'd been living on the island for generations. Or maybe it was that Sanctuary Island was home to a variety of misfits and oddballs who followed the golden rule about their neighbors' quirks.

Merry smiled back. She liked the way Mrs. Ellery always called her by her full name. "They're both good. Thanks for asking. And I hope Bosley will be up to playing by next Saturday! Alex will sob his eyes out if he doesn't get to pull on poor Bosley's ears at the park."

With plenty of fluttering and wispy hand wringing, Mrs. Ellery promised to see Merry and Alex in the park, got her marching orders from Ben on patient care— "Don't let him lick himself. Use a squirt bottle if you have to, or he's going to get an infection in a really nasty place"—and bustled out of the clinic with her faithful companion padding along beside her.

"You didn't have to do that." Ben crossed his arms over his chest, making Merry notice the muscles in his biceps and shoulders, the solid strength of him. The wide planes of his chest narrowed to a lean waist that made Merry's palms itch to touch, to see if it was as hard and ridged with muscle as it looked.

"Hello?" Impatience snapped in Ben's tone as he waved a hand in front of her face, and Merry jumped, heart racing. Crap, she'd been staring.

Desperate to distract herself from the heat pooling low in her body, Merry grinned and arched a brow. "I know Mrs. Ellery is a woman of the world—heck, she probably had more sex than you and me in our whole lives put together during the Summer of Love alone—but that dog is her baby. And trust me, no mama wants to think about her little boy doing the nasty to himself."

"I wasn't talking about your morality policing," Ben said, glowering down his nose at her. "I meant all this. The office."

"Oh!" Stupidly, Merry felt the urge to apologize choke up into her throat, but she swallowed it down. She had nothing to apologize for.

"This place is a hot mess," she said instead. "What have you been doing since your assistant left? Throwing your bills and diagnostic notes onto her desk and waiting for the elves to come at night and file them by magic?"

Ben rocked back on his heels while his eyes did a funny, shifty squint. "No!"

Merry laughed. "Oh, for the love of . . . that's exactly what you've been doing. Doc, come on. Just hire someone new."

"I tried," he growled. "You think I like living this way? I'm going out of my mind, and I've interviewed what seems like every empty-headed bimbo on the Eastern Seaboard to find a replacement, but now the agency won't send me anyone else."

"I wonder why." Merry studied the thunderous scowl on his handsome face. It was enough to scare the bejeebus out of any poor college kid looking for a summer job. "Have you thought about doing phone interviews?"

Grabbing a big black binder off the desk, Ben started flipping through it. "I need to get to my next appointment. If I can figure out what the hell it is. You got something to say, spit it out. I assume you didn't come over here to clean my office and critique my interview style."

Merry's mouth went bone-dry. Licking her lips, she fought to keep her head up and her tone as straightforward as Ben's. "No. I'm here to talk about your offer."

Ben paused his riffling through the appointment calendar, his gaze trained stubbornly on the page in front of him. "My proposal, you mean."

His sudden stillness communicated a level of nerves that, perversely, put Merry at ease. Hopping up to sit on the edge of the desk she'd cleared, she swung her booted feet and leaned back on her hands. "I thought about what you said, and you made some good points. So here's my counteroffer."

That got Ben to look at her. "I'm no expert, but I don't think that's how marriage proposals usually go."

"Tough bananas. If you want somebody who'll smile big and bat her eyes and agree with everything you say, propose to someone else. And I recommend you actually take her out to dinner first, at least once. Most girls would prefer you pop the question after a little courtship."

Ben's gaze sharpened thoughtfully. "Dinner! I should've taken you to dinner. Is the Firefly Café good enough, or would it have to be that fancy French place in Winter Harbor?"

"Don't be a dummy. There's nothing better than the Firefly Café," Merry told him. "But that's beside the point, because you didn't ask some other woman to marry you—you asked me. And I don't need any of that courtship crap, because if we do this thing, it's not going to be a regular marriage. It's more of a business deal. What's the phrase? A marriage in name only."

She held her breath, because that was essential—a deal breaker, in fact. Merry Preston had slept with plenty of guys for reasons that turned out to be pretty stupid, in retrospect, and she was through with it. Sure, Ben was hot—it would be impossible not to notice. But she'd fallen for good looks before, and she knew better now. That part of her life was over—she had more important things to focus on these days, like Alex.

"That sounds like you're saying no sex," Ben said, with his usual bluntness.

Taking that as her cue to be equally blunt, Merry laid it out for him. "If you're going to expect sex from me in return for financial stability . . . there's a name for a woman like that, and it's not a label I'm willing to carry. So I want it understood up front. If we get married, I'm never going to have sex with you. Ever."

To the casual observer, Ben would bet he looked calm and collected, unconcerned at the fact that the woman of his dreams was offering him everything he wanted in one hand, and taking back a big chunk of it with the other.

But Ben was a master at weathering emotional whiplash—he'd been told that as a fairly complicated, uneven-keel person, himself, he'd inspired plenty of it in others—and the important thing was to keep his eyes on the prize.

She was close to saying yes. A qualified "yes," to be sure, but this first "yes" was only the first step of a much longer journey. And without it, he had no chance at getting *any*thing he wanted.

So Ben shrugged instead of arguing, and said, "Makes sense. I wouldn't want you to do something you're uncomfortable with."

That had the added benefit of being true—Ben's dream was not, in any way, to coerce Merry Preston into sharing her life and herself with him.

He needed her to want him back.

Her eyes went wide, and he could tell he'd surprised her. Not very flattering. "Seriously?" Merry blinked. "Oh-kay . . . great."

"Good."

"Hold up." Merry shook her head. "For serious now, you get what this means, right? I'm okay with you . . . seeking comfort elsewhere. That's only fair."

"Fine." Ben shrugged. It was easy to agree to a contingency he never planned to take advantage of.

She threw her hands up. "Ben! Now who's not thinking it through? Let me spell it out. If we stay married, you will never father a child with your wife. Are you really willing to give up all hope of a legitimate heir?"

The words rocked Ben on his heels like a slap across the face. Merry couldn't know how close she'd cut to the bone, how much fathering another child was exactly the eventuality Ben hoped to avoid. "It's not a matter of giving up hope," he said starkly. "There's no chance of me fathering a child, legitimate or otherwise. Ever."

He would never take that chance again, with Merry or anyone else.

"Oh!" Red suffused her cheeks as her eyes went wide and moist with sympathy. "I'm sorry, I didn't realize . . .

I didn't mean to bring up something so painful and personal. But it's important we're on the same page about this, because it's a deal breaker for me."

"We're good. Is that your only deal breaker?" Ben asked abruptly, tightening his fingers on the appointment book until the plastic squeaked in his hands.

"Anxious about what else I might come up with?" Merry flashed a smile and her booted heel hit the desk leg with a rhythmic thud-thud-thud. "Don't worry, you'll like this next one. I'm willing to agree to the trust fund for Alex—I can't pass up the chance to give my son the best chance at life."

"Excellent." Fulfillment flooded Ben for a blissful moment . . . until he noticed the determination firming Merry's lips.

"But," she said, holding up a hand. "The trust should be in Alex's name only. I want a third party we both agree on to be his trustee. Someone good with money and with Alex's best interests at heart should hold the purse strings until he's old enough to take over."

"I nominate you," Ben said immediately. A huge part of the point of this was to make sure Merry was taken care of.

"No. I don't want your money. And I wouldn't know what to do with it, how to invest it and keep it safe for Alex. I was thinking somebody like Harrison Mc-Namara would be a good choice."

Harrison McNamara wasn't only Jo Ellen Hollister's main squeeze—he was also the manager of the local bank, and a smart, savvy businessman. Ben was unwillingly impressed with Merry's pick, even as he realized she was determined to deny him the satisfaction of taking care of her the way he'd imagined.

"That makes sense," Ben admitted grudgingly. "But

look, don't be a stubborn idiot about the money. I've got more than I need—you don't. If we get married, we share it. That's how it works."

"Your money is yours." Merry set her jaw, and Ben hated that he noticed how beautiful she was in her righteous determination. "This isn't nineteen fifty. It's not your job to support me. In fact, if we do this, I'll want to contribute to the household. Which means getting a job outside of working at the barn."

Ben pounced. "What about Alex? Are you going to let me hire a nanny to look after him? Because the chances of you finding an employer other than your mother who's happy to babysit? Virtually nil. And if you're going to keep working at the barn, too—"

"I have to," she interrupted. "Mom needs all the help she can get, setting up the new facility for the change-over to therapeutic riding, and I need to see it through with her. It means a lot to me."

As it happened, the planned Windy Corner Therapeutic Riding Center meant a lot to Ben, too—enough to have him volunteering his time and considerable skills as the on-call veterinarian—but he still marveled at the easy, open way Merry put it out there. As if she had no fear that revealing what mattered to her meant that it would be taken away.

"I was going to point out that a job in addition to working at the barn means long hours away from Alex." *And me.* "So maybe you should rethink that point. It's not like I need your help with the bills."

"I get it, you're Richie Rich." Merry shrugged helplessly. "But can't you see that I have to do my share and pay my own way, or all I'm doing is trading dependence on my mother for dependence on you?"

Ben had to look away from the plea in her blue eyes,

or he was going to crumble under the pressure. His gaze landed on the tidy surface of the desk, with its neat piles of paper.

"You're right," he realized, snagging a page off the top of the nearest pile. "I do need help with the bills. And the filing, and keeping up with my appointments and stocking the supply closet."

"What do you mean?"

Ben raised a brow. "I know exactly where you can work, for good money and flexible hours. And I can guarantee the boss won't mind when you bring your baby with you to the office."

Merry slid off the desk, eyes huge in her shocked face as she stared wildly around the office. "No! What? I don't have any qualifications, my work history is spotty, at best. This is a bad idea."

"It's a great idea," Ben told her. "In spite of your frankly terrible interview technique. And you had the gall to criticize *my* interviewing skills! Anyway, you're hired. I'm looking at the new office manager for the Sanctuary Island Veterinary Clinic."

Just as he was congratulating himself on finding the perfect loophole, Merry recovered enough to narrow her eyes and poke a stiff finger into the center of his chest.

"And you'll pay me exactly what you paid your last receptionist, right? No more, no less. No special treatment."

"Fine, take all the fun out of it," he grumbled. "And don't worry about special treatment. You'll have to learn on the job, and I need you up to speed fast. So you'll need to start as soon as possible."

"As soon as . . . an hour ago, when I cleared off this whole desk?" She smirked up at him, so full of mischief and loveliness, it caused a physical ache in Ben's hands that he wasn't supposed to reach for her.

He gazed into her eyes for a long, silent heartbeat. Ben yearned toward her as if she'd magnetized his insides, an almost uncontrollable force pulling him in her direction. But she'd said she didn't want that, didn't want him, and Ben would never force her.

She'd said she didn't want him . . . but a sudden flush painted her cheeks and the tips of her ears red. Her pearly skin showed every change in body heat, Ben knew, and as they stood there, mere inches apart, the flush spread down her neck. Her breathing hitched quietly, and when she swallowed, he was close enough to track the movement of her slender throat.

Her chest rose with an inhalation and her lashes fluttered slightly, but she didn't step away. Ben stared down at her, so close, so touchable, and he smiled.

He'd never force her . . . but he could tempt her.

"It sounds like we've got a deal," he murmured, very aware of the thickness of his voice. "All points agreed upon, all details hammered out. I'll get my attorney to draw up a contract, so you can look it over."

"Okay." Merry's gaze flickered to Ben's mouth for a bare instant, but it was enough to set off fireworks in Ben's chest.

"One last point," he said, bending near to brush the words against her temple. "About the no-sex clause."

"Nonnegotiable," Merry breathed, her blush intensifying. Hope kindled like a flame in the pit of his stomach.

"I'm not arguing," he assured her. "Merely stipulating an exception."

Suspicion crept into her tone. "What exception?"

With the same care and precision he used with his

frightened patients, Ben lifted his hands to her upper arms and skimmed the silken flesh there so lightly that he felt it when she shivered. "After we're married, there will be no sex . . . until you come to me and ask for it."

Chapter Six

"If your plan is to wait me out, Doc, you'll be waiting a long time," Merry declared. Well, she meant it to be a declaration, a firm and serious vow, but somehow it came out sounding all husky and needy.

Ben shrugged, his dark brows scrunched in that grouchy way that made Merry's fingers itch to smooth them out. "We'll see."

"We *will* see," Merry insisted, forcing herself to step back and out of the danger zone. "We need to be clear before this goes any further."

She paused. The blunt, brutal truth didn't seem to want to leave her mouth, but it was too important—if she held back and he got the wrong idea, she wouldn't be doing Ben any favors, in the long run.

Merry tilted her head and looked him straight in the eye. "I know we haven't talked about feelings much. It's all been about what makes financial sense and what's best for Alex, and I don't want to hurt your feelings or anything, but Ben, I don't love you."

She held her breath for his reaction, but his expression never even flickered. If anything, his grumpy scowl lightened up a bit. "I know that. I never expected you to."

"All right. That's . . . good." Knocked off balance, Merry couldn't help poking at him to find out more. "But what if you fall in love with someone later on down the road? I wouldn't want to stand in your way—we should have a plan for that."

"We can if you want," Ben said indifferently. "But it's not going to happen for me. I'm not built for it. I prefer a smart, sensible partnership with all the details spelled out ahead of time in a contract. I'll take that over the mess and chaos of love any day of the week, and twice on Sundays."

His face, as usual, gave nothing away. But there was a rigidity to his stance, a brittle stillness in the way he held himself, that hinted at old pain and deep regret. Merry, who had more than her share of both, decided to back off and let this drop gracefully. For now.

"Then I guess we're in agreement." Another thought popped into Merry's head. She couldn't believe she'd almost forgotten about it! "Oh, wait—I also want a trial period before we even think about starting adoption proceedings. A year."

Ben's eyes narrowed. "Six months is all you'll need. I'm going to be an excellent father figure."

"A year," Merry insisted. "For you as much as for us. Being a parent isn't fun and games all the time. We need to be sure this arrangement is working out before I make such a permanent decision about my son's future."

Jaw clenching, Ben dipped his chin. "Reasonable. But I'm not going to change my mind," he said, as if he'd heard everything she wasn't saying.

To her own surprise, Merry wasn't actually all that worried that Ben wouldn't be up to par as a dad—she'd seen him with Alex, and she'd felt the tenderness and care radiating off Ben whenever he held her little boy in his arms. They wouldn't be having this conversation at all if she hadn't.

But she was worried—terrified—about what would happen if she and Alex grew to depend on that tenderness and care, and someday down the line, Ben left.

She wouldn't put her son through the lingering, corrosive heartache of abandonment. The fact that Ben couldn't have kids of his own reassured her a little, in a sad way—Alex would be it, for him, and what mother wouldn't appreciate that?—but she had to be cautious. This was her son's future. She couldn't take any chances.

"One year," Ben said, as if making a mental note and recalibrating his plans. "Starting from today?"

So soon. Somehow, that one sentence made this whole theoretical discussion feel real. Merry swayed on her feet, a little light-headed with possibilities. "This . . . is actually happening, isn't it?"

"If you want it to." Ben tucked a hand into the pocket of his white lab coat and drew out a tiny black velvet box.

"Geez, count your chickens much?" Merry said faintly. "You must have been pretty sure I'd come around."

"I wasn't sure, but I had hope." Ben turned the box, so small in his long-fingered hands, and offered it to her on the flat of his palm, the same way he'd offer a sugar cube to a horse to keep from getting bitten.

His instinctive caution made her smile, even as she shook her head and backed away until her hips bit into the edge of the desk. "We don't need a ring—this isn't that kind of engagement, remember? No romance required."

"It's not romantic," Ben insisted, gesturing with the box impatiently. "It's part of the trappings. If we're going to do this, we're going to do it right. The whole point is to create a stable, normal environment for Alex. That means Mama gets a ring on her finger."

He shoved the box toward her, and Merry accepted it reluctantly. "I guess so," she said, then gasped when she opened the box and saw the ring.

Big and square, the diamond glittered in its old-fashioned setting surrounded by a constellation of tiny pinprick diamonds. The slim platinum band looked like two vines twisted into a braid. It was the most beautiful ring Merry had ever seen—not that she'd encountered a lot of engagement rings in her life.

"No," Merry said through numb lips. "I can't accept this, it's too much, too expensive—"

"Relax." Ben grabbed the ring from her nerveless fingers and slipped it into place on her left hand, where it winked at her seductively. "It didn't cost me a dime. This ring has been in my family for generations. My grandmother left it to me, and I know she'd be glad to have you wearing it instead of sitting around collecting dust in a safe-deposit box."

Merry held her hand up, dazzled by the prism of light the ring threw off in every direction. "You make a good point. Something this pretty deserves a happy life."

"My thoughts exactly."

Ben's slow smile transformed his lean, saturnine face, and Merry felt a warning tingle of feminine awareness. Before that tingle could blossom into a full-blown heat, however, the sharp ringing of the office phone shattered the moment.

Grateful for the distraction and the chance to get her head together, Merry grabbed for the phone. "Dr. Fairfax's office! How can I help you?"

Ben lifted his eyebrows. He looked impressed, and Merry preened a little. She did have an excellent telephone manner, if she did say so herself. Okay, so maybe she'd cultivated it during that brief period when she'd worked as a phone sex operator, but he didn't need to know that.

"Merry, honey, is that you?"

Her mother's tinny voice in her ear jolted Merry out of her contemplation of the many and varied jobs she'd held over the years. "Mom! Hi. What's up, is something wrong with one of your horses?"

There was a beat of silence where Merry could practically hear Jo deciding whether or not to ask what Merry was doing at Ben's office, answering his phone. In the end, Jo went with ignoring it. "Not one of ours, but Ben does need to get out here as quickly as possible. Is he available?"

"For an emergency, for you? I'm sure he is, but let me check." Covering the mouthpiece, Merry glanced at Ben, who nodded and went into the exam room to grab his bag.

"He's on his way," Merry told her mother.

"Could you come, too?" Jo sounded stressed, in a rush. "I can't take the time to explain right now but there's a lot going on here, and I could really use another pair of hands."

"Of course. We'll be there as soon as we can." Merry hung up, worry already eating at her. Jo said it wasn't one of the Windy Corner horses that needed help—so maybe she'd gotten word of trouble with one of the wild-horse bands that roamed Sanctuary Island?

"She wouldn't tell me what was up," she said as Ben reappeared, bag in hand and brows lowered back to their normal Serious Business position.

"Whatever it is, I'll handle it." Ben scowled over his shoulder when Merry followed him out the door.

"Don't even start," she cautioned him. "If there's trouble at Windy Corner, I'm coming with you."

"I can see how this is going to be," Ben grumbled as he tossed his medical kit in his truck and climbed in. "You work for me now. That means you're supposed to do what I say."

"I prefer to think of it as working *with* you," Merry said loftily, and hopped into the passenger seat. She'd get her car later. "Marriage is a partnership, I hear. And that reminds me, we haven't talked about our wedding vows yet. I don't mind going with the traditional vows—I can tell you're a bit of a traditionalist—but I'm telling you now, we'll be rewriting that line about me obeying you."

"Sure. We wouldn't want to start our married life with an immediate, obvious lie." The truck engine turned over with a cranky cough.

Merry beamed. "I'm so glad you see it my way! Now step on it, Doc."

Ben backed up with the smooth ease of a man more used to driving a truck with a horse trailer attached than without, and revved up the hill to the main road with a roar.

"Don't get any big ideas." He slanted her a warning glance. "I'm not making vows about obeying you, either. I'm going fast because I want to and my job requires it, not because you told me to."

Rolling her eyes, Merry buckled herself in for a bumpy ride. "Enough wedding talk. We can negotiate who gets to be on top later. Just get us to the barn, Doc. Mom sounded bad—like she'd seen a ghost. I've never heard her like that."

"You're worried. Don't be. Whatever it is, we'll get through it together." Ben didn't take his eyes off the

road, all his focused intensity on pushing his old truck
as fast as it could safely go.

But his words pierced Merry's soul as surely as if he'd
taken her in his arms and whispered them into her ear.

Together.

She had a fiancé. A partner in life. From now on, no
matter what happened, she wouldn't face it alone.

Taylor squinted through the windshield of her lovingly
restored and maintained VW Bug. What the heck was
happening out at the barn?

Parked out front and almost blocking the wide double doors of the big green-painted barn was a mam-
moth horse trailer, the kind that could hold up to a
dozen horses at a time. No one on Sanctuary owned a
trailer like that.

She'd already planned to head over to Windy Corner
as soon as school let out—she'd predicted, totally ac-
curately, that after the first full day of classes she'd need
the comfort and familiarity of Jo, the horses, and her
barn chores.

Taylor had spent the entire stupid day distracted by
trying to track down Matthew Little to apologize. But
for a tall, broad-shouldered guy, he was frustratingly
adept at disappearing.

Tomorrow, she promised herself as she pulled around
to the back of the barn to park in her usual out-of-the-
way spot. For now, it was time to find out what was going on to make Jo Ellen leave a tense, terse message on
Taylor's phone, asking her to get over to the barn asap.

She dug her dusty paddock boots out of the trunk
and swapped them for the black Converse All-Star
sneakers she'd worn to school. Chucks were wonderful
in many ways, but their white rubber-covered toes and

soft canvas uppers weren't the best protection against getting stomped on by big horse hooves.

Hefting the newly oiled English saddle out of her backseat, Taylor balanced it on her shoulder and started the hike up the hill to the barn. Before she got more than three steps, however, a tall, familiar figure appeared in the doorway.

Her mouth dropped open. "What are you doing here?"

Matthew Little stepped out of the darkness of the barn and into the clear afternoon sunlight.

Something flashed in his eyes—probably dislike— and had they always been that color? Almost eerily golden-green against his tanned skin and dark hair, his stare seemed to burn a hole through Taylor's chest.

"Don't worry. I'm not here to bother you." He sneered.

"You're not. I mean, you wouldn't," Taylor faltered, then cut herself off.

Get it together, McNamara!

The saddle on her shoulder slipped, and she jerked it higher, the weight of it pressing her down into the earth. Or maybe that was Matthew's gaze. "I'm glad you're here," she told him firmly. "I tried to talk to you at school today. But every time I saw you, it was like you were running away from me, ducking into the boys' room or turning a corner. Or surrounded by a bunch of girls."

She laughed a little, to prove how much she didn't care, but Matthew didn't laugh. He crossed his arms over his newly broad chest, making the muscles stand out distractingly under his tight T-shirt. "So?"

"So . . . nothing." Taylor gritted her teeth in annoyance as the damn saddle wobbled again. "What do I care if Dakota Coles and her posse of Goody Two-shoes cheerleaders want to drool all over . . . I don't care, okay?"

And she didn't care. She absolutely didn't have to fight the urge to stomp up to that giggling bunch of haters and snatch Dakota Coles bald-headed for having the utter hypocrisy to drape herself across the shoulders of a guy she'd made merciless fun of for years. Or to smack some sense into Matthew, who really ought to have better taste and sense than to be taken in by dum-dum Dakota's perfect platinum-blond curls and bleached-white smile.

"Okay." Matthew shrugged and turned, like he was about to walk away.

"It was annoying," Taylor blurted, and he stopped, head cocked. He was still listening. Taylor swallowed hard, her grip going sweaty and slippery on the leather of the saddle. "It was annoying because I needed to talk to you and get this stupid apology over with, so I can forget about it and move on with my life."

"Apology, huh?" Matthew did an about-face and sauntered down the hill toward her, his face unreadable. But she thought she detected a slight softening around his jaw, as if he'd unclenched his teeth.

That gave her the guts to ignore her jumpy nerves and lift her chin. "I *am* sorry," Taylor said. "I was surprised—but I shouldn't have called you that name. It was awful, a really crappy thing to do. I suck totally."

"Give me that." He reached for the saddle. "And don't go committing ritual suicide about it, or anything. You're hardly the first person to call me names."

Taylor surrendered her heavy burden reluctantly. "But I don't want to be that girl. Ever." Shoving at the loose, flapping cuffs of her black flannel shirt, she frowned down at the frayed hem of her too-long jeans. "I know what it's like to have people whispering and gossiping, acting like they know something about you when really, they don't know you at all."

She felt the glance he darted at her like the brush of fingers against her cheek. "I guess you do," he said quietly.

"So, Matthew," Taylor said, stressing his full name and curling her lips in a real smile for the first time all day. "Did you come out to the barn just to make me grovel?"

"Just Matt is fine. And no—I'm here to help my mom's cousin. He's visiting from the mainland, and he brought some horses from his farm to—"

From inside the barn came the shrieking whinny of an enraged animal, followed by the sharp bang of iron-shod hooves on the solid oak of a stall door.

"Is one of them a demon from hell?" Taylor asked, eyebrows shooting up.

Matt grimaced. "Sort of. It took Sam, my mom, me, and my new stepdad to get Java into the trailer, and I came along to help unload him."

"New stepdad?" Even in the midst of her need to see the demon horse and find out why it was here in Jo's barn, Taylor noticed that little nugget of info. Something bigger than a late growth spurt had happened to Matt over the summer, that much was obvious.

There was an unfamiliar confidence in his step, in the way he held himself, to complement the new strength in his shoulders as he easily balanced the unwieldy weight of her saddle. Maybe this stepdad guy had something to do with it.

"Yeah, my mom re-married." Matt smiled a little, and Taylor had to blink to clear her head. "An awesome guy from New York. He's got a motorcycle."

"So you're not mad about it?" Taylor couldn't help the question. It seemed like everyone in the universe had the same opinion about steps, from fairy tales to movies and books, as if every kid should be upset when a parent fell in love and added someone new to the family mix.

But Taylor had adored Jo Hollister for years. She wanted nothing more than for her dad to make it official with Jo. And permanent.

"No way! He's great, and he makes her happy. No-brainer, at least to me. I was the one who told him to stick around and fight for her, actually. If I hadn't stepped in, he probably would've headed back to New York and now they'd both be miserable."

"Grown-ups!" Taylor rolled her eyes. "Beats me why they're automatically supposed to be in charge of our lives, when they can barely figure out their own."

"True." Matt laughed, a deep sound that sent a tingle of excitement pulsing through Taylor's stomach. "They're kind of hopeless, sometimes. It's like they forget what it's like to be young and take risks."

She liked Matt. A lot. More than she'd liked anyone since . . . well. Since Caleb Rigby's dad shipped him off to military school to get him away from Taylor's "bad influence."

If she were smart, she probably wouldn't do anything to make herself a bad influence on Matt Little—but with Dad coming down so hard on her about everything lately, what choice did she have but to embrace her inner bad girl?

Taylor reached out to snag the sleeve of Matt's forest-green Henley between two fingers. He stopped in his tracks, staring down at her with a question mark in his eyes.

Swallowing past the dry scratchiness of her throat, Taylor tipped her head back to meet his gaze. "So . . . would you be up for a little more teenage rebellion? Or is a walk in the park after dark as bad as you ever go?"

The immediate flash of interest in Matt's hazel eyes

kicked Taylor's heart into high gear. She'd show him—there was more fun to be had on Sanctuary Island than boring, perfect Dakota Coles would ever know about.

If Taylor had to circle back to the wild side for a while to spend some time with Matt Little, so be it.

"Text me," Matt invited, digging his phone out of his pocket and handing it over so Taylor could key in her number.

She pretended her fingers weren't shaking as he shook his head with a grin and took off up the hill. Taylor watched him go, carrying her heavy saddle as easily as if it weighed nothing, and felt a shiver of electricity spark down to the tips of her toes.

Why did being bad always feel so good?

Chapter Seven

Ben stood outside the stall and studied the stallion, rage prickling like a cold sweat at his hairline.

The horse's ragged coat was the color of bitter cocoa, and his black mane and tail were snarled into knots that hadn't felt the touch of a comb in quite some time. There were other warning signs: the horse's hide was scored with a number of small nicks and Ben could count his ribs with every heaving breath. The prominent ridges of his spine and hip bones made Ben grit his teeth against the suicidal urge to rush into the stall and examine the animal with no further delay.

But the whites of the stallion's eyes showed as he tracked Ben's every movement, muscles shuddering with tension and nostrils flared to catch the scent of danger. And for a horse in this bad shape, the presence of any human beings undoubtedly equaled danger.

"Oh my God." Merry, who'd gone straight to her mother's office to check on Alex, walked up beside him and put her hand to her mouth as tears sprang to her eyes. Ben had to look away from her, he had to keep his cool.

Ice it down, Fairfax.

Ben ground his back teeth so hard, he felt like it would take a crowbar to pry his mouth open. So he kept quiet. There was nothing he could say to make Merry feel better, anyway.

This horse had been neglected and abused, over a long period of time. And until they both calmed down, there was no way Ben was going in that stall with him.

"Mom tried to tell me," Merry whispered, "but I didn't think it would be this . . . heartbreaking to see."

That was enough to unlock Ben's jaw. "What exactly did your mother say about this animal?" he demanded, distantly pleased with the coldness of the words.

Merry flinched as the horse kicked nervously at the stall door. She turned an accusing gaze on Ben. "This animal? What is there to say other than that he's in pain. Get in there and do something about it!"

"The animal isn't necessarily in pain," Ben said, every word falling toneless and dispassionate from his mouth. "In any case, it's likely he's existed in this condition for some time now. A few more moments to allow him to calm down won't hurt him."

"Wow." Merry shook her head. "Your sympathy is overwhelming, Doc."

"Sympathy won't get this animal treated," he pointed out.

"I can't believe you!" Merry put her hands on her hips and faced him down like an avenging angel. "How could anyone look at that poor horse and not be affected?"

If only, Ben thought bleakly. Pushing aside the stupid, small part of him that wanted to feel hurt at Merry's immediate assumption about his lack of empathy, Ben shook his head.

It didn't matter—in fact, it was safer this way. If

Merry thought he had no feelings, she'd never look deeper for them.

He filtered everything out of his voice but impatience. "Just tell me what Jo said."

Merry pursed her lips, eyes flashing with reluctance. "She was on the phone with someone about getting supplies to reinforce the crossbeams on this stall, so I didn't get much out of her. But she said the stallion will be staying here for a while—and I guess it belongs to a friend of hers?"

Ben perfectly understood the disbelief sharpening Merry's tone. He'd never be able to call anyone who treated an animal this criminally a *friend*.

"That would be me." The deep, gruff drawl came from behind them. Ben pivoted to face the stallion's owner, fists clenching instinctively.

You can't kill him, Ben reminded himself through the red fog clouding his view of a big guy—taller than Ben by at least six inches—with light brown hair and a close-trimmed beard.

"Sam Brennan," the lumberjack lookalike said, holding out a giant paw and flashing a smile that faded when Ben crossed his arms over his chest.

"You're the owner of this horse?" Ben felt his upper lip curling into a snarl, and he couldn't do a thing about it. So long, Ice Man.

Anger surged back to the surface, hot enough to boil his blood. Despite the fact a real fight between them would likely end with a broken nose for Ben, he was savagely tempted to haul off and punch this hulking stranger. So what if Sam Brennan was beefier than prime rib? Ben had grown up a nerdy kid with a knack for sarcasm and an inability to back down—he'd been in more than his share of fights.

Merry's hand on his arm was the only thing that

kept Ben from launching himself at this abusive horse owner. Her touch sent a wave of calm through Ben, allowing him to regain control of his runaway emotions.

Her stare was so intent, he could practically feel it boring into the side of his face, and when he met her gaze, the connection between them crackled with electricity. Then she stepped up to stand shoulder to shoulder with him, and Ben's heart jumped into his throat.

"His name is Java," Sam Brennan said, his brown eyes widening as he glanced from Ben's snarl to Merry's thundercloud of a frown. "And hey, whoa—it's not what you're thinking."

"What I'm thinking," Merry hissed, "is that you brought this poor, mistreated horse here for Ben to fix. And he'll do it—but I will be damned if you ever get your hands on Java again."

That's my fiancée going toe to toe with a mountain man twice her size, was all Ben could think for a long dazzled heartbeat, until Sam Brennan jolted him out of it by throwing his shaggy head back and shouting a big belly laugh up at the barn ceiling.

"Oh, I like you," Brennan declared. "By God, you are your mother's daughter. The younger one, right? Meredith."

Ben couldn't say he cared for the appreciative sweep of Brennan's gaze over Merry's soft, rounded curves and tumbled dark curls. Not that she was dressed for flirtation today, by any means—lately she'd traded the stretchy faux leather leggings she used to wear when he first met her for plain old jeans, and her black T-shirt was baggy and worn thin in spots. Ben was pretty sure that flaky patch on her shoulder was dried spit-up.

Sam Brennan didn't seem put off by any of that, which only made Ben hate him more. He didn't want to respect the guy for being able to see beneath Merry's new-mother exhaustion to the beautiful woman even she'd forgotten existed.

Ben angled his body between Merry and Sam, partly to block the man's view, and partly to keep Merry from being the one who lost her cool and jumped the giant.

"Good, y'all have met." Jo hustled out of the office, her long strides eating up the ground, her face intent and serious. "And Benji, you can see why we called you. What a mess!"

"Don't call me Benji," Ben growled automatically, then frowned in confusion. "And we might have gotten a name or two into the conversation, but I could use an explanation and some background before I start my examination."

Jo's gaze flew to Sam Brennan, and something dark passed over her expression. Sam said nothing, however. Just crossed his muscle-corded arms over his massive chest and waited with an air of silent calm for whatever Jo was about to say.

"Mom, what is this guy doing here?" Merry asked. "The way that horse looks . . ."

"I know." Jo leaned against the stall doorway, close enough to peek inside at the heaving, stamping stallion. "But that's what Sam does. He finds horses that are being neglected and abused, and he rehabilitates them."

That made more sense. Something pinged in Ben's memory. Turning a considering stare on Mr. Mountain Man, he said, "Sam Brennan. You run the biggest horse-rescue operation in Cabell County."

"I am." Sam nodded, his mouth flattening under the shadow of his beard. "For now."

"I'm familiar with your program. But don't you have a large-animal vet on staff?" Ben demanded.

"Used to. She quit. That's why I'm here. Java's . . . a special case. I couldn't trust him to just anyone—not that there are a lot of takers. Turns out most vets aren't willing to work on a vicious, half-crazed stallion who put his last owner in the hospital."

"Ben will do whatever it takes," Merry said with incomprehensible faith. "But how did you know to bring him here? How do you know Mom?"

Sam shot Jo Ellen a sideways glance. "Well, Java isn't the only reason I'm in town. My cousin Penny Little asked me to come down and spend a week with her son, Matt, while she's off on her honeymoon."

Jo Ellen cleared her throat. "That's okay, Sam, no need to cover for me. I've mentioned you to Merry and her sister before." She paused, her eyes focused on Merry's face. "When I told you about how I got my start learning about therapeutic riding and equine-assisted therapy."

Ben saw the moment the light bulb flared bright in Merry's brain. "Sam! With the horse-rescue program! He helped you during rehab."

Holding her head high and her gaze steady, Jo nodded. "That's right. Sam's the best—he's one of the good guys, I promise you."

That had Merry flushing faintly and offering Sam a sheepish smile. "Oh, geez. I'm sorry for the way I yelled at you, before."

Sam shrugged. "No worries. I've had worse, believe me. Now Doc, what do you think? I can't promise you'll get out of this with no broken bones—Java is a wild and woolly one."

Relieved to be called back to his main purpose, Ben allowed everything to drain from his consciousness except for the overriding need to figure out where the animal's pain was coming from and how to make it stop.

"First, a little more context from you," he said briskly, setting his medical kit on the large chest to the left of the stall door. "I understand you acquired the animal very recently, but tell me everything you know about the conditions he's been kept in. The more complete a patient history I have, the more I'll be able to focus my attention on the likely danger areas."

Ben's head was bent over his notebook, all his attention absorbed in organizing his notes and the questions he'd need to ask to be sure and get all the relevant details—so when Merry's slender hand landed on his arm, he was startled. The wink of his grandmother's diamond on her ring finger shot through him like an arrow made of heat and anticipation.

Gripping his elbow with surprising force, Merry tugged until Ben turned to face her. "Ben, wait. I have a bad feeling about this. It sounds really risky."

"This is what I do," he reminded her even as the concerned frown between her drawn brows warmed him down to his core. "That horse needs my help."

"I know." She flinched as Java punctuated her unhappy words with a ferocious snort and another slamming kick to the wall of the stall. "And I know you'll do everything you can to help him. But surely there's a procedure for this kind of thing—I mean, that poor horse is out of his mind with terror. Can't you tranq him or something, just to make him be still?"

"I can't risk a tranquilizer before I have a better idea of his general condition," Ben told her, as gently as he could. She seemed honestly worried, which was a novel enough experience on its own to have Ben's heart racing. "Plus, he's clearly severely malnourished, which could affect the strength of whatever drugs I give him."

Merry ducked her head, dropping her hand away from his arm. Ben immediately missed the pressure of her fingers. "I get it. It's fine, do your thing."

"I'll be careful." That was the most Ben felt he could

safely promise, and it was enough to make Merry meet his eyes. Reading the lingering fear there, Ben risked a small, teasing smile. "Don't worry—you're not going to get rid of me that easily."

Behind them, a short, sharp gasp reminded Ben that they were not, in fact, the only two people in the world—let alone the only two people in the Windy Corner stables. Glancing over his shoulder, he saw Jo Ellen's eyes riveted to her daughter's left hand.

Crap. The timing could be better, Ben knew. This was all happening a little more quickly than he'd anticipated.

"Ah," said Sam Brennan, in his deep, even-tempered drawl. "Looks like congratulations are in order."

"Merry?" asked Jo faintly. "What's going on?"

When Merry was thirteen, she'd been caught shoplifting underwear from Victoria's Secret. Facing her mother's white, tense face across the barn corridor now, Merry felt exactly the way she had when she'd left that pink-and-red-striped dressing room with four bras bunched up under her shirt.

But this was different, she reminded herself forcefully. She wasn't doing anything wrong here—she wasn't acting out like a petulant brat, hoping down deep that the pinch-mouthed, disapproving saleslady would call her father and tell him exactly what Merry had done, and force him to come pick her up.

He'd been working that day, of course. It was long-suffering Ella who'd ridden the bus out to the mall and collected her delinquent baby sister from the bored security guard.

This time, Merry was prepared to stand on her own and defend her choices. But as Ben turned, too, and put his arm around her, Merry got that same shiver that had thrilled her earlier.

She wasn't on her own in this.

"I've asked Merry to be my wife, and she agreed," Ben announced. "Now, can we get back to the business at hand?"

"What? No," Jo sputtered, her jaw going loose with shock. "Merry, is this true?"

The way her mother was looking at Ben's enfolding arm made Merry hyperaware of the way it was draped over her shoulders like a warm, protective shield. Suddenly uncomfortable with the implied intimacy—this wasn't exactly the way to keep Ben from getting any funny ideas about their wedding night!—Merry shrugged it off.

Ben frowned down at her, but she shook her head. "I don't want to start this thing under any false pretenses. That's no way to begin a marriage."

Some unnamed emotion tightened the corners of his eyes, but he shrugged and went back to his notebook as if the outcome of this conversation couldn't matter less to him. "Suit yourself. I've got work to do."

Sam Brennan, who'd been watching this whole exchange with every evidence of interest, jammed his hands in his jeans pockets and sauntered over to lean against the barn wall by the tack box. "I swear, y'all are better than a soap opera. I'm waiting to find out you're actually brother and sister or something."

Still feeling guilty about the way she popped off on him earlier, Merry gave the big guy a smile. "Nothing quite so dramatic. But I obviously do need to have a quick conversation with my mother, if you guys will excuse us."

Sam tipped his head in one of those gentlemanly

nods they must teach Southern boys in school. "Nice to meet you, Merry."

Her gaze slid to Ben, who'd clearly skipped class the day they were handing out manners.

Merry's brand spanking new fiancé had his head down and his hands buried in his beat-up canvas medical bag—he didn't appear to notice or care that she was about to have what promised to be, at best, a super awkward conversation with her mother.

She sighed and rubbed at her neck, feeling the after-effects of emotional whiplash. But then, she'd dealt out some mixed signals of her own, she realized. Gathering herself, she laid a careful hand on her fiancé's shoulder. "I'll see you in a few minutes. Come to the office and say hi to Alex—he'll cry if he misses you."

Ben grunted, refusing to look up at her. "Do me a favor—if your mother talks some sense into you and you decide not to marry me after all, just text me or something."

Stung, Merry backed off, tucking both hands under her arms against the sudden chill in the air. Her cheeks felt hot with embarrassment, and when she snuck a glance at Sam Brennan, he gave her a sympathetic grimace.

Great, even strangers could see how weird and strained things were between Merry and this man she'd agreed to marry.

Maybe this was a bad idea after all.

As if she'd said the words aloud, Ben's head snapped up like a stallion scenting danger on the wind. His sharp gaze pierced her heart. "Hey. I'm sorry. Give Alex a squeeze for me, and tell him I'll see him soon. Okay?"

And just like that, Merry felt the cold knot at the center of her chest melt in a flood of happiness. "I don't care what people say about you," she said, going for teasing and hitting husky instead. "You're not the biggest crank on Sanctuary Island."

Predictably, Ben scowled. "Yes I am."

"Nope. You're sweet as candy. You're the gooey, chewy nougat at the center of a chocolate candy bar."

"If I'm chocolate, I'm the bitter kind," he said grumpily.

"Nope," she told him, her spirits lifting. "You can't fool me anymore with that scowly mask you put on. Like with Java—I thought you didn't care about his suffering, but that's not it at all, is it?"

It was intensely satisfying to watch the dull flush of red darken the tips of his ears. "You're going to be hell on my reputation."

"You care," Merry said relentlessly. "You care a lot."

What had Ben gone through in his life, Merry wondered, to make him think he needed to convince the world he didn't give a crap about anything?

In the stall, Java seemed to have worn himself out a bit. He kicked at the door, but it was half the strength and force of his previous loud protests. Ben glanced at his patient and flexed his long, dexterous fingers.

"I have to be unaffected," he explained. "Horses are prey animals—their instincts make them sensitive to the slightest hint of danger. If I go in there angry and upset, Java will feel threatened . . . and with an animal like this, that could be very dangerous."

"I get it," Merry said around the lump in her throat. "I'm sorry I doubted you."

"I'm sorry you have to talk to your mom about all this by yourself. If you wait, I'll go with you." He grimaced. "But I can't swear I'll be much help. I don't do well with big emotional conversations."

"Oh, I don't know about that. I think you're doing

okay." Merry smiled at the look on Ben's handsome face. Surprised and pleased—it suited him.

Giving an amused Sam Brennan a good-bye wave, Merry marched down the hall to beard her mother in her den, feeling more confident than ever that she was making the right decision.

Maybe a life with Ben wouldn't always be easy or smooth—but it would certainly be interesting.

Chapter Eight

When she entered her mother's office, the first thing Merry's eyes went to was her baby's playpen next to the battered old desk.

Alex lay on his back surrounded by plush toys, kicking his little legs—and as she watched, he gave a mighty wriggle and rolled over onto his stomach. She rushed across the room to get an up-close view of even more kicking, and some funny swimming motions his chubby arms made as they waved through the air.

"Look at my big boy! Did you see that, Mom? He rolled over on his own."

Jo stood up from her desk and leaned over the playpen, a wide smile lighting her face. "What do you know! He'll be crawling before we know it, and then we'll have to watch out."

Jo paused. "Or . . . I suppose not 'we,' but you and Ben will have to watch out."

Merry swallowed. "Mom. I'm sorry you found out like that. I wanted to tell you, but it just happened, literally a few hours ago, and when you called with an emergency . . ."

"No, I get it," Jo said, holding up her hands. "Don't apologize. I was only surprised because . . . well, honestly, I didn't think you and Ben had figured out that you like each other yet."

Merry blinked. "What do you mean?"

Laughing a little, Jo sank back down into the swivel chair behind her desk. "You two have struck sparks off each other since the moment you met—but I was sure you were resisting the attraction."

"Attraction!"

Jo frowned. "Yes," she said slowly. "I . . . aren't you attracted to him? You must be, to have agreed to marry him."

"Well." Merry palmed the back of her neck, not sure at all how to deal with this. "Look, there are lots of reasons people get married—love and romance and . . . attraction. That's not all there is."

Jo, who'd been married and divorced once, and was currently in an on-again, off-again long-term relationship with a man who desperately wanted to marry her, snorted softly. "Believe me, I know. Marriage is complicated. But honey, help me understand. What exactly is going on between you and Ben? I didn't even know you were seeing each other, outside of his barn visits."

"We weren't," Merry admitted, dropping into the rocking chair they'd set up in the corner for when Alex needed soothing during the day. Merry pushed off with her feet and listened for the rhythmic creak of the runners against the hardwood floor. Maybe she was the one who found it soothing. "But we've gotten to know each other a bit, and I think we want the same things for the future. Is it the romance of the ages? Not at all— but I don't want that, and neither does he."

Jo arched a brow. "Are you sure about that?"

"Very." Merry was firm on this point. "I was totally

clear with him. He knows I'm not in love with him, and he's fine with that. And obviously he's not in love with me, either."

Jo had a weird look on her face, like she was suppressing a sneeze. Was she mad? Was she going to try to talk Merry out of it?

But as she filled her mother in on the rest of the details of the marriage negotiation, Merry remembered all the reasons she'd agreed to it in the first place. Riding the surge of confidence that she was doing the right thing, she finished with, "And the bottom line is that I believe Ben will be a good father to Alex. They've had a connection from the very first moment of Alex's life—that has to mean something."

"Maybe," Jo conceded. Worry lines bracketed her mouth. "But Merry, what about your connection with Ben? Because I agree that not every relationship needs to be about attraction and romance—but sweetheart, I want that for you. You deserve that kind of happiness."

Merry shook her head, rocking faster in instinctive denial. "That's not what I'm looking for. In fact, that's part of why I said yes to Ben. After all the men I've been with, all the failed relationships and terrible, stupid choices I've made when I was thinking with my body and my heart and not with my head—Ben is perfect for me. He's safe. Because I've learned my lesson about letting my hormones rule my life. I'm going into this for the right reasons."

"I understand where you're coming from." Jo appeared to be picking her words carefully, like one of the wild horses finding a path through the soft, squishy salt marsh. "And I don't want to imply that you don't know what's best for you and Alex."

"But?" Irritation sparked through Merry's chest.

"But . . . honey, I've seen you with Ben. You didn't

flirt with him in an obvious way, but I always thought you felt more for him than you were letting on."

"Well, I don't. There's nothing there except mutual respect and a shared desire to give Alex the best life possible. And that's good enough for me."

Even as she made her declaration, Merry was aware of a slight tickle of doubt. It was true that ever since giving birth to Alex, Merry's thoughts hadn't exactly been on sex. She'd even wondered if being a mother meant that she was simply over that kind of desire— and heaven knew, Merry was ready to move past that part of her life, which had never brought her anything but grief and pain . . . and Alex.

But in the back of her mind, a quiet voice reminded her of the wash of heat and jangling nerves when she looked at Ben, when their bodies brushed in the confines of his truck, or he bent close to tell her something. The way she felt about Ben wasn't exactly safe. On some level—the deepest, most physical level, Merry did want him.

And Ben hadn't exactly said he didn't care about sex.

He'd said he wouldn't push her. And then he'd challenged her to resist him. Then he'd leaned in, almost close enough for a kiss. And if their lips had touched right then, Merry was honest enough with herself to admit that she would have been lost in a haze of desire. Even now, her mouth tingled, almost aching for the feel of Ben's kiss, and everything low in her body tightened in a rush of lust as sharp and undeniable as it was dangerous.

What if Dr. Ben Fairfax wasn't as safe a choice as he seemed?

"Is this your first rescue exam?"

Ben slanted a glance at Sam Brennan's calm, inquisitive expression. Nothing much seemed to ruffle the guy.

"We don't see a lot of mistreatment of animals on the island," Ben said. "It's too small and close-knit a community."

"Self-selected for horse lovers, too," Sam observed. "Since everyone who lives here either grew up around wild horses or moved here knowing that the island doubles as a horse preserve."

"True." Ben certainly had. The island's warm embrace and protective stance toward the bands of wild horses who roamed its shores had appealed strongly to Ben. He'd needed that, when he first moved here with his grief and his failures still throbbing like open wounds. "I guess it's not like that everywhere in the world."

"Sanctuary Island is the exception to every rule," Sam agreed, with a fond chuckle.

Ben noticed that Sam's deep, resonant voice appeared to calm the stallion. Every time Sam spoke, Java's long ears flicked in his direction. "You seem to know an awful lot about it, for someone who doesn't live here," Ben said, to keep the guy talking while he started his visual exam.

"I mentioned my cousin Penny. She moved here a while ago with her son. I'm sure you've met her—she waits tables at the Firefly Café."

A vague picture of a sweet-faced young woman with masses of soft chestnut hair floated to the forefront of Ben's brain. He pictured her in the sea-green cotton dress that was the waitress uniform at the Firefly Café, and it looked right. Familiar. "Sure," he murmured, most of his brain focused on cataloguing the shivering stallion's many symptoms. "Good pancakes."

Intent on investigating the deep sway of Java's back,

the thick line of his spine pushing up against his hide, Ben moved slowly and carefully into the stall. Java hung his head and shuddered, worn out by his earlier tantrum.

"I'm more of a waffle man, myself," Sam said, as low and soothing as if he understood the part his voice was playing in this exam.

He kept talking, a smooth patter of words Ben tuned out completely—some nonsense about his cousin getting married and how much his nephew had shot up in height over the summer—while Ben immersed himself in the cool, challenging world of diagnostics.

Dull coat, but that could be lack of attention and unwillingness to stand still for a hosing down. Ribs, spine, and hip bones all prominent, indicating malnutrition, but subject is potbellied, pointing to parasitic infection. Tapeworm possible, evidence fungal infection on hooves due to standing in wet, marshy pasture. Result? Deworming protocols necessary, including quarantine during treatment . . .

Ben was so involved in following the clues, he forgot that he was working on a severely traumatized animal that outweighed him by hundreds of pounds. Until the large doors at the end of the barn slid on their rollers and banged open, startling Java out of his exhausted stupor.

Everything seemed to happen in slow motion. The slam of the door had Java jerking his hoof out of Ben's hands. Ben, crouched low to get a close look at the state of the animal's feet, moved to straighten up. But before he could, the hoof he'd been examining hurtled toward his face.

At the last second, he managed to turn his head. Pain exploded through his left temple in a sickening rush, the air all around him torn with screams of equine fury and shouts of warning—then the world went black and silent.

Ben came to as he was being dragged out of the stall, hands hooked under his arms and his heels scraping through loose hay and sawdust. Above him, Sam Brennan's fiercely determined face swam through Ben's field of vision as pounding feet and loud voices pierced the fog of pain clogging his brain.

He blinked, and when he opened his eyes once more, it wasn't Brennan's beard he encountered, but a confusingly upside-down view of Merry's pale cheeks and wide, frightened eyes.

"Ben! You're awake."

"Of course I'm awake," he grumbled, making a concerted effort to lift his head. Not a good idea. Ben let gravity have its way, only realizing his head was cradled in Merry's lap when she pushed tentative fingers through his hair to find the bright, shocking center of pain beside his left eye.

"It's okay, lie still. Mom is calling down to the dock to get an emergency water taxi to take you to Harbor General."

Ben groaned, stomach flopping at the very idea of going out on one of the small powerboats locals used for quick trips back and forth to the mainland. "No, I don't need it. I'm fine."

This time when he moved to sit up, Merry helped him. "You got kicked in the head by a horse! You're not fine."

"It was a glancing blow," Ben told her, blinking to focus his gaze on the circle of people standing around them. "I feel like Dorothy waking up after her dream of Oz. How long was I out?"

"Only a few minutes," Merry admitted. "But you were fully unconscious. You need to go to the hospital." Worry tightened her voice to a thin thread, and Ben felt something warm and precious uncurl in his belly.

"No hospital, no ferry, no water taxi." Ben was as definitive as he could be, considering the fact that he was pretty sure he couldn't stand under his own power yet.

"Why are you being so pigheaded about this?" Merry gave an exasperated huff.

"Oh, Benji specializes in pigheaded," Jo said with a smirk that somehow managed to look fond. "He's never taken a day off since he got to Sanctuary. Rain, snow, hurricane, a bad case of walking pneumonia—nothing stops Dr. Fairfax from making his rounds."

"Somebody has to keep Sanctuary going. It's not like there's a long line of people clamoring for the job. Trust me, the minute we get another vet on the island to take care of the housepets, I'll start taking time off." Ben grimaced, subtly flexing his leg muscles to check how shaky they were. "And don't call me Benji."

"Well, if you won't go to the hospital," Merry said, standing up and dusting herself off, "I'll just have to take care of you."

Ben glanced up at her in alarm. "What, right now?"

She arched a brow and crossed her arms over her chest. "Don't worry, I won't judge you for leaving your porn out or having stacks of empty beer cans around the place. I know it's your bachelor pad."

"Was my bachelor pad," he corrected, just to see the disconcerted smile tip up the corners of her pink mouth. "And I'm not worried about you seeing my house. It's perfectly presentable."

Okay, not the complete truth. Ben was worried—but

he was also not fool enough to pass up this golden opportunity to move his plans forward.

"Then it's settled." Merry sounded a little nervous, but the smile she sent her mother's way didn't show it at all. "Mom, my car is over at Ben's office, and I guess I'll need to pack a quick overnight bag, plus some things for Alex."

Ben let his attention drift while Merry and her mother hashed out the details—who'd drive, how to pick up Merry's car from the vet office, blah blah blah. He studied the other people who'd gathered around to gawk at the spectacle of Dr. Ben Fairfax laid out on his back with the beginnings of what promised to be a truly spectacular black eye.

Sam Brennan raised his brows in a silent acknowledgment of Ben's good luck in landing a woman like Merry. Considering Sam's heroic rescue efforts, and the fact that Merry was currently arguing with her mother about how long she'd be staying at Ben's house, Ben felt magnanimous enough to nod a silent thanks up at the big guy.

Beside him was a tall kid who looked vaguely familiar, like everyone who lived on Sanctuary was familiar even if he'd never bothered to speak to them. From the way the kid looked up at Sam Brennan with hero worship in his eyes, and the similarity in their coloring, Ben deduced that this was the cousin's son Brennan talked about earlier.

And beside the kid was Taylor McNamara, Jo's right-hand helper at the barn. She was watching Brennan's young relative with a naked interest that Ben was pretty sure would humiliate the crap out of her if he held up a mirror.

"Oh, wait. Merry, you and Alex can't go stay at Ben's house!" Jo said suddenly, jolting Ben out of his contemplation. "In all the excitement, I completely forgot. Your sister is coming home tonight!"

Ben's heart sank. There went his plan to use this visit to ease Merry and Alex into living out at his farm. But Merry and her sister were crazy close; he'd seen the wistful look on Merry's face when she got off the phone with Ella. There was no way Merry would want to miss Ella's homecoming.

Damn it. If there was anyone alive who could talk Merry out of this whole modern-marriage-of-convenience caper, it was her big sister.

Ben gritted his teeth and got his feet under him. He set his jaw against the sick, swirling pain in his head and stood up. "No worries. We'll all hang out and welcome Ella and Grady back to the island together. I'll bring the beer."

Merry was there beside him in a flash, her slender arm sliding around his waist and steadying him. When he inhaled, he could smell the clean green-apple scent of her hair. "Careful," she cautioned. "And also, don't be crazy. We can see Ella and Grady tomorrow! You need to go home and rest."

"Maybe Grady could stay with you," Jo suggested, clearly still hung up on the idea of having both her girls under one roof again. Not that Ben could blame her. "That's a best friend's job, right, Ben?"

"No. That's a fiancée's job," Merry said, and relief flooded through Ben. "I know Ella will understand that I can't make it tonight. Tell her I'll talk to her tomorrow?"

Hmm. Maybe Merry didn't want to hear what her sister would have to say about this engagement, either.

Feeling more hopeful than he had in a long time, Ben allowed Merry to help him gather up his medical kit and write out prescriptions for Java's care in a slightly shaky hand.

Merry and Alex were coming home with him. In spite of the ache in his head, nothing had ever felt more right.

Chapter Nine

It took way longer to actually get Ben moving toward home and rest than Merry wanted. First he insisted on being driven back to his office to call in his orders for the antibiotics and ointments he needed for Java's treatment. Then there was the trip to Jo's house to pack Alex's diaper bag, his toy bag, and, oh yeah, a few changes of clothes for Merry.

Now they were finally all strapped into her car and trundling way out to the far end of Shoreline Drive. Her precious baby boy was bundled into his Snap 'N Go car seat behind Ben. Silent, stern-faced, sharp-tongued Ben Fairfax . . . the man she was going to marry.

Nerves prickled at her, but she shoved them down with the ease of many years of practice. She'd made her choice, and there was no point worrying about it now.

If this turned out to be yet another in a long line of huge mistakes, well, Merry would just pack Alex up and hit the road. She'd done it before when she was on her own; she could do it again.

A pang hit her chest at the idea of leaving Sanctuary

Island. She'd been happier here than anywhere she'd ever lived.

But her happiness was nothing compared to keeping Alex safe and giving him what he needed to grow up better than Merry had. And one of the things she hadn't had was two loving parents.

So here she was.

"Turn here," Ben said abruptly, pointing at a roughly carved sign tacked to a pine tree. The words ISLEAWAY FARM were etched and shaded with black lettering, charming and rustic. But that wasn't the only sign.

As Merry slowed the car to accommodate the rocky gravel of the winding driveway, she saw at least five signs warning against trespassing on private property. "Not a big fan of company, are you?" she asked, sneaking a sideways glance at his drawn, tense face.

Looking as if the day had worn him out more than he'd like to admit, Ben tipped his head against the passenger seat's headrest. "I don't mind certain people's company," he allowed grudgingly. "But most of the world is better experienced at a distance . . . not on my front porch. And there are other considerations."

"Like what?" Merry asked, to keep him talking. She didn't want him falling asleep before she could maneuver him out of the car and onto a horizontal surface.

"You'll see in a minute," he replied with a drowsy, secret smile that did strange things to her insides.

In the backseat, Alex started up one of his achingly adorable nonsense conversations that mostly consisted of repeating "Ba!" over and over. Merry couldn't wait for the day when he actually connected what he was saying to a real thought, but she knew he wasn't quite there yet.

Ben, on the other hand, sat bolt upright in his seat

and swiveled to stare into the back of the car. "Is that his first word? Stop the car! We should be recording this!"

"Relax." Merry laughed a little, warmth tingling through her. Ben might not like most of the world, but he sure liked Alex. Not surprising, since her baby boy was practically perfect in every way. But it still made her happy. "He's only four months old! He doesn't know what he's saying, he's just talking."

Cocking his head down, Ben gave her a severe look from under his dark brows. "Maybe most four-month-old children—and in fact, most adults—talk just to hear themselves speak, but Alex is different. He's smart. Look at him! He's trying to communicate with us."

Merry flicked a glance at the rearview mirror. Her smart kid was scowling fiercely, almost growling "Ba!" at his own sock-clad feet as they kicked in the car seat. His arms were outstretched, chubby fingers spread to try and catch the elusive feet waving through the air, without a lot of success.

"What do you think he's trying to say?" she asked Ben, amused.

Ben gave her an irritated snort. "Maybe that his feet are too hot. Here, little man." He reached over the seat back and helped Alex remove his socks. Alex, as if determined to prove Ben right, kicked gleefully and shouted "Ba!" with every evidence of real joy.

"See?" Ben shot her a triumphant look. "Sometimes a man wants his feet bare."

Merry narrowed a mock glare in his direction. "Is this how it's going to be? You two boys ganging up on me?"

As soon as the words were out of her mouth, she wanted to call them back. Ben's connection with Alex was a huge part of the reason she'd said yes to this crazy scheme—she didn't want to do anything, ever, to shake Ben out of that.

Even if there was a tiny, dumb part of her that wished he'd look at her with the same level of intense interest, pride, and love he reserved for Alex, shining from his gray eyes.

But Ben didn't appear to be shaken by Merry's teasing. Instead, a slow, pleased smile creased his handsome face. "Not to worry, Mom. I don't think there's much chance of anyone taking your place in Alex's heart."

Merry, who hadn't worried about that for an instant, smiled back. "Even if I smother him and turn him into a momma's boy?"

Wincing, Ben squeezed his eyes shut. "Not gonna let me forget that anytime soon, are you?"

"Welcome to married life," she told him. "Where anything you say can and will be used against you the next time we fight."

"We won't fight," Ben protested, blinking owlishly. He was starting to drift again, Merry noted with concern. "That's the advantage of spelling everything out rationally and logically before the wedding. No misconceptions or disappointments later on."

Merry hoped that was true, although she couldn't shed the conviction that no amount of logic or rationality would be enough to prevent Ben from disappointing her someday. Everyone did, eventually—it was better to be prepared.

Before she could come up with a response, the car pulled up to a closed gate stretched across the driveway with yet another NO TRESPASSING sign hung on the top rung.

"I'll get it," Ben said, struggling with his seat belt. Which gave Merry plenty of time to roll her eyes, put the car in park, and hop out to deal with the gate herself.

"Not exactly how I pictured this," Ben muttered when Merry got back in the car.

Merry's heartbeat quickened even as she gave him a casual, "No?"

She liked that he'd thought about what it would be like to bring Alex and Merry home with him for the first time.

"I didn't think I'd be nearly blinded by a headache," he griped, then his eyes widened. "Watch out!"

Jerking her attention back to the drive, Merry instinctively wrenched the wheel and slammed on the brakes. The car screeched to a stop, narrowly missing a shocked-looking black-and-white nanny goat.

With an irate bleat, the goat scurried and hopped off the driveway, dainty cloven hooves skittering in the gravel. The goat had only three legs.

Merry blinked. "Is that why you had the gate closed?"

"One of the reasons." Ben sounded resigned as he rolled down his window. "Go on, Missy! She doesn't understand about cars. Sorry."

"No, it's fine," Merry said faintly, nudging the car back into a steady crawl across a wide, grassy yard dotted with tall pine trees. She could barely discern the outline of a house through the tree trunks. "Are there . . . more?"

"Missy's the only goat," Ben said, shifting in his seat. "But there are a few others."

He wasn't kidding. The drive up to the low front porch took less than five minutes, and in that time, at least seven dogs of varying breeds and mobility mobbed the car, barking their heads off. A giant calico cat with a short stub instead of a tail streaked out of sight under the porch steps, and when Merry parked the car, she was sure she caught the distinctive crow of a rooster coming from behind the house. "You have your own zoo!"

Ben stiffened, pausing in the process of getting himself unbuckled. "No cages," he pointed out tersely.

"A free-range zoo," Merry amended, hurrying around the car to help Ben out. He shook her off, though, and instead of arguing, Merry shrugged and bent over the backseat to grab Alex. "He's going to love this. Do you have any sheep? Sheep are his favorite."

There was only silence from Ben. Straightening up with Alex in her arms, Merry looked around to see Ben watching her with surprise brightening his eyes. "What?" she asked, fighting the urge to smooth her hair down. That was a lost cause, and had been for the last four months.

Ben stared hard at her, as if trying to read her thoughts. "You're not . . . weirded out?"

"By what?"

"All this!" Ben flung his arms out to the sides, and had a passel of excited dogs immediately jumping and pawing at his thighs, eager and enthusiastic about greeting their master after his long absence. "It's not exactly normal to have this many pets."

"Not for most people, I guess." Merry gazed around the yard, taking it all in. "But you're a vet. I think it would be weirder if you didn't love animals enough to keep a lot of pets. These guys aren't exactly pets, though, are they?"

Shoving the dogs down and away, Ben surreptitiously held his left hand curled into a loose fist at the right level for Cassiopeia to sniff. The small Doberman mix was the newest addition to his little pack, and she still depended heavily on rituals like the welcome-home scenting to feel comfortable at Isleaway.

"They're not house pets, if that's what you mean," Ben said, deliberately evasive. "I'm gone from home for long stretches of time. It's only practical to give them the run of the property instead of cooping them up in kennels inside."

"That's not what I meant." Merry moved around to the trunk of the car, clearly intending to juggle her squirming infant and his diaper bag while unpacking the rest of their luggage.

Ben shoved her aside as gently and firmly as he could. "Go on up to the porch," he told her. "I'll get the rest of this stuff."

"You're injured!"

"I'm not an invalid," he growled, scowling away the wooziness of leaning over to drag Merry's duffel out of the trunk. "It was a bump on the head, not a pair of broken arms and a severed spinal column."

"Fine, be a big dumb man about it. I'm only think-ing of your health and well-being." Merry dropped the diaper bag on the ground with an exasperated hmph and hitched Alex higher on her shoulder.

Ben watched them march up to the porch, his heart lifting with every step she took. Alex tangled his little Vienna-sausage fingers in the dark brown curls waving over Merry's shoulders, and stared around this loud, chaotic new universe with enormous eyes.

Ben slung the duffel strap across his chest, picked up the diaper bag, and waded through the swarm of furry, wriggling bodies to follow his own personal Florence Nightingale up the porch steps.

"I'm sorry," she said, the instant he stepped foot on the sanded pine boards of the porch floor. "I don't know what possessed me—the spirit of a shrewish, nagging wife, I guess. But I'm over it now, and it won't happen again."

Ben's chest clutched like a fist. "Don't apologize. I was a jerk, that's not your fault. I know you were trying to be helpful." He struggled for a moment, then forced out, "I guess I'm not used to needing help."

Merry, who'd been holding herself rigid and stiff, softened visibly. "I know. You're used to being the one who does the helping."

He felt uncomfortably exposed all of a sudden, as if Merry's low voice had the power to strip away skin, hair, everything external, and leave only raw nerves behind. Ben busied himself with unlocking the front door.

"Like with your menagerie out there," Merry went on, soft and relentless. "When I said they weren't pets, I meant . . . you didn't buy them from a breeder or a pet shop or something, did you?"

Ben shook his head, focusing on keeping his hand from trembling and jiggling the key out of the lock.

"They're rescues, aren't they," Merry murmured. "All of them."

"If you hate the animals, too bad. It's a package deal, they come with the house and the trust fund."

Ben heard the roughness of his own voice and regretted it as soon as he saw the way Merry's eyes widened. "I never said I hated them. Who could hate a bunch of rescue animals?"

"My ex-wife," Ben said, watching Merry closely. "She said I had a tendency to bring home strays—and at first, she liked it. Thought it was sweet or something, evidence of my inner goodness. But after a while, it got old."

As he'd hoped, Merry zeroed in on the key piece of new information. "Ex-wife? You've been married before?"

"Years ago," Ben confirmed. No point keeping it a

secret; it was bound to come up eventually, and it would seem odd if he'd never mentioned Ashley. "Nothing you need to worry about."

"I'm not worried," Merry denied, with a very worried frown wrinkling her brow. "I just . . . didn't know you'd been married before. It seems like the kind of thing you should know about your fiancé."

"That's why I'm mentioning it." Ben got the door open—time to oil that ancient lock again—and led Merry into the dark foyer. "Careful on the floors—I waxed the hardwood last week, and they're still a little slippery."

"Oh my gosh," Merry said as she lifted her gaze to the rainbow of light pouring in through the stained-glass window. "Ben. This place is . . ."

"My pride and joy." He laughed, but he was serious. "I moved to Sanctuary after the divorce, to get away from all the memories. And to escape my parents' embarrassingly unsubtle attempts to marry me off to one of the daughters of someone else in the tennis and country club set."

"I've never played tennis," Merry said faintly, her gaze moving over the furniture Ben had spent happy, solitary hours picking out from local craftsmen's shops.

"You haven't missed anything," Ben told her. "It's dull. I came here because I needed a change. I wanted a different kind of life than Ashley and I had in Richmond. And Sanctuary couldn't be more different if it were on another planet."

"Ashley," Merry murmured, then appeared to shake herself free of something. She turned bright, determined eyes on him, and Ben swallowed hard against the surge of joy it gave him to see her standing in his home. His private sanctuary.

"I'm glad you're here," he told her. It felt like the words were ripped from him against his will.

She flushed a pretty pink and tightened her hold on Alex, who seemed to have decided it would be fun to launch himself out of her arms in a backward swan dive. "Are you tired? You should lie down and rest. Alex and I will just . . . hang out here until it's time to wake you up and make sure you haven't lapsed into a coma."

Frustrated, Alex chose that moment to open his mouth and loose an earsplitting wail. Despite himself, Ben raised his brows in shock.

"That's some impressive lung capacity, right there."

Merry gave a rueful laugh. "Yeah, I think he's got a future as an opera singer, if he wants it. Alex, baby, come on. You're fine." She made a face in Ben's direction. "I'm sorry, it's been a couple of hours since he ate, he's probably hungry."

The crying continued unabated, Merry's cheeks going redder and redder. And Ben realized with a start that Alex must still be breast-feeding. Merry probably wanted privacy to feed her child.

"Oh! Let me give you the fifty-cent tour," he rapped out, striding off down the hall. He waved to his left. "Kitchen! On the right, dining room. And down here," he continued as he opened the last door on the left, "are the bedrooms."

He put her duffel and the bulging diaper bag at the end of the queen-sized guest-room bed. Giving the room a cursory inspection, Ben wondered if she could tell she was the first person who'd ever stayed in it.

"It's beautiful," Merry said, sounding as enchanted as anyone could with an armful of screaming infant. "Who decorated this place for you?"

Now it was Ben's turn to feel his cheeks burn. "No one."

Pausing in the act of reaching to finger the velvety nap of the wine-colored throw blanket folded over the foot of the bed, Merry shot him a surprised glance. "You did this yourself?"

He shrugged. "I like to support local artisans. There's a lady who weaves her own cloth up on Honeysuckle Ridge, and the guy who made all the furniture in here lives just down the road in one of the seaside cottages."

Merry stared at him over the head of her baby, who was snuffling into her neck like he might find a hidden nipple behind her ear. "I've known you for half a year. You've been on this island for, what? Seven years. But no one here knows you at all, do they? Least of all me."

Chapter Ten

As always, the act of feeding Alex did at least as much to calm her as it did to stop his tears.

The intense feeling of closeness, the private, intimate connection nourished something deep in Merry's soul as surely as it fed Alex his dinner. She loved the way he'd close his dimpled fist around the bunched-up cotton of her T-shirt, and the way his cloudy blue eyes would flutter shut in sleepy ecstasy. There was nothing on the planet softer than the fine-grained silk of Alex's rosy cheeks, or the wisp of black hair on his head.

Merry absently combed that hair into a messy faux-hawk feathering up from the center of his scalp and thought about what she'd gotten them into.

On paper, Ben Fairfax was quite the catch. Well educated, successful, rich, good with kids and animals, inconveniently hot, and also, apparently, a talented interior decorator.

So why was she having second thoughts?

This whole idea had felt so much safer and easier when she could think of Ben as that cranky, grumpy misanthrope who uncharacteristically adored her son.

Now that she was at his home—which would be their home if she went through with this, a thought that made her shiver hard enough to nearly dislodge Alex from his lazy sucking—Ben was acquiring layers. Nuance.

And Merry couldn't help but be intrigued.

Which was a bad sign. If her past with men was any indication, Merry being intrigued by Ben equaled Ben hiding some hideous secret, like a pierced penis, a current girlfriend, or the fact that he lived with his mother.

Merry knew herself well enough to know that she could *not* pick 'em. But Ben was supposed to be different. He was supposed to be the smart choice. Rational. Safe.

But how safe could he be when Merry's stupid, stupid body went up in flames whenever he was nearby?

As if Ben could sense the coldness of Merry's feet, a sudden knock sounded on the guest room door.

"Figured Alex wasn't the only one who might be hungry, so I heated up some soup. You want?"

Merry glanced down to check on Alex's progress with lunch, and found his head lolling back on his little neck, his pink mouth pursed in slumber. Moving carefully to keep from waking him, Merry stood up from the all-too-comfortable rocking chair in the corner and cracked the door enough to peer out.

"Yes, please," she whispered. "Give me a second, I'll be right out."

"Do you want me to take him?" Ben asked. "I promise I'll avert my eyes."

After four months of practice, Merry was adept at juggling a sleeping baby while twisting her clothes back to decency. But the hopeful expression on Ben's face had her twitching the door open wide enough to pass the limp bundle of Alex's blanket-swaddled body into Ben's waiting embrace.

Ben had his eyes closed, like the Southern gentleman he hid so well, most of the time. And Merry wondered if he'd expected her to reciprocate and not watch him, because when he felt the weight of Alex in his arms, the soft smile that curved his mouth was so private, so real. Merry was ninety-five percent sure Ben would be embarrassed if she knew he'd seen it.

But she couldn't help but be glad as she shut the door and pulled her bra and shirt back into place. Every time she started to question her decision, Ben's honest, loving reaction to her son shored up her resolve.

For a new mom who'd spent a good portion of the past four months feeling insecure and defensive about her mothering skills and her status as the person best able to care for her baby, Merry was surprisingly okay with letting Ben hold Alex.

She paused for a moment, arrested by the realization that on a deep level, she trusted that even if she wasn't safe from sizzling chemistry and aching desire for her fiancé, her son *was* safe with Ben.

It was as if a weight she'd been lugging around since before Alex was even born rolled off her shoulders and disintegrated.

Taking advantage of the few minutes of privacy, Merry checked out the adorable en suite bathroom, decorated all in shades of navy and cream with a luxuriously deep bathtub and separate shower stall. She couldn't wait to take a swim in that tub, to sink neck-deep in fragrant bubbles and relax with a juicy romance novel, and heck, while she was fantasizing, how about a box of chocolate truffles?

Merry unpacked quickly, piling clothes on top of the dresser rather than opening and poking through the drawers the way she wanted to. By the time she'd settled them in a little and taken a guilty, illicit moment to run a comb through her messy curls—why did she bother? In the face of Ben's perfect home and good manners, and the knowledge of his high-society background, Merry knew neater hair wasn't enough to make her fit in—it had been ten minutes since Ben knocked on the guest-room door.

She found her way back down the hallway to the kitchen, where a pot of what smelled like beef and vegetable soup steamed gently on a front burner. The stovetop was off, but the soup was still warm and there were a couple of bowls set out, waiting. But no Ben.

Not wanting to call for him and risk waking Alex, Merry wandered through the empty rooms of Ben's beautiful home. There was no upstairs, even though it looked like a two-story house from the outside, and when she found the living room, she realized exactly why. The ceiling soared high overhead, opening the room to a view that stopped her dead in her tracks to blink and stare.

The entire back wall of Ben's house was clear, sparking glass, a panoramic picture window that looked out onto a sweeping view of the ocean. The pine trees that crowded the front of the house and the driveway framed the window, which showed how the cabin had been perched just so, at the edge of a rise looking out over the endless expanse of blue-gray water. Afternoon sunlight sparkled on the waves, and Merry caught her breath as she imagined what a sunrise must look like from the wooden deck.

Merry fought down a spurt of panic. It couldn't be more different from her mother's ramshackle old family home, full of quirks and squeaky floorboards and tatty curtains. And Ben's house was certainly nothing like the succession of small, grotty apartments Merry had shared with her string of bad boyfriends back in D.C.

This place was gorgeous. Every detail had been chosen by a loving hand. Even the plump, overstuffed pillows nestled in the corners of the brown leather couch whispered about good taste and sophisticated style.

And here she was. Merry Preston, whose idea of style had always run more to punk-rock T-shirts and jackets held closed with safety pins. She didn't belong here.

Breathing fast and shallow, Merry quickened her steps in search of Ben and Alex. She was almost running by the time she retraced her steps down the hall to the bedroom where she'd noticed a closed door across from the guest room.

She knocked first, not wanting to walk in on Ben in a private moment, but the need to find her baby and . . . and . . . she didn't even know what. Leave this lovely place before she contaminated it with her bad hair, cheap jeans, and makeupless face? That need overwhelmed every other consideration.

Shoving the door open, Merry scanned the bright, airy room. Slightly more spacious than the guest room, it was obviously the master bedroom. A low, wide bed with cleanly modern lines dominated the center of the room, and on the bed lay Ben Fairfax, fast asleep and clasping a drooling Alex to his broad chest.

Merry's racing heart slowed as if it had been dipped in sweet, thick honey. Ben was sprawled out on the mattress fully clothed—he hadn't even managed to take off his shoes before he conked out. But he had managed to curl his strong arms in a loose, protective circle around Alex—who was in one of his favorite, and most hilarious sleep positions, facedown and tiny rump stuck up in the air.

The sight of the two of them together was enough to make a stronger woman than Merry go weak in the knees and gooey in the midsection. Merry decided she could be forgiven for the way every single thought other than "Awwww!" immediately fled her mind.

Looking at their peaceful faces, Merry felt the tidal pull of endless days and nights of interrupted sleep. She edged closer to the bed, drawn as if by the gravitational force of an entire planet, contained in the tiny form of her son and the much larger, more muscular body of Alex's living mattress.

The way her blood raced and her breath caught at the unquestionably gorgeous planes and angles of Ben's slumbering form gave Merry a moment of instinctive fear. Goodness, how she wanted him—and how afraid that made her.

But Ben cared about Alex. He was solid, strong, dependable—in short, he was different from the losers she'd been with before. He was no immature, insecure boy strutting around and puffing out his chest to prove his masculinity.

No, what Merry saw as she gazed down at the bed was her baby in the secure arms of a real man.

And as she smothered a yawn, Merry felt suddenly sure of exactly where she belonged.

Ben surfaced from sleep as if he were swimming up from the depths of the ocean, a slow rush of light and consciousness breaking through the comforting darkness behind his closed eyelids.

"Hey. Come on, open your eyes. I need to check your pupils," a husky female voice whispered directly into his ear.

Merry. He'd know her voice anywhere, in a crowded room in the dead of night—much less in his own bed with late afternoon sun slanting through the open blinds.

Disoriented, Ben blinked. Merry. In his bed.

Turning his head on the pillow, he was confronted by

a vision from fantasy. Merry was stretched out on top of the white hand-stitched coverlet, her entire body mere inches from Ben's side as she propped herself up with her head on her hand and leaned slightly over him.

Was he still asleep? This would be one of his better dreams.

"Merry," Ben whispered, part of him afraid even saying her name would break the spell and Merry would wink out of existence like a blown-out candle.

But she didn't disappear. She leaned closer, the fresh apple scent of her enveloping him in intoxicating heat.

Lost in the dream world, Ben reached up and threaded his fingers through the silken fall of her hair to wrap his hand around her nape. Her eyes went wide in the instant before he tugged lightly but firmly to bring her lips down to his.

Chapter Eleven

Her mouth was parted on a gasp, and Ben took advantage of the chance to deepen the kiss. She tasted better than she ever had in any of his dreams before—sweet and clear, but with a mysterious hint of dark spice that had him chasing the flavor with his tongue.

For a heart-stopping moment, Merry was rigid against him, but when Ben stroked her sensitive neck with the tips of his fingers and tipped his head to taste her more fully, she made a soft moan in the back of her throat. As she melted into the kiss, Ben reveled in the velvet of her mouth and the deep, drugging intensity of finally getting what he'd wanted for months.

His body awoke in a roar of heat, passion igniting and threatening to burn him from the inside out. Ben tightened his fingers in Merry's hair and she made a noise that had him hardening in a breathless rush.

He tugged her closer, every inch of his body aching to press her full length against him, but Merry resisted, continuing to hold herself carefully above him with her hands propped on the bed by his shoulders.

It almost hurt to break the kiss, but Ben's brain was

coming back online, rebooting much more slowly than his tight, throbbing body, and with the dawning of awareness came the knowledge that he'd already broken his promise not to push Merry for sex.

Not that she'd exactly run screaming from the room when he kissed her.

Relaxing back into the pillow, Ben fought to catch his breath as he stared up at Merry's flushed cheeks and glittering eyes. The deep hunger in her gaze knocked him sideways, rewriting everything he thought he knew about his relationship with Merry Preston.

"What's going on?" he rasped, half hoping she'd answer with another kiss.

Instead, worry darkened her searching eyes to deep midnight blue. "You don't remember? That doesn't seem like a good sign. You were kicked in the head by Sam Brennan's latest rescue project."

"And you came home with me to make sure I didn't fall into a coma and die," Ben finished impatiently. "Mission accomplished, but that's not what I was asking about. I kissed you. Should I apologize for it?"

Merry's pretty pink blush darkened to crimson. "No apologies necessary. Let's just chalk it up to the stress of the day and the weirdness of waking up all on top of each other like a pile of puppies."

The only thing that could've distracted Ben from taking advantage of the fact that he now knew Merry wanted him back was the realization of exactly why she'd pulled away. Ben stared down at the warm weight nestled against his side.

"Holy crap. Alex." Ben had been making out while the kid slept right beside him. He could only thank the good Lord that Ben had woken fully when he did, or poor Alex might've gotten a crash course in the facts of life a good fifteen years early.

Luckily, the realization that there was an infant snuggled between Ben and the woman he wanted more than he'd ever wanted anything was more effective at dousing desire than a cold shower.

Twisting onto his side, Ben carefully rested his hand on the impossibly small, delicate back of the baby snuffling into the front of his shirt. And for an odd, embarrassing moment, he once again had that disorienting sense of wandering into a waking dream.

Merry wasn't the only thing he wanted. The chance to be a father, to be there for Alex the way he'd never be able to for . . .

"He's fine," Merry said, still blushing. "I didn't want to wake him or smoosh him, but I never forgot he was there."

"I did," he said gruffly, guilt kicking him in the gut. "I am sorry—that wasn't the way I intended our first kiss to go. But to be completely honest . . . I can't regret it."

He snuck a look at her, frowning at the worried crinkle between her eyebrows. But when Merry caught his glance, she gave him a slight smile. "Our first kiss. And it happened mere hours after I swore I wouldn't sleep with you."

"We already slept together," Ben pointed out logically. "And it was awesome. In fact, do we have to get up?" He craned his neck to peer at the old-fashioned round alarm clock sitting on his carved bedside table.

Beside him, Merry shook her head, and he was thrilled to see that the lines of worry had been wiped smooth in favor of a real smile. "No, are you crazy! Whatever you do, don't get up. First rule of parenting: never wake a sleeping baby."

Trying not to laugh and jar Alex, Ben snorted softly. "Guess I've got a lot to learn about kids."

"I'm not fretting about that," Merry said, but something in her tone had him darting a wary look in her direction.

"Tell me what you're fretting about." Whatever it was, he'd think of a way around it. Ben studied the way her dark curls spilled over the white cotton pillowcases, the easy curve of her waist and the tilt of her head as she tucked a hand beneath her cheek and met his gaze.

"Tons of things," she said frankly. "I'd be nuts if I had no qualms. Marriage is a big step—and, let's face it, the women in my family don't have the greatest track records with commitment."

"Ella seems pretty happy," Ben pointed out, fighting down a chill of apprehension.

"But she and Grady aren't married!"

"They've been together a while now, though. And I don't know for sure so this isn't me breaking the bro code, but I wouldn't be too surprised if Grady pops the question before much longer."

Merry gave a delighted wriggle against the pillow. "Your best friend is totally gone on my big sister. And vice versa."

"So it's not marriage as an institution that you're afraid of," Ben deduced. "It's marriage and me."

"It's marriage and *me*," Merry corrected him, tilting her head. "I've made some truly terrible decisions when it comes to men, in the past."

Ben held his breath. Was this the right moment to ask about Alex's father? Since her arrival on the island, Merry had been vague and uncommunicative about the identity of the man who'd fathered her baby. All she'd say was that he was out of the picture, by his own choice, and that she had no intention of going back to him even to ask for help.

Not that she'd need to worry about that now.

"Our marriage is a smart decision," Ben reminded her firmly. "It's based on mutual respect and clearly defined, shared goals, not nebulous nonsense like emotions or hormones."

He watched as the line of her spine melted further into relaxation on the bed. He'd obviously been right to stress the lack of feelings rather than delving into her past. She wasn't ready to know how he felt. Maybe she never would be, and he could live with that.

"Mutual respect," she murmured. "I like that. You're a good man, Ben Fairfax, and you're not going to fool me into thinking you're not, ever again."

"Don't get carried away. I'm acting out of enlightened self-interest, not some kind of charitable impulse."

Backlit by the rosy glow of the setting sun pouring in the window, Merry was a dark silhouette haloed in pink light. He could barely make out her expression, but he thought she pressed her lips together.

"I hope that's true," she said carefully. "Alex and I . . . we can't be another pair of strays you take in, like your three-legged goats and cats with no tails. I'm done being rescued—I'm making this choice with a clear mind and heart, not out of desperation."

The comparison lanced through him like a scalpel, deadly sharp and painful in its accuracy. He couldn't deny that his savior complex was playing a part in this, but . . . "I'll say it again," Ben insisted, his voice oddly hoarse. "Respect. You have mine. And, for the record, I feel like I'm the one who should be thanking you. You're saving me from countless haranguing phone calls with my mother nagging me to get remarried and give her a grandchild."

"You said you can't have kids," Merry said slowly. "So why would your mother still be asking you about it? I mean, didn't you ever tell her why your previous marriage ended?"

The quiet and stillness of the bedroom, the lingering intimacy of the kiss combined with the closeness of sharing a pillow and whispering over the head of a slumbering baby—the walls surrounding Ben's memories shimmered and dissipated as if they'd been built from gossamer threads instead of rocks.

It was only fair, he realized. If he wanted to know more about Merry's past—and he definitely did, if only to satisfy his anal-retentive inner physician about the completeness of Alex's medical records—then Ben would have to be willing to tell her about himself. Give a little to get a little. And if he could divert Merry's attention to less painful secrets at the same time, so much the better.

But somehow, opening up to her still felt as tricky as shucking an oyster from its shell, and about twice as dangerous.

"If you're asking for more details on my marriage to Ashley, I'm willing to share them, within reason. Some things are private, though, and Ashley is a good person. She doesn't deserve to have our marriage rehashed and dissected behind her back."

Ben saw the immediate spark of interest in Merry's bright eyes. "So it was an amicable divorce. That's good, I'm glad—and I definitely don't want you to tell me anything that makes you uncomfortable. But I admit I'm curious about her. If she's such a good person, why aren't you still with her?"

And there it was. The tough question, the one Ben most wanted to avoid . . . but it was the only question that mattered, when it came to his past.

Grief swelled in his throat, thick and sudden, and

Ben struggled to choke it down. He got it under control by concentrating on the warm, twitching lump of Alex's small body beside him on the bed.

"I'm sorry." When he opened his eyes, Merry was leaning up over him once more, the same worry creasing her brow as when she'd checked him for signs of concussion. "I shouldn't have asked. Tell me when you're ready. Or never! It's none of my business."

Ben ignored the hoarse catch in his voice when he answered, "If not yours, then whose? Don't apologize, it's not your fault. It's just hard to talk about, even all these years later."

The worry in Merry's eyes shifted, turned inward in a way Ben didn't understand. "I get it," she said quietly. "There are some people, some things in life that you never get over. You can move on, and commit to new things, and you can mean it—but part of you will always belong to the past."

Before Ben could disagree, Alex stirred and kicked, waking from his long nap with a smacking of lips and a big yawn.

"Here, I'll take him," Merry said, lifting Alex into her arms. Relief at avoiding any more revelations about his past and the brush of her hands against Ben's chest made him long to grab her wrist and tumble her back down into the nest of quilt and pillows. But he'd already gotten away with enough today. He wouldn't push his luck.

At the bedroom door, Merry paused and turned to look back at Ben. "I want you to know that it's okay, and we don't need to talk about this again. I think I understand enough that your proposal makes a little more sense."

Aching with unspent desire, Ben hauled himself upright and frowned in the direction of the doorway. "What, exactly, do you think you understand?"

Merry gave him a smile as bittersweet as dark chocolate. "You want a marriage without emotions, and you're sure you'll never fall in love again, because you're still in love with your ex-wife."

Ben opened his mouth, a denial on the tip of his tongue—but he hesitated. What was so bad about the solution Merry had come up with for why Ben proposed? If it made sense to her and made her more comfortable, he'd be an idiot to contradict it.

God knew, he wasn't eager to explain the real reasons behind the wreck of his marriage to Ashley.

On the bed, Ben's jaw dropped, and Merry's heart surged into her throat. Was something else going on? But no, he closed his mouth on whatever he'd been about to say, and Merry's heart thumped back down into her chest where it belonged.

Merry glanced over her shoulder at the hallway. Escape beckoned. Raw and twitchy, all she wanted was to flee the intimacy of this moment and the enormous, oxygen-sucking overwhelmingness of Ben's presence.

Just for a minute. That was all she needed to shore up her defenses and catch a breath that didn't smell like Ben's complicated aroma of peppermint soap and fresh-cut pine.

Merry slipped into the hall, expecting Ben to call her back, half dreading it and half hoping for it—but he didn't.

Battling down a strange swoop of disappointment, Merry slipped into the guest bedroom and closed the door behind her. She settled in the rocking chair she was already starting to think of as the Nursing Station and got Alex going on his evening snack.

As Alex buttoned up his eyes and concentrated on doing his thing, Merry felt a buzz in her back jeans pocket. Contorting herself to retrieve her cell phone, she grinned to see a text from her sister.

Ella hadn't sent a message in words. Instead, she'd snapped a picture with her phone's camera and forwarded it, along with a series of seven excited exclamation points.

Looked like Ella had really and truly learned to stop taking life so seriously and to slow down enough to enjoy it now and then. Merry smiled down at the tiny image of her sister's dimpled cheek pressed close to the rugged jaw of her new love, ex-search-and-rescue guy Grady Wilkes. If she squinted, Merry could make out the windswept coastline and Sanctuary Island's ramshackle dock, unofficially nicknamed Summer Harbor.

Suddenly consumed with the need to talk to Ella, Merry hit number one on her speed-dial contact list before she could think too hard about the fact that she'd insisted on spending the night at Ben's partly to avoid dealing with her older sister's inevitable shock and disappointment with the whole quickie-marriage thing.

Every ring of the phone ratcheted up Merry's tension until finally, Ella answered with a breathless, "We're almost home! Are you coming to pick us up?"

Swallowing down a surge of emotion, Merry said, "No, sorry. Mom will be there, though, I'm sure."

She could hear Ella's frown over the crackly connection and the static of the ocean breeze. "You're sure. Don't you know? Aren't you at Windy Corner with Mom? What's going on?"

At that instantaneous note of concern and fierce protectiveness in Ella's voice, Merry couldn't help but smile. This was why she loved her big sister. Yes, Ella meddled, and yes, for years she'd been sure she could run Merry's life better than Merry did. But the fact was, Ella hadn't been completely wrong about that . . . and more importantly, when Merry was in trouble, there was no one on earth she could depend on more than Ella.

Merry knew, deep in her bones, as if it were written into their shared DNA, that Ella would always be there for her. No matter what.

That made it easier to say, "I left Mom's house. I'm at Ben's. We're getting married."

Closing her eyes, Merry pictured the shock on her sister's face. Ella wheezed out, "Good Lord, Merry. I leave you alone for a few months and you go completely nuts!"

"This is not me being nutty," Merry said. "At least, I don't think so. I actually think I might be making the sanest decision I've ever made in my life."

And then it all came spilling out, the words flowing as easily as they used to when Merry would get home from school, bursting to tell someone about her day— and there was fifteen-year-old Ella, making Merry's afternoon snack and waiting to hear all about it.

"So I said yes," Merry concluded, a little winded by the outpouring of explanations and background, justifications and reasoning. She was silent for a second, then said, "You think this is a terrible idea, don't you?"

"That depends," Ella said slowly. "Ben is a good guy underneath all the sarcasm and gruffness—I'll never forget how hard he fought for you and Alex, the night he was born. But Merry, all this stuff about keeping emotions out of it . . . do you honestly think you can do that? You're one of the most emotional people I know."

"Which has gotten me into every scrap of trouble I've had in my life," Merry pointed out, with an apologetic snuggle of her sleepy baby. *Even if it was worth it sometimes,* she told him silently.

"That's certainly true." Ella sounded thoughtful. The

fact that she wasn't yelling was a pretty big relief to Merry—Ella tended to react to worry and fear by attacking the problem, which sometimes translated to attacking the person having the problem. But Ella seemed to be actually considering the possibilities of this marriage, and a shiver ran like an electric current through Merry's whole body.

"Oh my gosh," she said numbly. "You're not going to talk me out of this, are you?"

"Is that what you were hoping for?" Ella asked. "Sorry to disappoint you, hon. But the days of me making decisions for you are over. I'm trying to turn over a new leaf here. So I'm not going to lock you up to keep you from marrying Ben, if that's what you want to do."

Surprise stole all the strength from Merry's body. Sagging back against the high, solid Nursing Station chair, Merry realized that until this moment, the engagement hadn't felt truly real to her.

Ashamed, Merry grimaced. "In some secret corner of my brain, I think I've been holding my breath, waiting for you to show up as the Voice of Reason and put a stop to the whole thing."

"That sounds like you don't want to go through with it," Ella replied, caution clear in her voice.

"No—I mean, I'm scared. It's a big step, and most women would probably be thrown if they found out that the man they're about to marry is still hung up on someone else."

Even saying the words gave her a pang she didn't understand.

"But that shouldn't bother you," Ella said, all rationality and logic. "Since you're not in love with Ben. Right?"

"Right." Merry bit her lip at how uncertain she

sounded. "That's not what this is about," she said more strongly, to remind herself as much as to convince Ella.

"Okay, then. Look, I'm not going to make this decision for you. But if you want my advice, here it is: listen to your heart. You have the best, biggest, most generous heart of anyone I know."

In the background of the call, Merry heard Grady's rough, playful "Hey!"

"Not counting you, dummy," Ella said, partially covering the speaker, but Merry could still hear her.

"Listen to my heart?" Merry huffed out a laugh, feeling as if the breath had been knocked out of her. "Boy, you *have* changed."

"I know I haven't always been the world's biggest advocate for it, but recently I've learned that life is more than a series of smart moves. Sometimes the smartest thing you can do is something a little risky and crazy. So what's your heart telling you, Merry?"

Merry swallowed hard, trying to listen for her heart over the soft, homey sounds of Alex's mouth working, the creak of the rocking chair, and the ocean breeze in the background of the phone call.

She sat and rocked and stared down at her son's tiny, round-cheeked face, and felt certainty drop over her shoulders like a cozy blanket.

"I'm marrying Ben Fairfax." It wasn't the first time Merry had said it out loud, but it might have been the first time she actually believed the words. "I think it's the smart move—and my heart . . ."

"Yeah?" Ella sounded choked up, which instantly got Merry's tear ducts working overtime.

"It's confusing," Merry gasped. "Because my heart has steered me wrong so many times. But this time, I don't know. For once, my head and my heart seem to be in agreement. Not sure what that means."

"Oh, honey," Ella said, sniffling. "I think it means my baby sister is about to be a bride! You have to let Mom and me help plan the wedding."

As Ella launched into planning mode, Merry leaned her head against the high back of the rocking chair, grinned up at the ceiling, and tried not to think about the fact that the decision to marry Ben was a three-way tie between her mind, her heart . . . and her willful, unpredictable body.

Chapter Twelve

Right up until the moment Sheriff Shepard pounced, everything was going perfectly.

Taylor was nothing if not a veteran at planning ways to get into trouble, and having a willing accomplice for the first time since her childhood best friend was snatched away by his overprotective dick of a dad pushed Taylor to new heights of creativity.

She hadn't stopped at enticing Matt Little out to her favorite spot on the island after curfew . . . she'd also snitched a three-quarters full bottle of rum from her dad's liquor cabinet.

Matt had resisted at first. "Come on," he'd said, leaning back on his hands in the gritty sand of Heartbreak Cove's narrow strip of beach. "Do we really need alcohol to have a good time?"

With his jeans rolled up to his shins and his strong-boned bare feet burrowing into the wet sand and gently lapping waves, Matt looked like the poster boy for wholesome living. Trying to ignore the squiggle of doubt in her own belly, Taylor shrugged and flopped down next to him before uncapping the rum.

"You don't have to. But I'm having some. After today, I could use a little help relaxing."

There, that was a pretty good cue. Casting Matt a surreptitious glance from the corner of her eye to see if he'd caught her drift, Taylor inhaled and swallowed at the same time. Gasping a cough at the sting of rum down her throat, she doubled over her raised knees, eyes watering.

Great. How many ways could she embarrass herself in front of this guy? But Matt didn't laugh and pound her on the back, or swipe the rum with a superior grin, the way Caleb might have. Instead, he laid one long-fingered hand gently over her spine and leaned closer with a concerned frown. "Hey, slow down. We're already breaking curfew, right? So there's no rush. We've got all night."

He didn't mean anything by it, probably, but the words still sent a hot shiver spreading out from that single point of contact between his palm and her back. His touch seemed to burn through the thin cotton of her tank top. Clearing her throat, Taylor breathed in and out for a slow minute, unwilling to sit up straight and risk Matt dropping his hand. But eventually he sat back anyway, so she did, too.

Doing her best to be nonchalant, Taylor took another, slightly smaller and more cautious sip, rigidly controlling her facial muscles against the automatic grimace. Despite her reputation, she'd never really gotten used to the harsh burn of straight liquor. "Fine, don't have any," she said, cradling the bottle to her chest as if it were precious. "More for me."

Matt sighed, audible even over the whisper of the waves at their feet. "Hand it over."

Cheeks burning with triumph, Taylor passed him the bottle. Electricity arced between them when their fingers brushed, and she imagined she could see white-blue sparks flying. The night was cool, at least sitting here in the breeze off the water, and for the first time all day, Taylor felt the twisty knot of emotion in her chest uncoil.

"I wasn't even sure you'd be able to come out to-night," she said, vividly aware of the warmth of his lean, denim-clad thigh mere inches from her bare legs.

"My mom and Dylan are still on their honeymoon."

"Does that freak you out?"

Matt made a face. "If I think about it too much, it might. But no, I mean—I'm happy for her. She deserves to be happy."

"Where's your dad? Do you see him often?" As someone who'd lost a parent to cancer, Taylor was half fascinated, half shocked by families that split up on purpose.

Ducking his head made a shadow fall across Matt's handsome face. "Nah. We talk on the phone sometimes, but I know my mom doesn't like it. She gets sad or something—tense—whenever she knows I called him."

"So don't tell her," Taylor suggested, digging her feet into the sand beside Matt's.

The look he shot her was full of wry amusement, and the way his mouth twisted made her want to lean over and kiss that smirk right off his face. "You're going to be a bad influence. I can tell."

That's right. And more fun than going to Bible study with stupid Dakota Coles and her self-righteous band of do-gooders. Snagging the rum bottle from Matt's re-laxed hand, Taylor lifted it to her lips. "What was your first clue?" she murmured against the glass rim.

Something hot and dangerous flashed through Matt's eyes like heat lightning stitching across the sky, and Taylor's heart slammed against her ribs.

Without breaking her stare, Taylor tipped her head back and swallowed another sip of rum. It went down easier every time, and she was starting to feel light-headed and a little dizzy.

Although that could just be the way Matt was looking at her, and the catch in her breath when he bent his head toward hers . . .

And of course, that was the exact moment that a pair of high beams flooded over them like a cartoon spotlight.

Hoping against hope that her luck would hold out and it would be Merry again, on another midnight lullaby tour of the island, Taylor squinted into the bright headlights as the driver's side door opened.

"Do you kids know you're trespassing?" asked a woman's voice . . . but it definitely wasn't Merry. In a single stomach-sinking instant, Taylor identified the voice as belonging to Sheriff Andie Shepard.

"Run!" Taylor dropped the bottle and scrambled to her feet and lit out for the line of trees at the edge of the salt marsh bordering the cove. After only a second, she realized she was running alone.

Looking over her shoulder, Taylor gasped. Matt was being handcuffed by the tall lady sheriff, his broad shoulders blocking her view of Taylor's escape. Indecision clutched at Taylor's throat, but when Sheriff Shepard crouched and picked up the half-empty bottle of rum, a numb despair settled over Taylor.

The thought of how disappointed her father would be nearly brought her to her knees, but she forced her legs to carry her back to the scene of the crime.

Maybe she was a bad influence, but she wasn't a bad person. She couldn't let Matt take all the blame for this adventure. Especially since it was really all her fault.

By the time she was following Matt into the one-room station house, Taylor's resolve was weakening. After one hissed, "Why did you come back? I would have covered for you!" from Matt while they sat in the backseat of the SUV waiting for the sheriff to get around to the driver's seat, they hadn't spoken.

With Sheriff Shepard's calm, stern presence in the front seat and Matt's tension-filled form beside her, Taylor hadn't been able to think of anything to say other than, "I'm sorry."

But being sorry was usually a waste of time, and Matt obviously didn't want to hear anything from her, anyway. He barely even glanced at Taylor as Sheriff Shepard uncuffed them and gestured to a pair of chairs in front of the battered metal desk in the corner.

Instead of sitting down at the desk, Sheriff Shepard leaned against it and stared down at them with an expression Taylor couldn't quite decipher. Regretful, maybe, as if she weren't enjoying hauling two teenagers in for processing . . . but calm, too. Regret wasn't going to stop Andie Shepard from doing her duty as she saw it.

"Tell me who I should call to come pick you two up," Sheriff Shepard said brusquely, hooking her thumbs in the belt loops of her tan uniform pants.

Taylor perked up. Maybe they weren't being charged after all! Thinking quickly, she wished with a sudden ache that she could call Jo. But with Ella's return to the island, Jo had both of her real daughters to keep her busy.

"Your parents?" Sheriff Shepard prompted. "Taylor, of course I know your dad."

Taylor froze in panic while the sheriff eyed Matt coolly. "But what about you, Mr. Little? I haven't seen your mom at the Firefly the last few days. Is she out of town?"

"Yes," Matt confirmed, his voice slightly muffled as he slouched low in the uncomfortable plastic chair. "My mom's cousin is staying at the house with me. You can call him. Sam Brennan."

Sheriff Shepard reached for the old-fashioned rotary phone on her desk, but before she could do more than put the receiver to her ear, Taylor unfroze and blurted out, "Don't call my dad!"

A flicker of sympathy flashed through the sheriff's bright blue-green eyes, but her voice was very firm when she replied, "I have to, Taylor. You know the drill."

Taylor winced. She did know the drill, but after the last time, she'd promised her father he'd never have to come down here to pick her up, ever again. She'd meant it with every inch of herself at the time, and she'd do just about anything to keep that promise now.

"No, I know," she improvised. "But he's out of town, too. Business trip."

Sheriff Shepard narrowed her eyes. "Then who should I call?"

Inspiration struck. "My sister," Taylor said, twining her fingers together to hide the fact that they were trembling a little. "Merry Preston. I have her cell number in my phone. Please?"

Studying her for a long moment with those uncannily ocean-colored eyes, Sheriff Shepard seemed to pierce straight through Taylor's mask of bravado to see the scared kid underneath. Taylor did her best to sit up tall in the chair and meet the sheriff's gaze head-on, but it wasn't easy.

When the woman nodded decisively and held out her hand for the cell phone, Taylor let out a silent breath of relief. Glancing over at Matt, she felt a pang at the obvious misery on his face.

Taking advantage of the sheriff's back being turned to make her calls, Taylor nudged her chair closer to Matt's. When he looked up, she tried out a smile.

He didn't smile back. "My mom is going to kill me," he muttered. "No, worse than that. She's going to be disappointed in me."

Gut wrenching with guilt, Taylor clutched at the plastic arms of the chair to keep from reaching out to him. "I'm sorry. The whole thing was my fault, it was all my idea. I'll take the blame."

For the first time since the sheriff showed up, a spark flared to life in Matt's worried hazel eyes. "Don't you dare. We're in this together."

"Together," Taylor echoed, giddy happiness unspooling inside her like a perfect line of computer code.

Maybe tonight wasn't a total disaster, she told herself with an unfamiliar burst of optimism. All she'd wanted was a chance to be close to Matt Little—and here they were, side by side. And if Merry extended her display of coolness about sneaking out to keeping this little incident from Taylor's dad, then she was golden.

But when the front door of the sheriff's office crashed open fifteen minutes later, it wasn't Merry's petite, slim form walking in beside a thunderously scowling Sam Brennan.

It was her father.

Taylor barely registered the fact that Jo Ellen Hollister was with him. For the space of a heartbeat, all she could see was the weary resignation in her father's eyes, the stern set of his mouth behind his salt-and-pepper beard.

"Mr. McNamara." Sheriff Shepard stood up, casting Taylor a look. "Home early from your business trip, I see."

"What business trip?" Dad stopped short, just inside the doorway, his stare locked on Taylor in a way that made her want to slide off the chair and down through the cracked linoleum floor.

Shaking her head, the sheriff crossed her arms over her chest. "Not important. It's good that you're here. Thanks for coming. You, too, Jo Ellen. And Mr. . . . Brennan, was it?"

"Sam Brennan. Matt, get your stuff. We're going home," Sam growled, drawing Taylor's attention. She stared at the way he was scowling at the sheriff, face hard as granite. He was almost unrecognizable as the big, gentle-eyed man who'd brought Java to Windy Corner Stables that afternoon.

If she met Sam Brennan in a dark alley in this kind of mood, Taylor realized with a half-pleasurable thrill, she'd run the other way.

Sheriff Shepard didn't appear to be intimidated, although her focus had narrowed to Sam's livid face. "I'm afraid Matt isn't going anywhere yet. Not until we have a little chat."

"What's there to talk about?" Sam planted his feet, solid as an oak tree. "Matt is a good kid. Never been in trouble a day in his life. This is obviously some kind of mistake. Or a case of overzealous police work. Slow night for crime in Mayberry, Officer? Bored of giving tickets to wild horses for running too fast?"

The fascination of this exchange was almost enough to distract Taylor from her own situation. Sam Brennan had balls of solid brass, going after Sheriff Shepard that way. Taylor was seriously impressed.

Sheriff Shepard wasn't. In spite of the fact that she didn't move or flush or clench her hands into fists, Taylor was willing to bet the sheriff's fingers were itching to go for her gun. She kept it all locked down, though, her voice as cool and unruffled as the surface of Lantern Lake at dawn.

"As duly elected sheriff of Sanctuary Island," she stressed slightly, "I'm aware of Matt's record. Or lack thereof. But that doesn't change the fact that he was caught trespassing on the wild horse preserve property at Heartbreak Cove. With a bottle of rum."

Sam stiffened, so clearly angry that his brown hair almost seemed to stand on end. "He wasn't alone, was he?"

"Wait just a minute," Jo broke in, hands on her hips. "What are you implying, Sam?"

For an instant, Sam looked tempted to back down, but then he shook his head. "I'm sorry, Jo. But you've mentioned your girl's issues in the past—the trouble she's been in. You know the rum was probably hers. Matt doesn't deserve to get dragged into that."

"Sam, don't." Matt spoke up, sending another thrill through Taylor, but the thrill was dampened by the knowledge that Sam was actually right. She'd messed up, big-time.

As if they hadn't even heard Matt, the four adults kept arguing. Taylor's dad jumped in with, "You weren't there. For all we know, that boy is the one who talked my daughter into this escapade. It's been a long time since Taylor was in any trouble, she's matured a lot in the last year." He paused, scrubbing a defeated hand over his mouth. "At least, I thought she had."

"Gee, thanks for the vote of confidence, Dad." Taylor sank down in her chair, feeling lower than the gritty sand on the bottom of her shoes.

But she should've kept her mouth shut, because now Dad was looking at her. Facing the full force of his disappointment was enough to make Taylor feel lower than dirt.

"What happened, Tay?" Jo asked softly. "I thought things were going so well."

Anger burned through her, cleansing as fire, and a lot easier to handle than guilt and regret. "Of course you think everything's going great now. You have your real daughters back."

"Oh, honey."

Taylor got a sick kind of satisfaction out of the hurt, horrified look on Jo's face.

"Your real daughters, by the way, totally suck," Taylor told her. The betrayal actually stung. Taylor latched on to it, glad for the chance to be the injured party. "I thought Merry was marginally cool, but no—she ratted me out the first chance she got."

Surprisingly, it wasn't Jo who defended Merry, but Dad. "She did exactly the right thing by calling me. I would've hoped you'd have the guts to face the music for this stupid stunt instead of imposing on a woman who's got her hands full with a concussed fiancé and a newborn."

Taylor sucked in a breath. She'd completely forgotten about Doc Fairfax's injury. She was officially the worst.

"And the worst of it is that you broke your word to me," Dad said, relentless. "After what happened with the Rigby boy, you promised me you'd abide by my rules about dating. You looked me in the eye and promised me."

Eyes burning and throat closing around a knot of desperate shame, Taylor cried, "It wasn't a date! We're just friends."

Which was true, even if she'd hoped for more, but she couldn't bear the weight of yet another broken promise. Refusing to even glance in Matt's direction, Taylor kept all her attention on her father's face and the slight softening she saw there.

But every cell in her body was aware of Matt going tense and still beside her.

Sheriff Shepard spoke into the highly charged silence that followed. "Let's all take a breath, here. Taylor and Matt are both in trouble. I have to charge them both with trespassing and underage drinking."

Chaos erupted as Dad and Sam Brennan tried to outshout each other and Jo did her best to play referee, but Sheriff Shepard shut them all up by raising one hand and clearing her throat.

"The law is clear," she repeated, inflexible as steel. Her blue-green gaze darted to Sam Brennan for an instant as she said, "Taylor and Matt might be good kids, but they broke the law. And while some of you may feel that the rules shouldn't apply to you or your family, I'm afraid I can't agree."

Another uproar. Beside her, Matt groaned and slumped over his knees. Guilt ripped at Taylor's heart.

But just as she opened her mouth, prepared to enrage her father by at least taking the blame for the bottle of rum, the sheriff pinned her with a look. She shook her head slightly, and Taylor's mouth snapped closed.

"They'll both be charged," Sheriff Shepard said, "but since they're both minors, there's every likelihood of Judge Barrow opting for rehabilitation over a harsher sentence."

"I bet you hate that," Sam Brennan snarled through clenched teeth. "Just think, if you'd only waited a few years to throw the book at these kids, they could be tried as adults."

Finally, a snap of temper flashed in the sheriff's eyes. "Mr. Brennan. I'm sure it's more comfortable for you to blame me than it is to take any responsibility for the fact that you were supposed to be looking after your young relative in the absence of his mother, but I don't appreciate your tone."

A muscle ticked under the close-cropped beard scruffing along Sam's jaw. "I don't give a damn what you appreciate. Do what you have to do, fine us or whatever, but I'm taking Matt home now."

Sheriff Shepard reached across her desk to grab a stack of paperwork. "Fill this out. I'll be in touch. Or someone from the courthouse will."

Sam and Taylor's dad both took the papers. Dad, an old hand at this, signed his name and handed the paper back, but Sam sat down to read carefully through every line of the document releasing Matt into his custody.

"Thanks." The sheriff nodded at Jo and Dad, then cocked an eyebrow at Taylor. "You can go. And I hope this is the last time we see each other like this."

Taylor locked eyes with the sheriff and straightened her shoulders. She'd hated the previous sheriff, a fat, old guy who'd pursed his mouth disapprovingly whenever he saw Taylor around town. But she liked Andie Shepard. Taylor liked that the new sheriff talked to her like she was a grown-up, not a dumb kid who couldn't understand what she'd done or what the consequences might be. It made Taylor want to act like it.

"I swear, I've learned my lesson," Taylor vowed, meaning it with all her heart. "No more breaking the law."

Something like amusement flickered in Sheriff Shepard's gaze as she accepted the signed papers from Sam Brennan. "Good. How about you, Matt?"

"This has been a big, stupid mistake." Matt kept his face turned away, his profile as hard as stone. "A mistake I'll never make again. I'm done with all of it."

A chill roughened the skin of Taylor's arms as Matt turned and followed his cousin out of the sheriff's office without a backward look. She knew what Matt meant. She was the mistake. And he was done with her.

Chapter Thirteen

Despite what Ben had told Merry about his reasons for entering into this marriage and adoption scenario, he wasn't exactly chomping at the bit to tell his parents about it.

They *should* be thrilled. After what happened with Ashley, his parents ought to bow down and kiss the ground at the prospect of a new daughter-in-law, complete with son and heir. He'd told them after the divorce that it would never happen—so this ought to be a dream come true for them.

The problem was, Ben had gotten divorced, quit his surgical residency, finished vet school, and moved to Sanctuary Island all to break away from his lifelong pattern of living his life to please his parents and make *their* dreams come true.

It was possible that an immature, resentful part of Ben didn't actually want to make his parents happy. He knew that wasn't likely to win him a nomination for Son of the Year, or even a nod at the Basically a Good Person Awards, but he hadn't talked to his parents except for Thanksgiving, Christmas, and their anniversary in years. And that had seemed to suit all of them perfectly well.

So he'd dragged his heels until a week before the wedding to tell them about it. Not that there'd been a lot of time for heart-to-heart phone calls since the engagement. Even with Ella and Grady back on the island and fully committed to helping them get this marriage off the ground in as little time as possible, it had still been a hectic whirl of days filled with wedding arrangements, meetings with lawyers, babyproofing his house, drama with Merry's sort-of sister, Taylor, and oh right, his veterinary practice.

Just because Ben's previously empty life was suddenly bursting at the seams didn't mean he could abandon his practice. As the only vet on Sanctuary Island, Ben had a responsibility not only to his paying customers, but to his four-, or in some cases three-legged friends as well.

And not only that, but he had a brand-new assistant to train. Or maybe it was the other way around, because most of Ben's workday was spent avoiding the office and the wild look in Merry's eyes as she tried to make heads or tails of his "filing system." Dramatic air quotes supplied by Merry.

So if Ben skipped out on things like setting a menu for the big picnic Jo Ellen was insisting on throwing in lieu of a reception, who could blame him?

Jo had decided to make the party open to the entire town and have it in the square at the center of downtown, which Ben balked at until Merry gave him a searching, serious look and said, "Actually, it was my idea—I thought it would be good for business, and make things easier for you if the whole town gets the chance to congratulate you all at once, in a giant lump. Was I wrong?"

And of course, she wasn't. As happy as Ben was about this marriage—and despite the myriad ways it could all turn into a pile of cow plop in the blink of an eye, he was happier than he'd been in years—he didn't particularly care for the idea of being on display.

That's what it felt like to be congratulated. He dreaded the knowing looks and smirking smiles. He hated the idea of people he barely recognized except as "Cat owner, semi-interesting case of feline immunodeficiency virus" or "Five head of sheep, yearly vaccinations" knowing anything real about him.

But getting married on Sanctuary Island, it turned out, was one of those life events that turned a private man into public property.

Merry was right. It was better to get it over with all at once instead of dragging the congratulations and smiles and backslapping out over the entire next year. Besides, Sanctuary Island loved a town festival, and chances were good that he'd be able to fade into the background after the party got going, and no one would notice.

Except, quite possibly, Merry.

In the wake of her first night in his home and the misunderstanding he'd deliberately let stand, Merry had been . . . polite. Friendly, even, but she'd preserved a careful distance that perversely gave Ben hope. That kiss had changed things, had forced them both to acknowledge the explosive chemistry between them. If Merry wasn't ready for the next step, that was okay. Ben could be patient.

After that first night, she'd never really gone back to her mother's house. Instead, all her belongings and Alex's began a slow migration over to Isleaway Farm—a suitcase full of clothes here, a high chair there. Ben didn't say anything about it, he merely stood back and let it happen, counting every new toy, discarded shoe, and stack of baby bottles cluttering up his pristine home like a miser hoarding gold.

And every now and then, he caught Merry studying him a lot more intently than her casual friendliness seemed to warrant. Each time her gaze slid away from his, her long lashes lowering to fan out over her pinkening cheeks, that hope surged in Ben's chest.

This relationship was so new, so fragile, Ben was determined to protect it. In this case, that meant avoiding a certain familial phone call until Merry marched up to him after dinner and shoved his cell phone into his hand.

"Why haven't you called your parents yet?" she demanded.

"I've been busy," Ben protested, fighting back a wince at how lame that sounded.

Merry thought it was pretty lame, too, if her narrowed gaze was anything to go by. "The whole reason you proposed was to get them off your back by getting hitched. Surely telling them about the marriage is part of the plan. Why are you dragging your heels about this? Is there something you're not telling me?"

Ben licked his lips, aware that his mouth had gone dry as the sand at low tide. He couldn't have Merry getting suspicious now, just when everything was coming together. "Give me the phone, I'll call them right now."

But Merry stepped back, holding the phone up out of his reach. "Ben. What's going on here?"

"Nothing, it's just I know they won't be able to make the wedding anyway. Not with their schedules. So what's the rush?"

"The rush is that they're your parents! You said us getting married and you adopting Alex would make them happy." Doubt darkened Merry's pretty face like someone had hit the dimmer switch on her inner glow, and Ben panicked.

"It will," he insisted. Not necessarily a lie—his parents might be happy for him, simply because Ben was happy. There was a first time for everything. "I've been putting off calling them because we're just . . . not close. Anymore. It's been hard."

He tried not to hate himself for using that excuse, even when Merry's face softened exactly the way he'd predicted it would. "I get that. It's tricky figuring out how to relate to our families as adults, isn't it?"

Ben knew he could leave it at that, and Merry would smile and stop pushing, and everything would be okay. But somehow, he found himself saying more.

"It's not only that. My parents—they're very busy people. Both doctors, both active on the boards of hospitals and charities. They never had much time to spend at home."

Pulling out the chair across from Ben's, Merry perched on the edge and leaned her forearms on the table so she could give him her undivided attention. "And you felt . . . neglected? Unloved?"

"No, my parents love me." Ben allowed himself a slightly ironic smile. "In their own unique ways."

Merry frowned. "As a parent myself, the only way I can imagine loving my kid is with everything I am and everything I have. I love everything about him."

"Ah, but that's just it." Ben shrugged. "It was never about me. My parents love me . . . but not the real me. It's more like the idea of me they each carry in their heads, the way they wanted my life to turn out. Their love for me is a reflection of their own ambitions—my actual presence is not required in their lives. In fact, they're happier when I'm not around. When I talk to them, well, the reality of me doesn't mesh with their fantasy of Benjamin Alexander Fairfax the Third, noted surgeon and scion of the wealthy Fairfax family."

Merry pressed her lips together, something sparking in her blue eyes. "Personally, I prefer Dr. Ben, small town veterinarian and noted crank."

It was the perfect response. Ben felt a pressure he hadn't even noticed release from around his rib cage, and he grinned across the table at his fiancée. "I'm not bitter about it. My parents are fine people, they gave me every opportunity in the world. I had it a lot better than most. I know that."

"But it would be nice to feel as if your family knows you, through and through, and loves you anyway," Merry finished.

A lump formed in Ben's throat, but he managed to say, "Exactly. There's nothing like having someone in your life who gets you."

That made Merry smile, a slow, sweet stretch of those pink lips, until happiness seemed to shine from every pore of her perfect skin. Wordlessly, she held the cell phone out to Ben, and he took it.

"Okay, I'll call them. But we're not holding up the wedding long enough for them to clear their schedules and get here," he warned, closing his fingers over the cold edges of his phone. "No more delays."

They'd waited two weeks only because Jo shrieked at the notion she could organize a buffet dinner for the whole town in less than seven days. And because Merry had wanted to give her father a chance to see if he could get enough time off to make it to the wedding.

He hadn't managed it. Or hadn't tried, Ben wasn't sure what Merry believed. All Ben knew was the resigned set to her sad face when she got off the phone with Neil Preston.

Neither of them was exactly batting a thousand when it came to their families.

"They don't have to come to the wedding," Merry said, "but I want to meet them. Alex should get to know his grandparents. All of them."

Impulsively reaching for Merry's hand, still extended across the table to him, Ben clasped her slender fingers and brought them to his mouth. He pressed a kiss to her palm and felt the way her fingers trembled. "Thank you."

"You're welcome." She pulled her hand away, but it was a slow movement. Almost as if she were as reluctant to let go as he was. Encouraged, Ben watched Merry retreat to the guest room to put Alex down for the night, then went out to the front porch and made the call he'd been dreading.

Shivering in the frosty chill of a late September evening, his butt going stiff and numb at first contact with the cold porch swing seat. Yeah, that felt like the appropriate setting for dealing with his parents.

"Son." Tripp Fairfax's deep bass voice boomed into Ben's ear, hearty and grating. "To what do we owe the honor? Your mother and I are on our way out to a function."

If Ben closed his eyes, he could picture them perfectly. Standing on the antique Persian rug in their chandeliered foyer, his father was tall and lean in his black-tie duds, with a dignified receding hairline in tasteful steel gray. Pamela Fairfax would be at his side, pulling on a pair of cashmere-lined gloves and arching a quizzical, perfectly plucked brow at the delay.

As a kid, Ben had snuck out of bed nearly every night to peer through the banister railing of the wide staircase and catch a glimpse of his beautiful, poised parents sailing out the massive front door to one of their "functions." Charity benefits, political fund-raisers, ballet galas, art gallery openings, hospital donor meet-and-greets . . . Tripp and Pamela Fairfax kept a busier social calendar than the heads of state of some of the smaller European nations.

"I won't keep you long," Ben said through a throat gone oddly tight. Damn, he shouldn't have talked about his family with Merry, should've kept it shoved down and buried like he usually did instead of letting those emotions surface. "I know how busy you are."

"Yes, well, we have obligations, Benjamin," Tripp said sharply, as if he'd heard something critical in Ben's tone. "Our position in society—"

Duty, honor, appearances . . . and, of course, the all-important sanctity of the Fairfax family name.

Already tired of this conversation, Ben cut through the bull. "I'm calling to let you know I've decided to get remarried."

There was a moment of silence broken by a static thump or two, and when the breathless voice came back on the line, it was Ben's mother. "Really? Oh, darling! That's wonderful! Tell me everything. How did you meet?"

Ben stiffened against the eagerness of his mother's tone and the onslaught of questions she was sure to ask. The edges of the phone dug into his palm. "She came to the island to stay with her mother, who owns the stables here."

"The horsey set," Pamela Fairfax said, a touch of disdain twisting the words into a sigh. "So athletic and dull, always inviting one to fox hunts and keeping packs of dogs. Ugh. Well, I suppose it could be worse. What's her name?"

"Meredith Preston."

"Preston," Pamela mused. "Who are her father's people? I don't know anyone by that name."

"You don't know them," Ben said, impatience making his words terse. "They're not FFV."

His mother's voice went soft and hurt. "There's no need to take a tone. You behave as if we're terrible snobs, and we're not! We don't expect everyone in our circle to be on the First Families of Virginia register."

Guilt scored over Ben's nerves, even as he silently grimaced at the blatant lie. He'd personally heard his parents rip a new surgeon at his father's hospital to shreds after learning of the man's "low" antecedents. In high school, Ben had been expected to choose his dates from a strict list of white-gloved debutantes, all from the very best families, every single one of whom could trace her lineage back to the wealthiest early colonists to settle in Virginia.

But Pamela and Tripp Fairfax, snobs? Certainly not!

"Sorry," Ben said tautly, "and I'm glad you don't care about Merry being FFV, because she isn't. She's not a Daughter of the Confederacy, either. She wasn't a debutante, and she doesn't own a string of pearls. Her baby's rattle isn't even sterling silver."

"A baby! This woman has a baby? You mean . . . she's divorced?" Pamela hissed, sounding ridiculously scandalized for a woman on the phone with her own previously married son.

"I never said she'd been married," Ben pointed out. "But yes, Merry has a four-month-old son. Whom I'm planning to adopt, legally and officially, once we've been married a year."

His mother gave a thready, high-pitched noise that made Ben roll his eyes. "Come on, Mom. Try to be happy for me. I might not have chosen one of your pale, colorless society girls, but Merry makes me happy. And, bonus, she comes complete with the grandson you've always wanted."

"That's not what has your mother so upset, and you know it." His father had clearly commandeered the phone when Pamela wilted in shock. "How could you do a thing like this? I realize you have never had the proper care and concern for what's expected of a Fairfax, but this is beyond anything I ever expected, even of you."

Ben's breath caught as if he'd been gut punched. It didn't matter how old he got, how hard he worked to convince himself he didn't care about his parents' weighty expectations—it still hurt to come up short.

This time, though, he didn't even understand what he'd done that was so unacceptable.

He'd assumed his parents would be surprised, perhaps even dismayed by Merry's situation—they could be ridiculously feudal and eighteenth-century about things—but he hadn't been prepared for this level of dismay.

Hardening his voice, he shot back, "I thought I was expected to carry on the family name, above all else. And when Alex becomes my son, he'll be Alex Fairfax. Your legacy is secured. Even if you can't be happy for me, I thought you'd at least be pleased about that."

"Pleased." The word strangled out of Tripp as if he were choking on it. "That our only son plans to bestow the Fairfax name—a name that has been synonymous with good breeding since before our ancestors left the court of King Charles the Second!—on a nameless bastard child, with God only knows what sort of people in his background."

The phone creaked as Ben's fingers clamped tight. "Do not. Call. Alex. A bastard."

The absolute ice in his voice stopped his father's angry tirade. Tripp sighed in Ben's ear, low and weary. "Son. I know how much you enjoy throwing the opportunities your mother and I provided you back in our faces. We've been patient with this latest rebellion because, as much as you might not like to believe it, we do understand that what happened with Ashley and the baby . . . that was difficult. You needed time to hole up and lick your wounds. We understood."

Ben swallowed, his finger hovering over the button that would end this call. But Tripp moved on hurriedly, his voice going even gruffer. "Now, do I wish you'd manned up and stuck it out with Ashley? Yes."

"You made that perfectly clear when she filed for divorce."

"And I won't apologize for that! She was grieving, she wasn't in her right mind, you should have fought harder—but that's over and done with. She's moved on, and for the last several years your mother and I have been waiting to hear that you were through sulking and were ready to come home and take your proper place in Richmond society."

"That's what I'm trying to tell you," Ben argued, struggling to keep the pleading note out of his voice. "I may not be moving back to Richmond and the life you wanted for me, but I am moving on. Here on Sanctuary Island, with the family I've chosen. There's no other place I belong."

"My God, you're serious about this." The disbelief in his father's tone rasped along Ben's raw nerves. "Please tell me there's still time to change your mind. And that you're making this woman sign a prenup!"

"Oh, she signed it," Ben said with relish. "We wrangled around about the terms for days, but she did finally sign on the dotted line."

"Thank the good Lord." Tripp sighed. "So at least your money is safe from this golddigger and her bas— child."

His father's near slip of the tongue fully justified Ben's bitter satisfaction at what he got to say next. "Oh, the money is safe, all right. Tied up nice and tight in a trust fund for Alex, to be administered by his mother and myself, with the help of the local bank manager, until he comes of age. And by the way, the wedding is in a week. If you can't smile and make nice, you're not invited."

Ben didn't wait to find out if his father would recover enough command of his tongue to be able to do more than gurgle "A week!" Instead, he mashed his thumb down on the end button and collapsed forward.

Staring down between his knees at the worn wood of his farmhouse's front porch, Ben rested his head in his hands and systematically got his breathing under control. Best to avoid a rage coma right before one's wedding.

A tap on the windowpane to his right brought Ben's head up. He stowed his phone in his pocket and ran his hands through his hair as he mustered up a smile for Merry's concerned face through the glass.

She disappeared from view, and in the next instant, the front door opened to reveal Merry giving him worried eyebrows as she cuddled Alex against her shoulder.

Mother and child glowed in the warm golden light spilling out of the house, like some ridiculously corny portrait representing "homecoming" or "welcome." Or "love."

Ben stared at the two of them and felt his throat close around a lump of emotion too big to name.

"He wouldn't go down," Merry said. Nerves

thrummed through her soft voice, and when she pressed a quick kiss to the baby's downy cheek, Ben saw the tremor she tried to hide. "I think he wanted to wait up for you."

The last week had also been a crash course in what it meant to live with an infant. Basically, a lot of crying, eating, voiding from both ends, and sleeping. Rinse and repeat daily. But there were peaceful moments, too.

Ben had learned to treasure the particular clutching fussiness Alex exhibited when night fell—the way the baby made fists and rubbed his eyes, tiny mouth furled like a rosebud. The way he arched his back and kicked his legs until Merry or Ben lifted him out of his play-pen and brought him up to be soothed against a steady heartbeat.

"I'm glad," Ben said, pushing to his feet as the swing creaked and swayed behind him.

Merry stepped out onto the porch and immediately shivered.

"It's cold out here!" Ben waved at the open door. "Go back inside where it's warm. I'll be along in a minute to help with Alex, I promise."

"Thanks." But Merry hovered, still, halfway over the doorstep. "Did it . . . not go well? I thought you said your parents would be pleased."

The fear in her voice brought all of Ben's early act-ing skills to the forefront. He smiled widely at her. "No, it did! They're thrilled, and of course they can't wait to meet Alex."

"Oh, good! I thought . . . you looked so upset. Ben, if this marriage isn't what your parents want, if it won't get them off your back like you thought, it's not too late to change your mind."

"What?" Ben sat up straight, alarm ringing through him like a bell. "No. I promise, they're happy."

"Okay. So why aren't *you* happy?" She was close enough now for Ben to smell the milky, powdery baby scent that clung to her. He breathed in deep and let it fill him with borrowed peace.

"My parents confirmed it. They won't be able to come to the wedding," Ben told her, perfectly truthfully. They couldn't come, because they hadn't been invited. "It . . . hit me harder than I thought it would, I guess."

"I know what you mean." Merry's sympathetic smile twisted in Ben's gut, his conscience screaming at him about using her own paternal disappointment to distract her from asking about his. "There are some things you can't prepare for, no matter how much you tell yourself you're supposed to be a grown-up now."

"No matter what happens," Ben said, the words burning at the back of his throat with how deeply he meant them. "I'll always be there for Alex."

Merry swayed toward him, just slightly, like a reed in the breeze. Shifting on her shoulder, Alex made a fretful noise and twisted to reach a chubby, imperious arm out to Ben. Heart in his throat, Ben gave Alex his index finger to practice his fine motor skills on.

"I know that," Merry said, with a certainty that rocked Ben down to his bones. "Why do you think I'm marrying you? I'll tell you this much, it's not for your recordkeeping or your accounting system."

She grinned, and just like that, the September night didn't feel quite so chilly.

I'm marrying you.

It was actually happening. Ben Fairfax was about to get more than he'd ever thought he could have, and nothing was going to happen to get in the way.

He smiled back and opened his arms to receive the squirming bundle of baby boy. With Alex happily grinding snot into the collar of Ben's shirt, Ben felt confident enough to put a friendly, nonpressuring arm around Merry's shoulders.

She leaned into him as they went back into the bright, warm house together, and shut the door against the cold.

Chapter Fourteen

In the midst of one of the most beautiful, clear, sun-dappled autumns coastal Virginia had ever seen, the day of Ben and Merry's wedding dawned gray and dismal. A chill fog lay over the island like a shroud, turning the winding roads and wild fields into a dangerous maze of blind curves and hidden sinkholes.

"Good," Ben said, glancing out the window over the kitchen sink as he rinsed out his coffee mug. "Maybe everyone will stay home and we can get married in private."

Merry shook her head, fighting a smile. She didn't want to encourage Ben's grumpiness, but it was hard when she was bubbling over with a hectic mixture of nerves, excitement, anticipation, and last-minute plans.

In fact, she was on the phone with her mother at that very moment, half tuning out the recitation of who was bringing the flowers and where they'd be placed, the potluck items she'd been promised by various towns-folk, and what Jo had still to bake before meeting Merry and Ben at the courthouse at eleven.

Covering the mouthpiece with her fingers, Merry

watched as Ben sat down to continue his grand experiment of introducing Alex to solid foods. In this case, mashed sweet potatoes Ben had boiled the night before.

After the phone call to Ben's parents that Merry had insisted on and then regretted when it seemed to make Ben so sad, they'd gone back in the house to put Alex to bed. Of course, once he'd gotten his way and had both Merry and Ben hovering over his crib, tucking him in, Alex went down without a fight.

Hesitant to bring up the whole parents-and-family talk again, but not quite ready for the evening to be over yet, Merry had followed Ben out of the guest room instead of turning in.

She was still glowing from the promise Ben had made, to be there for Alex. The words that were engraved on her innermost heart as her deepest wish, and he'd plucked them out of thin air and handed them to her.

The connection between Merry and Ben had strengthened over the past two weeks. There was nothing like seeing a person first thing in the morning, with pillow creases on one cheek and his dark curls tousled by sleep, to forge a new intimacy.

But that night, in the cozy comfort of the welcoming old farmhouse Ben had put so much work into, Merry felt a tug she couldn't deny. As if he felt it, too, Ben had turned to her suddenly enough to make her gasp.

The moment had felt fragile, suspended like a shimmering soap bubble between them. Merry's mind was a blur of home and warmth, sweetness like maple syrup trickling through her veins. Every breath seemed to pull her closer and closer to him.

The little voice in the back of her head that usually piped up to caution her about getting too close was silent, for once . . . but just as she was about to tilt her head and lift her lips for the kiss she could almost taste, Ben stepped back.

"I think Alex is ready for solid foods."

She couldn't have been more startled if Ben had poked her in the eye, Three Stooges style. Merry broke the surface of her daze, blinking to clear the film of desire from her vision. "Oh?" she'd managed, not very intelligently.

"I've been taking notes," Ben assured her, holding up one broad, long-fingered hand to enumerate his points. "He's been able to support his own head for several weeks now, and is able to maintain a sitting position for seven to ten minutes at a stretch. He's more than doubled his birth weight. And I noticed him eyeing your shrimp and grits yesterday, indicating that he's becoming interested in solid food."

Merry shook her head and tried to remember the many parenting books and child development guides she'd frantically devoured during her pregnancy. "Between four and six months is a good time to start trying solid foods, I think. But I haven't noticed Alex making chewing motions during feedings—that's supposed to be one of the big signs."

"He'll figure it out," Ben had said confidently. "Alex is above average in intelligence."

As far as Merry knew, Ben had no factual basis for this belief, but she was hardly one to argue. She was pretty sure Alex was the most perfect, wonderful, clever baby ever to draw breath.

So here they were on the morning of their wedding, sitting at the kitchen table and watching Alex push orange mush out of his mouth with his little tongue. Thus far, he'd ingested maybe a teaspoonful of sweet potatoes—and that was a generous estimate. The rest of the half-cup serving decorated Alex's chubby cheeks, stuck together the wisps of dark hair on his forehead, and smeared over Ben's hands and down the front of his blue plaid shirt.

Day Six of the Solid Food Experiment wasn't going well. But Dr. Ben Fairfax—meticulous, precise, crotchety, impatient Ben—never lost his patience. Never, not by a flicker of an eyelash, did he betray an ounce of frustration or annoyance. Not even when Alex's excitedly flailing hands knocked the spoon hard enough to send sweet potatoes sailing through the air to splat against the pretty dogwood-patterned wallpaper.

Merry suppressed a snort of laughter that had Ben narrowing his eyes at her. She gave him her best Innocent Angel face, but he didn't appear convinced.

"Merry? Hello, are you still there?" Jo's frazzled voice sounded in her ear.

With a guilty start, Merry fumbled the phone before she managed to get it back up to her mouth. "Yes! Sorry, Mom. I'm here—but we're feeding Alex, and he's determined to get the sweet potatoes all over everywhere except into his tummy."

"You and Ben are in the same room together! But it's the day of the wedding, it's bad luck," Jo fretted.

Resisting the urge to roll her eyes, Merry said, "Mom, it's not like that with us. And anyway, Ben doesn't believe in luck. Don't worry about it, we'll be fine."

As she said it, she realized that she actually believed it. Lighter in heart than she'd been in days—maybe in months or years—Merry breathed out a long sigh, and with it, all her doubts and worries.

"And Mom. Thank you for everything you're doing. I know you don't completely approve of how fast this is all happening, or my reasons for saying yes to it—and yet you're still working like crazy to help me make it happen. That means a lot to me."

There was a charged silence on the line, full of emotion. Jo cleared her throat, but it didn't help. Her next words were husky and thick. "I wasn't there for you when you were younger. But I'm here for you now. I hope you know that."

The sincerity in her mother's voice made Merry's chest hurt. "I do know that. And this marriage—it's not about getting away from you. I hope *you* know *that*. All I want is the chance to have a real relationship with you that isn't about the past, and isn't about me relying completely on you in the present. I don't think I can be a good daughter—or a good mother— unless I take this step toward independence. Does that make sense?"

Jo sniffed wetly, making Merry smile. "It does. Darn it. I loved having you and the baby around the house—but I understand that you need your own life, and if you think Ben will make you happy, then I'm nothing but glad for you, sweetie."

"Our lives are intertwined now, no matter who gets married," Merry pointed out. "Ben and me, Grady and Ella, you and Harrison—we're still family. We're all here for each other."

"Like when Taylor got in trouble and called you, and you knew you could call me."

A vise of guilt tightened around Merry's chest. "I know she was mad that I called you instead of showing up myself."

"Maybe at first, but she understood," Jo reassured her. "And even if you hadn't been dealing with Ben's concussion, it was the right thing to do, notifying Harrison and me."

"You're her parents," Merry said softly. "And after everything that's happened, all the changes Taylor's had to adjust to, she needed to know that when she was in trouble, you and her dad would drop everything to come and help her."

"Shoot, I hate this stupid phone!" Jo's voice was choked, bringing an answering ache to Merry's throat. "I wish you were right next to me so I could hug the life out of you."

"Me, too," Merry whispered, and for the first time since Alex was born, she meant it. This was the right thing to do. Already, things were better with her mother. "I'll see you at the courthouse in . . . gosh, only a couple of hours now. I'd better start getting ready."

She glanced at Ben, who blinked up at her with a stripe of sweet potato under one eye like a dash of war paint, making his clear gray eyes brighter than she'd ever seen them.

"And goodness knows," she said huskily, never taking her gaze off Ben. "It's going to take me the full two hours to scrub my boys clean."

Merry hung up to the sound of her mother's soft chuckle, her gaze trained on the two men in her life. "What a mess you both are," she said, oddly out of breath.

Ben grinned, his teeth bright white in a face tanned by working outdoors in sunny paddocks and pastures. "Are you volunteering to wash us off?"

A pleasurable tingle sparkled through her. It reminded her of flirting with her first crush, the fun and freedom of banter before everything got so heavy. "To take you outside and hose you down, maybe."

"Do you hear that, Alex?" Ben addressed the cooing, bouncing baby in his high chair. "Your mama is a hard-hearted woman. Threatening you with the hose! What do you think we ought to do about that?"

Alex bounced, banging his open palms on the high chair's tray, blue eyes wide with the joy of Ben's full attention.

Ben nodded as if Alex had replied. "I couldn't agree more. You're a scholar and a gentleman."

And before Merry could do more than blink, Ben had plucked Alex out of his high chair and swooped him toward her, both of them covered in sticky sweet potato puree and grinning with manic glee.

Shrieking in half-pretend horror, Merry darted away, leading them on a chase through the house before finally letting herself be caught, strategically, outside the bathroom where they'd set up Alex's baby tub.

"Okay, you've got me." She panted, thrilled down to her bones at how fun it was simply to play with someone this way. "Now what are you going to do with me?"

Without warning, heat flashed through Ben's gray eyes, turning them to molten silver. The blaze of very adult desire burned away the teasing, childlike playfulness like a bonfire.

Hands trembling with something Merry couldn't name—though she knew it wasn't fear—she reached for her gurgling, clapping baby. "Here, I can do bathtime, if you want to start getting ready."

But Ben only curled Alex closer to his chest. Alex's tacky fingers tangled in the overlong waves of his hair. "No way. I got this thing dirty, I'll clean it up. That's the kind of values we want to teach Alex in this house. Right, kid? Right."

It was funny. Merry had never been a baby-talk person. She didn't like it when adults talked down to children, even very small ones, as if they were lower life-forms incapable of understanding.

She knew all too well that kids understood and took in much more than the adults around them believed.

But now that she had her own baby, she understood where the baby-talk impulse came from. Confronted with that perfect, round, innocent face, her voice seemed to jump into the breathy upper registers without conscious volition. She still tried to use real words instead of the nonsense syllables she'd heard other mommies coo at their little ones, but it wasn't always easy.

For Ben, though, it appeared to be completely natural to speak to Alex as if he were a rational person, capable of understanding. And Alex, for his part, listened with the kind of rapt attention that made Merry's heart swell with pride, his dark blue eyes tracking Ben's expression and the movement of his mouth.

"Thanks. You're really wonderful with him," she said. "I'm not sure what we did to deserve this chance at being a happy family with you—but I'm thankful for it."

Merry's words hit him like a swift kick to the temple, the utter wrongness of it enough to make him dizzy.

"Don't thank me." The words came out harsh and stark, and Ben tried to modulate his tone. "I mean it. I'm the one who should be thanking you. These past weeks with the two of you living here . . . this house has never felt so much like a home."

She ducked her head as if she didn't totally believe him, but he could tell she wanted to. He didn't know precisely what fear or self-doubt held her back, but he could guess.

In that moment, Ben vowed to himself to do everything in his power to make her feel so safe and wanted at Isleaway Farm that she'd never even consider leaving.

"Okay, well. I'm going to go get showered and figure out what to wear. Since, you know, the traditional white dress isn't really an option." She gave a half laugh, combing her slender fingers through the unruly curls of her naturally dark hair. When he first met her, Ben remembered, she'd had it dyed magenta, the deep, dark pink at the heart of a rose.

"Wear whatever you want," he told her. "Whatever makes you feel most comfortable. Wear a white dress if you want to, and I'll make mincemeat out of anyone who looks at you sideways."

"You're sweet to me," Merry murmured, eyes wide as if it still surprised her.

Feeling as uncomfortably exposed as if he'd unzipped and dropped his pants in the hallway, Ben scowled. "I'd marry you in a white dress, black leather pants, or in pajamas. I really couldn't give a crap what you wear."

Interestingly, instead of increasing Merry's tension, the sharpness of his retort caused her shoulders to loosen and her blue eyes to sparkle.

"Gee, thanks," she said with a wry twist to her mouth, but Ben could tell she meant it.

This was the kind of thing that made him want to give up on trying to understand women. When he made an attempt at niceness, she tensed up. But when he was his usual jerky self, she relaxed.

Ben did the only thing he could. He retreated.

"Women," he whispered to Alex as he carted the orange-spackled kid into the bathroom and started the water running over the small, shallow plastic tub they'd set up in the deep sink. "I'm relying on you to help me decode your mother, buddy. Deal?"

Alex, who'd learned that if he smacked his hands together, everyone around him smiled and laughed and generally acted as if he'd cured cancer, clapped. Ben took it as an acknowledgment of their gentlemen's agreement. He stripped Alex out of his sticky onesie and dipped him, toes first, into the warm, shallow water.

"Fifty weeks from today, you'll be my kid for good. Alex Hollister Fairfax. S'got a certain ring to it, yeah? I think so."

Alex smacked the water in enthusiastic agreement,

and Ben caught his breath at the spear of pure happiness that shafted through his midsection, so sharp and clean it was almost a physical pain.

He gazed down at the wet, slippery baby discovering the joys of splashing water everywhere, and tried to push through the ache of holding everything he wanted in the palm of his hand.

Well, almost everything. But Ben could be patient. He could wait for Merry to come to him.

Couldn't he?

Chapter Fifteen

The entire town of Sanctuary may have been invited to celebrate this sudden surprise marriage between the irascible country vet and his friendly, vivacious bride. But for the wedding itself, Merry and Ben had decided to only bring a few witnesses down to the courthouse.

In a bright, airy room on the second floor of the red-brick building, surrounded by crumbling crown molding, threadbare lace curtains, and their closest friends and family, Merry and Ben signed the paperwork that made them husband and wife.

They'd opted out of the ceremony, deciding to keep it as simple and straightforward as possible. The justice of the peace, a middle-aged woman whose standard poodle Ben had treated for kennel cough last year, seemed disappointed not to get to read out her list of "Do you take so and so" type questions, but Ben was relieved Merry didn't want to mess with it.

He was having a hard enough time keeping his runaway emotions in check without having to swear in front of legal representation and his new wife's family that he'd love and cherish her till death did them part.

As it was, the entire surreal encounter with Judge Barrow took less than ten minutes, including the witnesses' signatures, and before he knew it, the whole group of them were decanted out onto the front porch of the courthouse, blinking and dazed in the midday light.

Ben was surprised at how different he felt about being married this time around. Possibly it had to do with how long he and Ashley had dated before their wedding back on the mainland. This thing with Merry was still relatively new, even if they'd known each other for months.

It made sense that this time, he looked across the crowded porch at the woman he'd just pledged his life to, and all he wanted was to be even closer to her. The ink wasn't dry on their license yet, and Ben already wanted more.

"Well," Jo said, cradling her grandson high on her shoulder. "That sure was the fastest I ever saw two people get hitched."

"Makes you wonder why anyone spends months and thousands of dollars planning a big, long church wedding," Ella added stoutly, wrapping an arm around Merry's shoulders. Grady raised his brows in a way Ben took to mean that Grady was skeptical that this whole experience had in any way let him off the hook for a big church wedding whenever he and Ella finally tied the knot.

From the way Ella was hugging her sister, Ben wondered if he were missing something important. Maybe Merry had always wanted to waft down the center aisle between pews lined with folks oohing and ahhing over her giant white-marshmallow confection of a dress. Maybe she was secretly sad and feeling deprived of her chance to fulfill some mysterious girlhood dream.

But when Merry glanced up and caught his eye, Ben

saw only a deep contentment in her expression. "I guess some people get married for the wedding and the dress and the gifts and the party. Me . . . I'm looking forward to the actual marriage."

The soft strength of her words hit Ben like a pillow to the solar plexus, a burst of feathers and all the breath left his lungs for a second. "Me, too," he managed to say. "In fact, all things considered, maybe we ought to go on home with Alex and let y'all celebrate without us."

"Oh oh oh, no you don't." Grady threw one of his big handyman's hands around Ben's chest and hustled him down the courthouse steps, laughing. "You're not getting out of this that easily."

"Whose side are you on?" Ben grumbled, shoving at his stupidly muscle-bound best friend. Ben was taller by a few inches and had enough muscle on him to wrestle a six-month-old calf to a standstill for shots, but Grady was even bulkier. He was broad, especially through the chest and shoulders, and easily weathered Ben's half-hearted escape attempts as he navigated the two of them along the walkway toward the town square.

Against Ben's hopes and wishes, the sky had cleared and brightened to a sparkling blue. Fresh, clean sunlight speared through the red and gold leaves of the tulip poplars dotting the square, dancing over the picnic tables spread with mismatched, multicolored tablecloths, steaming pots and casserole dishes.

At the end of the line of tables, right beside the white gazebo, stood a small folding card table. Ben felt his jaw drop. Sitting on that table was the tallest, most lopsided wedding cake he'd ever seen. It was at least five creamy white-frosted layers, and each one seemed to slant at a different angle and in a different direction.

"Dear Lord," Ben said blankly, hanging back while the rest of the wedding party collided with the loud, raucous rabble of well-wishers. "There must be Super Glue in the frosting. That's the only explanation for how the layers haven't slid apart and right onto the ground."

"Be nice." There was an amused twist to Grady's mouth that told Ben his friend was holding back laughter. "I heard Miss Emily made you that cake herself from a special family recipe."

Ben groaned and covered his face with his hands. "Crap. Ever since I set her crazy pet llama's leg, she's been threatening to bake me a cake. I guess this was the perfect opportunity."

"Can't say no to a slice of your own wedding cake!" Grady was enjoying this way too much.

Glowering at his supposed best friend, Ben said, "One hour. That's how long I said I'd stay, and I'll keep my word. But in exactly one hour, I'm making a break for it. And I expect you to back me up."

Some of the glee on Grady's stubbled, hard-jawed face faded into a more serious expression. He clapped one big hand on Ben's shoulder, hard enough to shove him forward a step. "I've always got your back, Ben. No matter what."

"No need to act like I'm about to go off to war or something, you big sentimental drama queen." But despite his eye roll and muttering, a tickle of warmth nudged at Ben's heart. Letting his gaze veer off into the crowd, Ben spotted Merry by the gazebo steps, holding a clapping Alex up to survey the commotion.

His family. The warmth around his heart blazed into a full-blown fire of joy so intense, it stole his breath.

"Anyway," Ben muttered without taking his eyes off his wife—his *wife*—and the boy who would be his son. "It's your turn next, boyo. I hope you're taking notes. Because this? This is how it's done."

And with that, Ben plunged into the crowd, shaking

hands right and left, dodging the puckered lips of every grateful old lady with an ailing pet and the back slaps of every farmer whose herd Ben had inoculated. He walked the line of picnic tables, barely registering the cornucopia of side dishes that made up their potluck wedding feast: everything from the humble shredded carrot and raisin salad he'd had a secret love for as a kid to a tray of fancy puff pastry tartlets stuffed with what looked like creamed spinach studded with slivers of dark red country ham.

The moment Ben broke free of tiny, wizened old Dabney Leeds and his querulous questions about his poor bulldog's watery eyes—the bulldog in question staring up at them in abject misery, stuffed into a doggie tuxedo complete with a black satin bow tie on his collar—a breeze rustled through the trees and sent a shower of autumn leaves swirling through the air.

Merry and Alex stood a step or two above the crowd, looking up at the shower of leaves, and Alex reached out both chubby arms to try and capture one as it sailed past.

He missed, his face clouding over with the beginnings of tears, but Ben snagged a perfect bright yellow specimen out of the air and presented it to him. Alex clapped, immediately distracted by trying to rip the crunchy leaf to shreds.

"You know he's only going to try and eat that," Merry said, laughing. Pink stained her cheeks, high and pretty.

"Since Alex hasn't yet worked out how to keep food in his mouth when it's delivered on a spoon, I'm not too anxious." Ben put a hand on the gazebo railing and stared up at them.

The longer he stared without saying anything, the more Merry's blush deepened. Eventually, she said, "This isn't awful for you, is it?"

"What? Oh, the party." Ben shrugged. He'd actually
managed to forget his deep-seated discomfort in public
gatherings for the past few moments. Standing here
with Merry and Alex seemed to drive it away. Or maybe
it was the fact that even the pushy, friendly, outgoing
Sanctuary Island residents appeared to have enough decency to give the newlyweds a few moments of semipri-
vacy in the midst of the reception.

Whatever it was, Ben was going to take full advantage
of it. "I'm fine. How are you, over here all by yourself?
I thought you'd be surrounded by a constant throng of
your mother's friends."

"It's amazing, isn't it?" Merry's eyes shone. "Everyone here is so kind and welcoming. I can't believe I
haven't even lived a full year on the island—I feel like
I've been here my whole life. I wish I had been."

Her brilliant glow dulled for a moment, and Ben
knew she was thinking about her absent father.

"You're here now, and for the foreseeable future,"
Ben said firmly. "That's what matters."

"The future," she echoed, a smile spreading across
her delicate features. "You're right. The future. And we
can make it whatever we want it to be."

Ben stepped up onto the bottom stair of the gazebo.
With Merry on the stair above, they were eye to eye.
She hadn't worn a frothy white princess gown, but she
wasn't in pajamas, either. He liked the gauzy long skirt
of the dress she'd chosen, blue silky material so pale it
was almost ivory, with sleeves to her elbows and a criss-
crossing bodice that pulled his gaze to the shadowy
valley between her lush round breasts.

She'd done something different with her eye
makeup, too, a darker Cleopatra-esque outline that
made them seem enormous and depthless, electric blue
pools that drew him in and made him long to drown.

On another woman, the sexy makeup might have been too much for such a sweet, innocent-looking dress, but on her, it wasn't—it was simply, perfectly Merry: a blend of mischievous vamp and aching purity that had Ben leaning in to kiss her soft, smiling mouth before he knew what he was about.

"Kiss, kiss, kiss!" The chant of the jubilant crowd filled Merry's ears as Ben's lips covered hers. Giddy and off-kilter, Merry let the moment wash over her, let the desire for closeness melt her into Ben's solid, wiry frame. She knew he was strong enough to hold all of them up if she lost her balance.

It wasn't their first kiss. He'd pecked her on the cheek at the courthouse, and there was that time when he was basically asleep and didn't know what he was doing . . . but, in a way, this was the first time they'd kissed with both parties conscious, unconcussed, and aware of what they were doing.

Maybe that was why it seared Merry to her core.

Even knowing how much she'd grown to like Ben and his cranky ways, how much she looked forward to the sight of his wide shoulders and narrow hips filling the office doorway when he came back from a call, the shivery way her body responded to the nearness of him, no matter how she pretended otherwise . . . none of that prepared Merry for the surging swell of desire that engulfed her at the first touch of Ben's lips.

Everything low and deep in her body tightened and shuddered, a cascade of pleasure over nerves she'd thought deadened by the pain of labor and delivery. Since giving birth, hell, since discovering she was pregnant, Merry's body hadn't felt entirely her own. The growth of new life inside her had brought home the truth that her body was meant for more than her own wants and needs . . . and once Alex was born, it was hard to go back to living alone in her body. Hard to think of it as all hers once again. Hers to give, hers to share, hers to enjoy.

But as Ben's mouth opened hungrily over hers and his tongue licked into her like a dancing flame searing every nerve, Merry reconnected with her body . . . and the bliss it could be made to feel.

The hard planes of Ben's chest brushing hers, the hard muscle of his shoulder under her grasping hand, and above all, the hungry slant of his hot mouth sent Merry's mind into a whirl of shocked sensation.

She kissed him back as if her life depended on it, as if she were learning how to kiss for the first time, eager and enthusiastic with the newness of it all. A guttural noise ripped from Ben's throat, and Merry quivered at it like a dizzy virgin.

Only the cheers, catcalls, whistles, and stomping feet of the assembled population of the entire island kept Merry from having her way with her new husband right there on the gazebo steps in front of God, Alex, and everyone.

Alex!

She broke the kiss with a gasp, the chill autumn air burning her lungs for a head-clearing instant. Pulling back far enough to stare into Ben's storm-gray eyes, she said the first thing that popped into her head. "I can't believe how often we seem to make out with my kid right in between us."

Ben lifted a hand to cup Alex's head. His long, slender surgeon's fingers were gentle against the curves of the baby's skull. "Hazards of being new parents. I bet most couples with a baby wind up stealing kisses around the kid."

"But most of them aren't newlyweds," Merry retorted, a little breathlessly. She was used to having to tilt her head back to meet Ben's gaze, and this straight-on view of his sculpted face was overwhelming. With his tumbled dark curls, razor-sharp cheekbones, and perfect raven's-wing eyebrows, he could be a model or an actor. It was inconceivable that this gorgeous man was wandering around a tiny town like Sanctuary, rescuing animals no one else wanted, an incredibly eligible bachelor ready for the taking.

Not anymore.

The possessiveness of the thought rushed through Merry like a tidal wave, dangerous and inevitable. Feeling the sucking drag of the undertow threatening to pull her under, she tried to remind herself that this wasn't how it was supposed to be, between them. Ben didn't want her messy emotions.

"Anyway, don't get used it," she forced out. "We're not like that."

"Oh?" Ben licked his bottom lip, and Merry couldn't help dropping her gaze to the movement of his tongue over the full, kiss-reddened mouth. "What are we, then?"

That pulled her up short. As much time as she'd spent defining what they weren't, Merry hadn't quite worked out what they were. "We're . . . friends. Almost definitely. Even though you drive me crazy sometimes, and other times I think you need a good swat to the seat of the pants."

The twinkle in his eyes brightened. "Anytime, sweetness. But everyone who came out here today to celebrate with us would probably say we're more than friends."

"They don't know the whole story, though," Merry argued. "Besides, I thought you said this party wasn't even about us, that Sanctuary will take any feeble excuse to throw together a potluck."

"That's definitely true. Last spring, the town lost its collective mind and put on a festival to celebrate the sighting of the first red-breasted robin. But this is different. You know what Miss Emily said to me when I thanked her for the cake?"

Merry leveled him with a skeptical brow.

"Okay, okay," he admitted, quirking his mouth. "Geez, woman. You know me too well. Anyway, when I asked Miss Emily what in the blazing hell she was smoking when she put that frosted monstrosity together, she didn't even get mad. All she did was grin and kiss me on the cheek." He turned his face to show her the smudge of virulent apricot pink in the vague shape of a smooch. "She told me she was happy I wasn't alone anymore. That I'd found a partner."

Without thinking, Merry licked her thumb and smoothed it over the lipstick mark to wipe it clean. "A partner. That works for me."

Today, they'd committed to stand by each other, through thick and thin. And wasn't that what partners did? They were there for each other, to lean on and support in turn. To cheer the victories and commiserate over the failures, and offer advice in the tricky situations life threw at them.

She could trust Ben with that much, Merry thought.

"Toast!" someone yelled, to an accompaniment of applause and cheering, and Merry realized how long they'd been standing silhouetted against the backdrop of the gazebo as if they were posing for their nonexistent wedding photographer.

"That's not my job, is it?" Ben asked, panic spasming across his face.

Merry laughed. "How can a man who's never backed down from telling anyone what he thinks of them be afraid of public speaking?"

"It's not public speaking I mind," he said darkly. "It's how everyone here is waiting for me to break down and cry with joy, or something. All those expectant smiles give me the willies."

Merry angled her head to gaze out over the assembled crowd of well-wishers, people she barely knew yet who had left their houses and taken time out of their lives to bring a covered dish down to the town square and help turn this somewhat impromptu business arrangement into an actual wedding party.

She saw a lot of smiles. Several people had brought their pets; Mr. Leeds and his long-suffering bulldog, an older lady Merry thought she recognized from the Firefly Café with a Persian cat on a leash, and there was a family with a young black lab puppy sporting a plastic cone of shame to keep him from licking at the shaved patch on his hind leg.

The lanky boy who'd gotten in trouble with Taylor had set up a pair of speakers on a folding chair by an open space of green grass. A blonde Merry didn't know leaned over the back of the chair flirtatiously while Matt scrolled through the iPod he'd attached to the speakers. With a grin up at the flirty girl, he picked a song, something jazzy with a lot of brass that made Merry want to dance. She wasn't alone. While she watched, Grady Wilkes pulled her sister to her feet and over to a level patch of grass. The two of them wrapped around each other like honeysuckle vines, swaying in place.

Merry saw Harrison McNamara whirl her mother into a quick two-step, Jo throwing her head back to shout a laugh up at the twinkle lights strung from the trees. And over by the nonalcoholic punch, Taylor McNamara stood ladling neon-pink liquid into plastic cups and casting sideways looks at Matt and the girl by the speakers.

When Merry gave her a smile and a thank-you wave, Taylor only shrugged, but Merry thought she detected a pleased tilt to her pointed little chin. They were going to be okay. Merry would make sure of it.

There were a lot of faces she knew, and more she didn't, but she had a feeling it wouldn't be long before everyone on this little island was out on the makeshift dance floor. "Speech!" Ella called, laughing up at her from the safety of Grady's arms.

"Thank you all for coming," Merry said, as loudly and clearly as she could. "My husband and I—"

She had to pause for the eruption of shouts and whistling, the stamping of feet and raising of plastic cups. Every breath of this perfect afternoon was like inhaling pure oxygen, life-giving and sustaining. "We appreciate it more than we can say," Merry finished, her heart pounding. She felt as if she'd finally come home.

Through the yells and laughter, the shouted congratulations and wishes for their happiness, Merry saw a sleek black car drive slowly up Main Street and park across from the square. Shading her eyes against the brightness of the afternoon sun, she squinted curiously to see who would emerge. Part of her fluttered nervously—the silly part that never stopped hoping her father would wake up one day and be interested in her—but the man who got out of the driver's side was too short and squat. Even from a distance, she could see that he wore a dark uniform and a cap, like a chauffeur out of a movie.

"Oh no," Ben groaned. He went rigid at her side, stiff and unhappy.

"What?" Merry asked, just as the chauffeur guy walked around to the back of the car to open the door for an older couple to climb out. The woman was slim and stylish in a classic pink wool pantsuit, and the man whose arm she took turned to stare over the town square like a king surveying his great, unwashed populace.

"Brace yourself," Ben said grimly. "Those are my parents."

Chapter Sixteen

Merry frowned in confusion. "Why should I brace myself? It's wonderful that they were able to make it in time for the reception! Isn't it?"

The ache of her own father's absence tightened her voice, and Ben had to force himself to uncurl his fingers from the fists that wanted to punch a hole through the gazebo wall. Because this was not going to be pretty.

Stay cool, he told himself. He was going to need to be cool to get through the next hour. His parents were here, invading his private island haven, crashing the happiest day of his life—and he wasn't going to be able to hide the truth from Merry.

"Listen." He turned to her, grasping her shoulders for emphasis. "When I said I invited my parents to our wedding, and they were sorry they couldn't make it? I lied. I didn't invite them. And they're about to make both of us very sorry."

"Why wouldn't you invite them?" she gasped. "And why would you lie about it?"

"Because they're horrible," Ben said impatiently.

"What, you think I turned out the way I am by accident? No. Trust me, these people are awful, and I didn't want them around you and Alex."

"If they're so horrible," Merry hissed, exasperated and embarrassed, "why go to all the trouble of marrying me to provide them with a grandson to carry on the family name?"

Caught out, Ben shook his head. "Just because my parents suck doesn't mean I'm happy to see the family name die out. Besides, that wasn't the only reason—but it was one I thought you'd be able to sympathize with."

She opened her mouth to argue with him, but Ben cut her off with a naked plea. "Can we talk about this later? I swear, I'll answer any questions you have about my relationship with my parents."

"Fine," Merry said, eyes flashing. "But this isn't over. And Ben? This is not a great way to start our married life—with you getting caught in a lie."

"Believe me," he said bleakly. "I know." He turned back to survey the two people picking their way through the newly fallen leaves blanketing the village green.

Heads turned as the newcomers made their way through the crowd of revelers. Harrison McNamara stepped in their path as if he wanted to greet them, but Tripp and Pamela Fairfax were old hands at ignoring what they didn't want to see. They swept past the dignified bank manager without a sideways glance, all of their glittering attention focused on the gazebo.

"What do you want?" Ben snapped, instinctively curling a protective arm around Merry and drawing her close. She was tense against him, her body all planes and angles. "You show up at my wedding, unannounced and uninvited—"

Merry jerked away from him with a reproachful glance before turning to his parents. "What he means to say is, welcome to Sanctuary Island. We're so glad you could be here to celebrate with us."

Tripp Fairfax stopped a few feet from the pavilion, his bushy brows lowered over the judgmental stare he leveled at the simple, homespun decorations . . . the harvest bouquets of red and gold leaves, the strands of cheap Christmas lights hanging from the trees. "Tell me we're not too late," Tripp said heavily. "To put a stop to this insanity."

"Oh, sorry. Was I unclear?" Sarcasm layered over Ben's voice as thickly as the buttercream frosting on their monstrosity of a wedding cake, but he couldn't stop it. "When I said you showed up at our wedding uninvited, I should've said you crashed our wedding *reception*. The wedding itself is over and done with, legal and official and nothing you can do about it. So you may as well head home."

Beside his father, Ben's mother closed her eyes at the news, one perfectly manicured hand pressed delicately to the pale pink lapel of her ladies-who-lunch suit. "Oh, Benjamin."

Fine tremors ran through Merry's entire body, and Ben ground his back teeth, wishing he could spare her this. *You made me call them*, he longed to say, like a child refusing to take responsibility. But none of this was Merry's fault.

Ben forced himself to calm down. If he could behave like a rational adult, maybe the example he set would convince his parents to follow suit. "Since you're here . . . Mother, I'd like to introduce you to my wife. Meredith Preston Fairfax."

Merry flinched again, but this time, Ben thought it was more due to surprise. It was the first time he'd said her married name aloud, and he was surprised himself at how much he loved the sound of it. She recovered quickly enough to say, in a high, tense voice, "I'm pleased to meet you?"

His mother pressed her lips together, looking sad and torn. But his father didn't even bother to acknowledge Merry with so much as a frown—he stared straight at Ben and said, "You are determined to ruin this family."

Ben felt the shock that ran through Merry's body before he strode down the gazebo steps to go toe-to-toe with his father. "That's it," Ben snarled. "You don't get to come here and pass judgment and be disapproving. I've lived just fine without your approval for a long time. I didn't need it when I left Richmond and moved here, or when I started the animal hospital, and I certainly don't need it now that I've found Merry and Alex."

"Benjamin!" Pamela sucked in a shocked breath. "How can you talk like this? How can you do this to our family?"

It was harder than he expected to ignore the genuine hurt in his mother's voice, but Ben couldn't afford to back down. "If you think I'm ruining your family, fine. Disown me. I've got a new family now."

Something flashed in his father's steely gray eyes, pain mixed with a grudging respect. Tripp shook his head. "Don't be so quick to cast me off, son. I've given you everything you've ever had, including the time and space to form this ill-advised attachment—and I can take it all away, just as easily."

"All you've ever given me is the knowledge that no matter what I do, I can't live up to the idealized image of me that exists in your head." Ben lifted his chin. "Face facts, Dad. There are some things in life you can't control. I'm one of them."

"I've never wanted to control you." Tripp pinched the bridge of his aquiline nose. "Such dramatics. I merely want you to live up to your full potential. Is that such a crime?"

Sincerity rang through his father's words, and Ben steeled himself against it. He knew his dad truly did want the best for him. But Ben's idea of what was best differed dramatically from Tripp's.

Still, in the interests of providing positive reinforcement, Ben backed down from his battle-ready stance. "I know, Dad. And I appreciate the opportunities you gave me when I was younger. But at some point, you have to be willing to acknowledge that I'm not a child anymore. I get to choose the life I want to live."

Tripp's gray eyes hardened to stone. "Not when you prove yourself unable to make rational choices."

"I don't mean to interrupt," Merry said, causing the entire Fairfax family to stare at her in surprise. Her shoulders drew up nervously, but she continued on, undaunted. "I'm sorry you're not happy about us getting married. But I think you should know that we have been totally rational about this decision. This marriage is not something we've entered into lightly or, or blinded by emotion. Honestly, it's more about practicality than anything else."

For the first time, Tripp Fairfax's gaze settled on Merry, drifting down to rest for a moment on the quilt-swaddled baby squirming in her arms. Ben felt everything inside himself gear up to jump down his father's throat the moment he uttered a single word to make Merry feel like crap.

Showing the self-control and diplomacy that stood him in good stead as the chairman of the board of the largest, most profitable hospital in Virginia, Tripp said, "Ms. Preston, I don't doubt your motives. From your perspective, of course this marriage makes sense."

It was fairly mild, for Tripp Fairfax, but Merry stiffened all over, a flush burning across her cheeks. "Think whatever you want; call me a gold digger if it makes you happy, but while you're at it, you might consider the fact that without this marriage, your son won't get the one thing he wants—and that he says you want, as well. A son to carry on the family name."

Tripp tilted his head to one side, scrutinizing Merry with curiosity. "How do you figure?"

Merry marched down the gazebo steps like an avenging angle, all flowing hair and righteous wrath. Ben watched her, transfixed. When she was close enough, she hissed, "How can you be so insensitive? I'm talking about the fact that Ben can't have biological children of his own!"

Ben winced as his father's eyes filled with comprehension.

Uh-oh.

"You think Ben is incapable of fathering a child?" Tripp mused, all but stroking his beard as he glanced between Ben and Merry. "How interesting."

"We're done here," Ben said, sidestepping quickly to reach his wife and put his arms around her trembling shoulders. "Mom, Dad, it's been lovely as always, but you missed your window to mess up the wedding, so it's time for you to go. Now."

"It's a public park," Tripp pointed out. "You can't force us to leave."

"Oh yes we can." Grady stepped up beside Ben, burly and intimidating. He was joined by Harrison Mc-Namara and his teen daughter, Taylor, brandishing a punch ladle, along with huge, intimidating Sam Brennan, flanked surprisingly by Andie Shepard in her tan sheriff's uniform.

One by one, the townspeople of Sanctuary Island, Ben's adopted home, came forward to stand with Ben and Merry—Miss Emily crossing her thin arms over her withered chest threateningly, old Mr. Leeds pulling a growling Percy by the leash.

They ranged themselves around the newlyweds and faced down the leaders of Richmond society with raised chins, clear eyes, and no hesitation.

"You'd better leave," Ben told his mother, softening his voice with an effort. "You don't belong here."

"Neither do you!" Pamela exclaimed, blotting at her damp eyes to keep her mascara from running.

"Yes I do." As the words left Ben's mouth, he realized they were completely true.

He belonged on Sanctuary Island. The people of this community accepted him for who he was, grumpy and antisocial and utterly dedicated to keeping their pets healthy. These people were ready to defend him, no questions asked.

"This isn't over," Tripp warned him, straightening his striped tie with a snap of his wrist. "We've taken a room at a waterfront inn across the channel in Winter Harbor, and we'll be staying until you come to your senses. Your mother and I aren't giving up on you, even if you appear to have given up on yourself. Come along, Pamela. Let's leave these people to their . . . hoedown."

He turned on his heel and stalked back to the car with Pamela tripping along at his side.

Ben let out a long breath. At his back, he felt the tension ebb out of the assembled mob of townsfolk.

"They're gone." The relief in Merry's voice clutched at his heart. "I can't believe it. Thank you, everyone!"

"Yeah, thanks," Ben echoed, slapping Grady on the back and showing a smile around the crowd, but it was hard to keep it up, even as everyone around them cheered.

This felt like a victory, but it wasn't. Not really. He knew his father better than that.

"They're gone for now," he said, tamping down on the dread in his heart while the rest of the party went back to partying. "But not for good."

Merry held herself carefully, as if a single wrong word might shatter something. "That's fine. I needed them to get out of here and leave us alone for the night, at least, to give me the chance to ask you a question."

Ben's heart dropped into his gut. "And I promised to answer your questions."

"You did. So here it is." She took a deep breath, as if steeling herself, and narrowed her vivid blue eyes on Ben's.

"What did your dad mean when he asked if I thought you were incapable of fathering a child?"

There it was. The crack in the wall behind which lurked every dark thing in Ben's past, every memory he'd banished, every emotion he'd successfully repressed.

Momentarily speechless, Ben stared down at the take-no-prisoners look on his new wife's face, and did the only thing he could think of: he told the truth.

"Technically, there's nothing to prevent me from fathering a child. I let you think there was, because I wanted to avoid this exact conversation."

Merry went white, with either fury or hurt. Ben couldn't tell, but he hated it either way. "God, Ben. Maybe your parents are right. This marriage was a mistake."

Ben reached for her hand. He had to stop her from leaving like this. "No! It wasn't a mistake."

But Merry kept shaking her head—in fact, all of her was shaking. "What was I thinking, marrying a man I barely know?"

"You know me," Ben assured her through the ache in his throat.

She looked away. "I thought I did. But it turns out I'm missing some pretty key pieces of the puzzle."

"Give me a chance to make it right," Ben demanded, not relinquishing his grasp on her cold fingers. "I promised to answer all your questions and, this time, I swear I won't leave anything out. No matter how much I hate talking about it."

Merry's mouth was turned down in an unhappy curve, but she'd stopped trying to pull away from him. "Ben . . ."

Sensing her weakening, he pushed forward. "One thing, though. This is a conversation we need to have at home."

"Why?" Her voice rose in suspicion. "So you can weasel out of it again?"

"No." Ben tried for a smile, but it felt all wrong on his face. "Because I don't want to cry in front of the entire assembled population of Sanctuary Island. They wouldn't be scared of me anymore, and I'd have to be extra mean to make up for it. As a thank-you for helping scare off my parents, let's spare them that. What do you say?"

Concern lit a hesitant glow in Merry's eyes, and Ben could admit to himself that he was glad to see it. If she could still worry about him, there was hope. At least enough to make it worthwhile to dig through the worst memories of his entire life.

"Fine." Merry glanced away. "I'll wait until we get home."

The simple fact that she still called the house at Isleaway Farm "home" beat back some of the darkness in Ben's brain. He smiled, and Merry wrinkled her nose at him.

"You get a reprieve, but all is not forgiven, and certainly not forgotten," she scolded, switching Alex from one arm to the other, the way she did when she'd been carrying him for too long.

"Understood," Ben said, reaching tentatively with both arms. It was an undeniable relief when Merry handed over the baby without hesitating.

She rolled her shoulders and pinned Ben with a challenging stare. "Really, you deserve to be punished. And I think I have just the punishment."

Ben braced himself. "What?"

"You have to let Taylor take wedding photos of us feeding each other cake. And then you have to dance with me."

The vindictive satisfaction in her voice and the twinkle in her eyes, along with the warm weight of the boy in his arms, filled Ben with a rush of disbelief so overpowering, he nearly staggered under the onslaught.

"Brutal," he managed. "But I notice you're punishing yourself, too—you'll be choking down that cake right alongside me, and you're the one whose toes are liable to get broken when I step on them on the dance floor."

"I figure I'm partially responsible for this situation," Merry said as she led him over to the table that held the towering white cake. "You offered, before, to tell me about your first marriage, but I didn't want to hear it. Stupid."

"Don't call yourself stupid," Ben growled without thinking.

Merry smiled faintly. "Don't worry, this time I won't let anything stand in the way of hearing the whole story. If we stand any chance of making this marriage work, we have to be honest with each other. Even when it hurts."

Swallowing down a spurt of unease, Ben nodded. Merry pressed a quick kiss to Alex's head, and Ben inhaled a swift, surreptitious breath of her fresh apple scent before she set off to find Taylor.

Honest even when it hurts.

Ben wasn't sure he could promise that. There were some truths that were never meant to be spoken aloud, and some that Merry might never be ready to hear.

For instance, the fact that Ben was fairly certain he was head over heels in love with his wife.

Chapter Seventeen

"In spite of everything," Merry said, sighing as she kicked her sore bare feet up onto the polished wood coffee table, "we managed to have kind of an awesome day."

The party had lasted long into the evening. Merry and Ben had eventually handed Alex off to be cooed over by a revolving rotation of relatives and friends, while they made the rounds. She'd added "thanking every single person individually" to Ben's punishment roster, which he'd taken with as good a grace as could be expected—i.e., a minimum of scowling and grumping, and only a few cutting asides when he was forced to deal with some of his more troublesome (or, in Ben's words "idiotic") clients.

Merry had ruthlessly suppressed her laughter, and wondered exactly when the sharp side of Ben's tongue had started to tickle her funny bone.

Now they were home, Alex was sleeping the sleep of an infant who'd endured more squeezing, dandling, and cheek pinching in one afternoon than in the entire four months of his life, and Ben was making tea in the kitchen.

"You have a gift," Ben told her, handing off a steaming mug that wafted minty steam.

"We said no gifts!" Merry groaned, struggling to sit upright in indignation. "I didn't get you a wedding present."

Ben laughed and settled onto the other end of the couch. "That's not what I mean. You have a gift for happiness. No matter what happens, you seem to come through it with a smile."

"Oh." Merry made a face and blew a cooling breath over her fragrant tea. "My sister's the one who went through therapy—and I say 'went through therapy' as if it were an ordeal, but I'm pretty sure if she ever gets married, her ex-therapist will be one of her bridesmaids—but even I know that 'gift for happiness' is another way of saying I tend to hide from the bad stuff in life."

"Is that such a bad thing? Personally, I find repression to be an effective coping mechanism."

Merry snorted. "That doesn't surprise me after meeting your parents, the king and queen of the WASPs."

"It's true, my family isn't big on openness and communication. Or, you know, feelings." Ben stared down into his mug as if lost in thought.

There wouldn't be a better opening. Merry took a cautious sip of her tea, even knowing it would burn her tongue, to buy time to pluck up her courage. This man she'd married was a mystery, an enigma, a Rubik's Cube of contradictions. She wanted to get to the bottom of him, to plumb his depths and learn his secrets—and that meant bringing up things he clearly didn't want to talk about.

But after today, and the threatening way his father talked about taking this life away from them, Merry needed to know.

"So . . . about that promise you made at the reception," Merry began, cringing inside at her own tentativeness. Why was this so hard?

Maybe because she was already in deeper with Ben, emotionally speaking, than she'd ever thought possible when she agreed to their so-called simple business arrangement.

He blew out a breath and planted his feet in the deep-piled rug, curling his toes into the cream wool. Merry found her gaze drawn to those masculine feet. They were sort of stupidly sexy, poking out from the frayed hem of the jeans he'd changed into the minute they walked through the door.

"Right," Ben said, pulling her away from her embarrassing sudden-onset foot fetish. "Any question you want to ask. Go."

Merry, who'd been thinking about this off and on for hours, knew exactly where to start. "What were you going to tell me about your relationship with Ashley, when it came up before and I shut you down?"

"Straight for the throat, no warm-up, huh?" Ben leaned over the mug cupped between his agile surgeon's fingers, his elbows braced on his spread knees. Shooting her a glance from under the thick fall of wavy brown hair over his forehead, he said, "You sure you wouldn't rather start small, work your way up?"

More than anything else, Ben's reaction told her she was tugging on exactly the right thread to start unraveling his past. "Start talking, Doc."

"I used to hate it when you called me that." He smiled slightly, returning his gaze to the fascinating stretch of rug between his feet. "Now I kind of dig it."

"Ben . . ."

"No, you're right. No more messing around. So, Ashley. We met at a hospital fund-raiser during the first year of my residency. My father is on the board, and I realized almost immediately that he'd orchestrated the whole thing—but for once, I didn't mind his interference, because Ashley was . . . perfect."

Perfect. Merry drew her legs up onto the sofa cushion under her and took a soothing sip of tea.

"She was blond and cool, not like most of the giggling, ex-sorority-girl daughters of my parents' society friends. Ashley is smart—she's the head of development for a local nonprofit fund that subsidized working artists. My mother loved her because she came from a good family; my father wanted to attract Ashley's father to donate money for a new hospital wing; but I didn't care about any of that because I was in love."

He shook his head at himself, as if he found the entire concept of being in love unbelievable now.

"So what went wrong?" Merry asked into the hush.

"Nothing, at first. We got married, I was promoted to chief resident, she cut back on her hours at the art fund . . . and got pregnant."

It wasn't as if Merry hadn't been prepared for this. It stood to reason that if Ben had proof of his ability to father children, he'd gotten it during his first marriage. But somehow, it was still a shock. Merry bobbled her mug and bit back a curse as she lifted her hand to her mouth to suck hot tea off her skin.

Her entire body was engaged in the act of listening, every atom of her being rerouted to her ears as she strained to catch Ben's next words.

"The pregnancy was normal. Easy, even. Ashley never had morning sickness, and she kept up with her yoga and lap swimming until the week she gave birth."

If Merry hadn't hated Perfect Ashley, who Ben was still hung up on, already . . . but with a shiver of presentiment, Merry knew she couldn't hate Ashley. Not with what was surely coming next.

"The baby was born exactly on time. I was in the delivery room, and since I'd already done my labor-and-delivery rotation, the attending even let me be the one to catch the baby." There was no wonder or joy in Ben's deadened voice, only sorrow, and Merry had to bite her lip to keep from begging him to stop talking. But now that he'd started, Ben seemed unable to stop. He told the story in a steady stream of distant words, as if it had happened to someone else.

"She looked healthy, ten fingers and toes, no obvious issues. Ashley cried. I might have, too, I don't remember. We named her Justine, after Ashley's mother. Justine Elizabeth Fairfax."

He paused there, long enough for Merry to count out five heartbeats as blood pounded in her ears. "It's a beautiful name," she finally said.

Ben jolted, blinking at her as if he'd forgotten she was there. "Yeah," he said, setting his mug down on the coffee table with a loud crack. She caught a glimpse of his eyes and caught her breath.

His eyes weren't numb or distant—they were infinite pools of rage and grief. "That pretty name looked great on her tombstone."

"Oh, Ben." Merry covered her mouth with her hand, frozen on the sofa. Should she put her arm around him? He looked as if he'd throw off any comforting touch, the line of his broad back vibrating with tension.

"She lived four weeks and five days. Four weeks and five days of tests, procedures, and specialists. She never left the hospital."

Heart breaking, Merry tried to imagine the extended terror Ben and his wife experienced in those days. She couldn't. Her brain simply refused to go there.

"Failure to thrive," Ben murmured. "Do you know what that means?"

Merry shook her head mutely, her vision blurred by tears.

"It means," Ben continued, soft and ruthless, "that she didn't grow. She actually lost weight after birth, even though Ashley fed her constantly. Her body refused to retain or efficiently utilize the calories she took in. She wasted away in front of us for four weeks and five days because of a chromosomal abnormality so rare, it only affects one out of every six thousand live births. It's like being struck by lightning. No way to predict it, no way to prevent it, no way to cure it. Nothing to do but stand outside the NICU and watch her fade."

The remembered helplessness in his tone was horrible, annihilating, and Merry couldn't stay respectfully on her side of the couch any longer. "You can push me away if you want," she said, scooting over to wrap her arms around his bent shoulders. "But I hope you don't."

He was icy marble under her touch for a long minute. Finally, he turned his head, just far enough to press his face to the side of Merry's neck. She clutched him closer in relief, fisting her hands in the loose cotton of his soft waffle-knit Henley and burying her nose in his hair.

"She died," he gasped thickly. "My baby girl, my Justine."

"I'm sorry, I'm so sorry," Merry kept whispering, over and over, feeling as if she'd been turned inside out. God in heaven, no wonder he hadn't wanted to relive this nightmare by telling her about it.

Ben's arms crept around her waist, hesitant at first, but soon he was holding on to her as if she were his only anchor in a stormy sea, tight enough to make her ribs creak in protest. His shoulders spasmed, he shook, but his face where it pressed against her neck was dry. He didn't cry.

That was okay, because Merry was crying enough for both of them.

Eyes swollen and burning, Ben let the flood of Merry's tears wash his grief back down into the depths of his soul. No amount of sobbing would ever wipe it away completely, he knew, but as Merry's hitching breaths ghosted over his head, Ben felt lighter than he had in years.

Repression might be a valid coping strategy, but there was something to be said for getting it all out there.

Sitting up took effort. Every part of Ben's body wanted to mold itself to Merry's, to melt into her and mesh together until he absorbed some of the sweetness and good humor of her outlook, her giant and generous heart, into himself.

"You can probably guess the rest," Ben said, sinking back into the sofa cushions, still close enough to feel Merry all along one side. He was exhausted by the emotional roller coaster of the day. "Ashley and me . . . our marriage didn't survive the death of our daughter. Ash got remarried four winters ago; I hear she's got a healthy toddler and another on the way."

Merry let him go so she could lean over and grab a tissue from the box on the end table. Blowing her nose, she shuddered out a long breath and pulled herself together. "Then," she said, frowning, "nothing went wrong with Ashley's other pregnancies."

Ben tensed. "Obviously not."

"So that's what your dad meant. You could father as many perfectly healthy kids as you want—there's no reason to assume lightning would strike twice in the same place."

"Doesn't matter." Ben cut off that train of thought

with a sharp gesture. "I'm never putting myself, or any woman I care about, through that again."

"But Ben, you can't blame yourself." Merry resettled with her legs under her as she stared earnestly at him and mouthed the same platitudes Ben had heard a hundred times from his parents, his friends, the doctors and nurses at the hospital. Even Ashley.

Unwilling to listen, Ben shifted restlessly. "I do blame myself. Justine—she never even had a chance at a life. I was supposed to be there for her, to protect her from everything. I trained to be a doctor, and when it mattered most, I couldn't heal my daughter. I was helpless."

Even Ben could hear the raw anguish in his rough voice, but instead of backing down or hurrying to placate him, Merry shook her head. The expression on her beautiful face was exasperation, tinged with fondness and a heartbreaking edge of empathy. "Oh, Doc. You pride yourself on rationality, you place reason and logic above emotion every time—but about this? Even you can't be rational."

And somehow, that single observation struck Ben like a tuning fork to the skull, reverberating all through him.

He sank deeper into the couch cushions, boneless with shock. "You're right," he admitted for the first time since he said good-bye to his baby girl. "I'm not being rational about this."

"And maybe you won't ever be." Merry put a gentle hand on his knee, sympathy softening her husky voice. "At least, not enough to take a chance on having a baby with me. And if that's the case, I'll understand. Just so long as you let go of the guilt and try to accept that the tragedy of Justine's death was not your fault."

Ben swallowed hard. "How did you get so wise?"

Merry ducked her head, hiding her eyes, but when she looked up again she was wearing a small, tremulous smile. "After Alex was born, you came around to see him every day. You were always so gruff when you first arrived, but when you saw how fat and happy he was . . ."

Ben struggled for a brief moment, then gave in. He'd gone this far, he might as well spill it all. "Alex was the first birth I attended, since Justine. It's meant . . . so much to me, I can't even tell you how much, to be part of his life. And yours."

They were still sitting so close, he could feel the way her body inclined toward him inside the circle of his embrace. In all the horrible aftermath of Justine's birth and painfully abbreviated life, Ben had never felt connected to Ashley this way. Which was completely his fault—he'd built thick, impenetrable walls around his heart to avoid dealing with the gut-wrenching horror of the situation. That much was true.

But it was also true that Ashley had never turned to him. Not once. They'd each been locked in their own separate cages, prisoners of grief and anger, and when Justine's death released them . . . they'd found they could no longer bear to even look at one another.

Every glimpse of Ashley's pale, shocked face had threatened to pull him back into that prison once more.

Ben stared at Merry's flushed cheeks, her nose pink from crying, her eyes bright with the remnants of tears she'd shed for him because he wasn't able to cry for himself. And he realized he'd never felt more free.

"What you went through," Merry began, then cut herself off with a choking breath. "I can't even imagine it. Thank you for telling me—I think I understand everything much better now."

"Oh, good." Ben barked a hoarse laugh, scrubbing his hands over his scratchy five o'clock shadow. "When you've got me all figured out, let me know."

"It might take a while." Merry slid over to rest her head on his shoulder. "You're pretty tricky."

"Luckily, we're married now. So you've got as much time as you need."

She buried a yawn in the front of his shirt. "True. I'll get started in a minute."

Her breaths evened out, deep and slow, and Ben felt peace drop over him like a fleecy blanket. He yawned wide enough to unhinge his jaw, and stretched one arm out to shut off the lamp and click on the baby monitor. He listened for a moment, but the only sound from Alex's room was a snuffled sigh.

Feeling as if he'd been given a precious gift, Ben maneuvered Merry carefully until they were lying spooned together, Merry's slim back to his chest. Her head was pillowed on his bicep, which was going to cut off all circulation to his arm in less than half an hour, but Ben didn't care.

He was exactly where he wanted to be.

Chapter Eighteen

Merry blinked awake between one breath and the next, cradled against the warmest, most comforting mattress she'd ever experienced.

A mattress that rose and fell beneath her, emitting a steady tattoo of measured beats against her cheek.

Her eyes flew wide. Oh, right. She was lying on top of Ben.

Every inch of her skin was suddenly and vividly roused to the sensation of being pressed up against Ben's powerful form. With her head tucked down against his chest, his sinewy arms curled loosely around her, Merry breathed in his spicy evergreen scent and tried not to think about how their legs were tangled together.

She'd fallen asleep in the loose, gauzy dress she'd worn to get married, and while she'd enjoyed it as a pseudo-bridal gown, it was less than ideal as a nightie. The filmy material had slithered up in the night to tighten around her thighs and leave her legs bare. Every breath shifted Merry's naked calves against the frayed denim of Ben's jeans in a way that sent shocking tendrils of heat curling up her spine.

Ben rocked slightly beneath her, his abs going granite hard beneath her hand, and one of his jean-clad thighs slid between hers. Merry swallowed her surprised squeak at the wave of desire that crashed over her when her hips slotted perfectly against Ben's.

Gravity and the dreamy lethargy of her body melted her into an unthinkable intimacy with this man she'd sworn never to touch.

Merry squeezed her eyes shut, but that only made the sensations more urgent and impossible to ignore. She felt something deep inside unfurl and stretch in a molten glide toward the source of pleasure.

Ben.

This was crazy. Was she ready for this? Her body was different now, after giving birth—would she even be able to please Ben? Did she want to try?

But the moment she bit her lip and did a slow-motion wriggle to get her hands braced on either side of Ben's hard-planed chest, ready to push herself up off the couch and away from temptation, Ben's surprisingly long, dark lashes fluttered. He opened eyes hazy with sleep, and smiled up at her.

Merry's heart tightened as if someone had tied a ribbon around it and pulled hard on the ends. Half asleep, with bright moonlight washing through the window and silvering his skin and hair, the first thing Ben did was smile when he saw her.

"Merry," Ben said, licking his lips in an absentminded, wondering kind of way. "My smart, wonderful new wife."

Staring down at him, entranced, she forgot all about getting up. "We fell asleep," she murmured, intensely aware of every shift and tense of Ben's awakening muscles. "You should've kicked me awake and made me go to bed."

"What for? I've slept on this couch plenty of times. It gives good sleep."

A smile tugged at the corners of her mouth. "It must. I don't usually nod off so easily." She sniffed, her nose a little stuffy, and memory came rushing back. "Especially not right in the middle of a majorly emotional conversation! Oh my gosh, Ben, I'm so sorry! You really should have pinched me or something."

Ben's laugh was low and deep. Merry could feel it in his abs, in the tightening of his muscles, before she heard it. He lifted one arm, bent at the elbow, over his head and tangled his fingers in the unruly waves of his hair. "And miss the chance to have you drool on me? No way."

Merry struggled upright in horror. "I did not drool! Oh no. Did I drool?"

Her position, braced over him on her hands, pushed her center of gravity lower, where his thighs cradled her hips.

Sensual awareness flashed through Ben's moon-dark eyes before he smiled up at her. "Only in a cute way. Besides, anyone would've zonked out after the day we had. Think about it. We started the day with a food fight, segued to a legally binding ceremony linking us for life, with a side of good old-fashioned parental disapproval, and finished up with me breaking apart into a million pieces on the couch."

"It is a lot to process," Merry agreed, unable to resist the urge to smile back at him.

There was a beat of silence, long enough for her to truly understand the new, uncharted level of intimacy they'd tumbled into, almost by accident.

"I'm glad you're here," Ben said suddenly. "In case I haven't mentioned it lately . . . I'm really happy you said yes."

"Me, too." And . . . she was fighting a blush, hoping the room was too dark for him to make it out.

But of course Ben, whose sharp eyes never missed anything, frowned and reached up to brush her cheek with the back of his fingers. "What's wrong?"

"Nothing." Merry ducked her head. She could get up, retreat to the safety of her bedroom and Alex's soft snuffles in his bassinet, but . . . she felt strangely safe already. "I've never been here with a guy before. This is new territory for me."

"What, napping on a couch? Yeah, that does sound a little tame for Miss Meredith Preston."

His voice was softly teasing, but Merry couldn't help taking it seriously. She wanted him to understand. "No, I mean . . . intimate."

He arched one of his brows, dark and devilish in the moonlight. "There's a baby sleeping on the other end of that monitor that proves otherwise."

Merry slapped at his chest with playful annoyance, wholeheartedly grateful for the way Ben always seemed to know when to lighten the mood. "Not like that! I mean, yes. I have had my share of . . . encounters. Some would probably say more than my share. My sister, the armchair psychologist, has lots of theories about lack of paternal involvement—which is about half a click away from telling me I'm searching for a father figure, which, ew. I'll cop to having some daddy issues, but I don't think it's as simple as that."

"Or maybe it's a lot more simple." Ben shrugged against the cushions, the move settling him deeper into the sofa. His searching gaze never left her face. "Maybe you simply enjoy sex. Which, by the way, is completely natural, not to mention biologically useful."

What a weird conversation. Merry settled back to rest her chin on Ben's cotton-covered sternum. "I guess

I used to enjoy it. If not the sex, always, then the close-ness. Even the illusion of it was enough sometimes. At least for a while. I don't know, it's hard to think about it now—I feel like such a different person from that girl who went out to a different club every night and had all those boyfriends."

"I wouldn't mind seeing you in your clubbing gear," Ben said, waggling those brows like a cartoon villain.

"Oh, I was a sight to behold." Merry huffed out a laugh. "Crazy hair in a rainbow of colors, leather pants so tight I basically had to paint them on. And my eye out for any guy that caught my fancy, who made me feel special, or could help me forget whatever drama I was worrying about that week. And I won't lie, at times it was fun. I loved the pounding music, the sweat and energy and anonymity of losing myself on the dance floor. But when I got pregnant . . . I couldn't afford to lose myself anymore. I had to be present, all the time. I had to pay attention. And now that I'm a mother . . ."

"What?"

She shook her head, letting the loose fall of her hair hide her face. "Being Alex's mother is the most impor-tant thing I've ever done. The stakes are crazy high. I can't afford to mess it up."

"Merry . . ."

"I know, I know." She shook back her hair, sum-moning up a smile. If it was a little shaky, hopefully the glamour of moonlight would help her out. "Every parent messes up. You read me this riot act once already."

"That's not what I was going to say." Ben sat up in a rush of controlled power, his muscles tightening and contracting in a way that sent weakness through all of Merry's limbs.

She was too busy gasping to put up a fight when Ben

manhandled her into straddling his lap in the center of the couch. "Okay, yes, I think you're setting yourself up for failure if you're aiming for perfection—but what you said about the clubs and the dancing, what you were looking for out there . . ."

"I had to grow up. I couldn't keep disappearing into a dream of music and sex and false, fleeting closeness."

He stared into her eyes, their faces so close together that she could feel the sweet rush of his breath against her mouth. "I get that. But Merry, don't let motherhood turn into another way to hide, another labyrinth to lose yourself in."

Merry reared back, scowling. "What?"

One of Ben's hands cupped her jaw, delicate and precise, the tips of his long fingers stroking the devastatingly sensitive spot behind her left ear. "I mean," he breathed out, pulling her down to him. "You're not only a mother—you're a woman, too. A beautiful, vibrant woman who deserves to be fulfilled in every way a human being can be."

A full body shiver enveloped her, tingling and prickling over every inch of her skin as her blood heated and thickened. Her heart throbbed in time with the pulse beating between her legs, primal and shocking and irresistible.

In a flash of heat lightning, Merry felt her body wake up, more vital and needy than ever before. Throwing her arms around Ben's neck, she hauled herself up and kissed him with every ounce of hungry joy inside her.

Ben swallowed a groan of triumph when Merry surged into his arms. Her mouth was open and wet, voracious, and he returned the kiss like a starving tiger mauling its prey. Their bodies crashed together, locked in a struggle as old as time. He had to get her naked, he needed to see her, to know for once and for sure that this was truly happening.

He'd always intended to get here, eventually—but he hadn't dreamed it would be on their actual wedding night.

Conscience pricked at him insistently, an annoying mosquito he tried to brush off as he licked into Merry's velvety mouth, but this was too important. He had to be sure.

Framing her impossibly fragile skull with his hands, Ben broke the kiss with a gasp. "Hold on. I promised . . . wouldn't push. Promised I'd wait for you to be ready."

Her lips were swollen and slick, her breath panted out in staccato bursts, but her eyes were clear. Hot. "Oh, I'm ready, Doc. Feel free to examine me, if you need to be convinced."

But Merry's slender fingers went to work on Ben's buttons, not her own, and when he raised his brows at her questioningly, she grinned. "It'll be a mutual examination."

"You want this," Ben said. It wasn't a question, exactly—but he searched her face for her answer.

It came in the softening of her wicked grin, the lazy hooding of her midnight-blue eyes. "I want you," she said, throaty and steady and sounding very much as if she knew her own damn mind and body.

Right. That ought to be enough for anyone's conscience.

And as Ben stripped off his shirt and bore her back onto the couch, her legs wrapped around his hips like ivy vines and her body soft and yielding, it was more than enough.

It was everything.

The moonlight turned her pale skin to cream, pure

and perfect in all its supposed imperfections—the heaviness of her breasts, the slight roundness of her belly, the lushness of her hips and backside. Merry's body was a banquet, and Ben savored every morsel.

He memorized her sighs and low, throbbing moans, the way she moved and the bright, greedy pleasure she took in every touch. If Ben could have made it last forever, he would have. But as dawn broke outside the windows, heralded by his ancient rooster Philbert's ear-splitting crow and a wavering cry from the baby monitor, Ben dropped one last kiss on Merry's slack, drowsy mouth and let her sleep.

Dragging the quilt off the back of the couch, he covered the luminous skin he'd tasted and caressed, and snagged his jeans off the floor. His foot slipped on an empty condom wrapper as he struggled into his jeans, and he nearly fell back on top of Merry.

Finding his balance, Ben checked his wife. Still out cold, although her eyelids flickered at the sound of another staticky cry from the baby monitor. Better get a move on.

He padded swiftly and silently down the hall to the guest room, stopping short in the doorway. Alex had given up on crying, and instead appeared to be entertaining himself by rocking back and forth on his back until slowly, while Ben watched, the little genius rolled over onto his belly. Kicking excitedly, Alex made the jerky swimming motions that Ben knew were helping him prepare for crawling and scooting in the coming weeks.

Proud enough to bust the buttons of his shirt, if he were wearing one, Ben moved to stand over the crib. "Oh, kiddo. You are going to be into everything once you start being independently mobile. And you know what? I can't wait."

At the sound of his voice, Alex cooed and banged his hands against the crib mattress. Grinning, Ben reached over the railing to lift the kid into his arms, sleep-warm and bright-eyed.

"You slept through the night," Ben told him. "Excellently done. For that, I think you deserve canned peaches in syrup for breakfast. Don't tell your mom, she'll worry about the sugar. But we know a little sugar will only make you sweeter, right, buddy?"

One of Alex's hands gripped the hair behind Ben's ear, tight and secure. "Da da da da," he said distinctly.

Ben's heart clenched with happiness. Rationally, he knew Alex didn't mean anything by it—at eighteen weeks, he hadn't yet assigned meaning to the random syllables his tongue was beginning to form—but even if "Dada" wasn't actually his first word, it would be a word Alex used eventually. And the meaning he assigned to the name would be Ben.

He held the boy close and allowed himself to remember a tiny, frail baby girl who hadn't lived long enough to call him anything.

For the first time in years, the memory was soft and sweet, tinged with melancholy, yes—but not a sharp, jagged knife between the ribs. Talking about Justine, telling Merry about her, had helped.

And although Alex could never take Justine's place, holding the sturdy little boy close and hearing his high, piping voice helped, too.

An unfamiliar feeling of contentment, pure and satisfying, poured through Ben like warm honey. The emotion had a name, and here in the quiet of dawn after a night of passion, Ben allowed himself to say it out loud.

"I didn't think I could have this—but here you are. We're a family now," he told Alex, who pulled his hair enthusiastically in response. "I love you. And I love your mother. But that'll be another little secret, okay? Mama's not ready to hear it yet. But someday . . . maybe sooner than I thought."

In the living room, Merry absently drew the quilt closer around her shoulders against the morning chill, and stared down at the baby monitor in her hand.

Chapter Nineteen

"And now everything's different, right?" Ella's voice carried the standard older-sister tone of all-knowingness.

Merry hated to admit it, but sometimes she actually found it comforting. It helped that once Ella discovered the love of her life on Sanctuary Island, she'd mellowed out quite a bit from the uptight, controlled workaholic Merry grew up with.

"Yes, but not necessarily in a bad way." Merry shrugged to settle the straps of Alex's baby carrier more comfortably on her shoulders before hooking one booted heel over the bottom rung of the paddock.

Inside the ring, Jo was putting the demon stallion, otherwise known as Java, through the slow, painstaking exercises Sam had written out for them before he headed back to his horse rescue operation on the mainland.

He'd worked with Java before he left, enough to get the stallion past the point of attacking anyone who entered his stall, but they still had a long way to go before Java would even be reliable enough to turn out in a pasture with Jo's other horses . . . much less for someone to get on his back and hope to stay there.

Jo currently had the dark horse on a thirty-foot longe line, encouraging the nervy, stamping stallion to travel in simple circles at the end of the rope, with Jo at the center giving quiet clicks of the tongue. Every time Java moved slowly past their section of fence, Merry saw her sister's grip on the top slat go white-knuckled.

When they first got to Sanctuary, Ella had actually been afraid of the horses, but with Grady and their mother's help, she was coming around.

"He's not going to bolt," Merry said comfortingly. She pointed to the end of the line, folded over itself in Jo's hand. "Mom's got him under control. And anyway, we're outside the paddock. He can't get to us."

"I know that." As if realizing how defensive she sounded, Ella rolled her eyes at herself and appeared to make a conscious effort to relax. "I don't know how you can be so calm. That's the horse who gave your husband a concussion!"

"You can't hold a grudge against an animal acting out in the exact way he's been conditioned to behave." Merry followed Java's slow, halting progress around the circle with a keen eye. He'd filled out a bit in the weeks since he arrived at Windy Corner Stables, and his gait had improved. The gleaming sheen to his clean, well-brushed coat only made the multitude of scars in his hide stand out more clearly, but he looked a lot better. "Besides, Ben is completely recovered. He's out on an emergency call on the other end of the island right now."

"Anyway," Ella said, determinedly steering them back to the point. "I would think it doesn't suck to find out that not only is the man you married good in bed—he's also head over heels in love with you."

"Who said 'head over heels'?" Merry demanded. "No one said 'head over heels.' In fact, no one said 'in love,' either. He could've meant, like, family love. Affection and fondness, caring about each other. That would be nice, too."

"Sure. The kind of family that's so fond and affectionate, you spent hours kissing and caressing every inch of each other's bodies."

"I never should have told you any of this," Merry moaned. "I regret everything."

"Everything except marrying Dr. Ben Fairfax and riding him like a pony on your living room sofa."

"Gah!" Giving up on getting anything useful or helpful out of her sister, Merry made a tactical retreat back to her desk in the tiny, dusty barn office.

Rolling her shoulders in relief—Alex was getting so big, it was quite the workout to lug him around in the baby backpack all day—she settled into her squeaky chair with her baby happily gumming on a teething ring in the playpen beside her.

One grant application, four IRS forms, and a phone interview with yet another occupational therapist later, Merry resurfaced to see Taylor trudge past the open office door.

The teen's shoulders were rounded, and she kicked angrily at the sawdust covering the floor as she walked.

"Taylor?" Merry called. "Is everything okay?"

Taylor popped her head in the door. "Fine," she said, unconvincingly.

"Listen, I still feel bad about snitching on you to Mom and Harrison," Merry began, but Taylor shook her blond head.

"No, you had a lot going on, important stuff. I get it."

Merry frowned. "You're important, too. And maybe I lost my chance to be someone you could turn to when you're in trouble, but I want you to know—I'm still here. I'll do whatever I can to help you. Whether our parents figure their lives out and get married or not."

Taylor shrugged, but Merry thought she looked pleased. "Speaking of getting married," she changed the subject breezily. "How's married life treating you?"

"Oh, you know." Merry felt her cheeks heat but tipped up her chin to brazen it out. There was no reason to be embarrassed! Stupid fair skin. "Just spending my Sunday trying to talk a therapist into moving to a tiny island in the middle of nowhere."

Brightening with interest, Taylor leaned on the door frame. "Hey, Sanctuary is an okay place to live."

"You and I know that, but it's been tough to convince the outsiders I've talked to. Plus, it's a very small pond I'm fishing in already. We need a licensed occupational therapist who's familiar with equine-assisted therapy practices—or maybe a hippotherapy specialist—and that person needs to also be willing to step up and help us staff out the rest of the therapy program, because I'm really not qualified to be hiring . . ." Merry cut herself off before her spiraling anxiety could choke her.

"Sorry," she said, grimacing at the wide-eyed look on poor Taylor's face. "You don't need to hear about all that. Suffice it to say that there are quite a few bottlenecks on the way to turning Windy Corner into a therapeutic riding facility."

"No, I do want to hear about it," Taylor protested. "I want to be involved. If there's any way I can help . . ."

Touched, Merry smiled at the girl everyone in town thought was such a hellion that she'd never care about anyone but herself. "Oh, don't worry, Taylor. We're going to need you and your expertise with the horses, once the therapy clients start showing up. You're a part of this—we're in it together."

"It's a really good thing Ella thought of," Taylor said abruptly, standing up straight. "I never said, after our . . . misunderstanding about the plans. But I'm glad we're doing this. It's important, and we're going to help a lot of people."

"Misunderstanding" was a nice word for what ensued after Taylor poked around this office and unearthed Ella's discarded plans to turn their mother's stately home into a bed-and-breakfast. Taylor had used the plans to make trouble between Ella and Grady, who was very much against the idea of tourists tramping all over his secluded island haven, but everything had turned out all right in the end.

Once everyone saw Ella's real plans for the therapeutic riding center, the bank had extended a loan and they'd gotten down to the hard work of turning Ella's business proposal and sketchy drawings into reality. Until they were up and running and actually bringing money in, however, any penny they could pinch helped.

"I'll tell Ella you said so," Merry said. "She'll like that."

Taylor made a face. "Ugh, I guess I should tell her myself. Being a grown-up sucks a lot of the time, doesn't it?"

Shifting in her chair sent an echo of remembered pleasure throbbing through muscles sore from lack of use. Merry felt a smile curve her lips. "You're doing a pretty good job at it, from what I can see. And there are a few compensations."

"Yeah, like being allowed to talk to a boy outside of school." Taylor kicked moodily at the battered wood of the doorway.

"Ah, man troubles. My favorite kind!" Merry kept

her voice as light and easy as she could. She and Taylor had come a long way from the open hostility of those early days on the island, and the last thing she wanted to do was scare the girl off. "Come in, come in, and tell me all about it."

"I'm supposed to be mucking out stalls." Taylor glanced down the barn hall behind her, clearly reluctant.

"Sure, if you'd rather shovel horse poop than dish about boys . . ."

That decided Taylor. In seconds, they were installed on the battered couch against the far wall of the office and Taylor was saying, "See, there's this guy. Matthew Little. I like him, and I think maybe he liked me, for a minute—but I screwed it all up."

"Yeah, I guess a trespassing and underage drinking charge can put a damper on a fledgling relationship," Merry said sympathetically. "No judgment—I got into way more than my share of trouble when I was your age. And even older and supposedly more mature."

Taylor's mouth twisted in a wry grin. "Thanks. But actually, I don't think it was the trip to the sheriff's station that turned Matt off. I think it was my dad and all his overprotective bull about how boys always lead me astray."

"Your dad is kind of scary, in a tall, dignified way," Merry pointed out. "Maybe Matt just needs to be around him more, and they'll each learn to tolerate the other."

Taylor's sulky gaze dropped to the floor. "Well," she said, drawing the word out like stretching taffy. "It might not be only Dad's fault that Matt won't return any of my texts . . ."

"Ah, now we're getting to it." Merry leaned in. "Come on, spill."

"I told my dad—in front of Matt and the sheriff and

everyone—that we weren't dating, that we were just friends." Taylor tripped over her own story, the words were tumbling out of her mouth so fast. "But right before the sheriff showed up, I think we were about to kiss. Maybe. I don't know! But Dad was so mad about me breaking my promise not to talk to boys outside of school, and I'm already such a huge disappointment to him, it just popped out. And now I can't take it back. But even if I could, I'm still not allowed to date! It's just a mess."

"Hmm, that's a tricky one," Merry admitted.

"Matt ignores me at school," Taylor said glumly, picking at a loose seam in the couch cushion with her short fingernails. "He's all buddy-buddy with that fakey-fake Dakota Coles and her posse of prissy cheerleaders. He's in with the good-kid crowd now. Why would he even want to hang out with me?"

"Because you're awesome. And he likes you! I saw the two of you together out at the barn, there were some serious sparks flying, girl."

A hint of a grin tugged at Taylor's reluctant mouth. "You think?"

"I know," Merry declared. "Take it from me, one semireformed bad girl to another—even the nicest boys get bored with being good all the time. Mark my words, he'll start talking to you again."

"Judge Barrow did sentence us to community service. We'll probably be picking up trash, pulling weeds, or grooming the trails around Heartbreak Cove after school. Just the two of us."

"Sounds like the perfect opportunity for a nice long chat, to me," Merry said, waggling her eyebrows. "And your dad can't object, because it's court-mandated community service. Definitely not a date."

"That's true." Taylor straightened away from the doorjamb, her face brightening as if she'd caught sight of the light at the end of the tunnel. "Thanks, Merry. I'll start thinking about what I want to say, once I have him alone."

She seemed to hesitate, then all in a rush, Taylor continued, "For whatever it's worth, Merry, I think you're totally qualified to find the right person to help with the therapy stuff. I mean, I think the reason people like you is that they can tell you listen to them. Like, really listen. So thanks. For listening to me."

Throwing a quick, fierce arm around Merry surprised shoulder, Taylor squeezed once and then jumped up from the couch.

"You're welcome! And hey, let me know if you want to test out some potential conversational openings ahead of time," Merry called as Taylor bounced out of the office and down the hall to do her chores.

Is this what it's like to be a big sister? To know the right thing to say and how to solve life's problems?

If so, I could get used to being on this side of the sister relationship.

Of course, being a younger sister had its good points, too, Merry reflected as she went back to her notebook filled with fund-raising ideas. She stared down at the tip of her blue pen idly doodling in the margins, and saw that she'd unconsciously drawn a pony with Ben's wavy dark hair lounging on the living room sofa at Isle-away Farm.

Happily, there was no one in the office to see her fierce blush, or the satisfied smile she felt steal across her face.

Because as embarrassing as Ella's teasing was, she'd been right about one thing.

Merry didn't regret going back on her vow not to sleep with Ben. She'd objected to the idea originally, not only because she couldn't stand the thought of him expecting sex from her in exchange for his name and his trust fund, but also because after Alex's birth, she saw her body in a totally different way.

Her breasts were functional—they provided sustenance. Her body was a vehicle for life, for the comfort and support of the life she'd created. It hadn't belonged to Merry alone since the moment she felt Alex's first fluttering kick inside her.

But being with Ben had pulled her back into her own body in a major—and majorly pleasurable—way. He'd reminded her of what she could feel when she let herself go, and she wanted to feel it again.

Soon.

The emergency call turned out to be one of Grady's false alarms about the wild horse band.

Grady, who'd appointed himself the unofficial protector of the wild horses after he moved back here five years ago, had a terrible habit of riding out alone to check on them, seeing something out of the ordinary, and assuming that veterinary care was urgently required.

"They've adapted over centuries to these exact living conditions," Ben reminded him as they hiked back through the frostbitten marsh to the side of the road, where he'd parked his truck. "You don't need to call me out here for every little sniffle and sneeze."

"To be fair," Grady protested, "the foal has big scabs all over his lower legs. And it's Tough Guy—Ella would flay me alive if anything happened to him."

Tough Guy was a five-month-old bay colt who'd had

an inauspicious start to life when his dam ran into trouble during the birthing process. Grady and Ella had found her and, with Ben's coaching over the phone, had helped her give birth to a healthy boy.

So even though contact between the band of horses and humans was strictly prohibited, in order to protect the animals and keep them from losing the instincts they needed to survive in the wild, Grady and Ella felt an ongoing and personal interest in this particular colt.

Ben could understand that, which was why he tempered his voice. "He's got mud rash. That's it. The wild horses live in salt marshes on an island—they're going to get damp. It's very common, so untwist your panties and take a deep breath."

Narrowing his hazel eyes, Grady cocked his head to one side as he absentmindedly scratched under the leather of his horse's bridle. "That was almost . . . sympathetic."

Ben snorted and kept his gaze focused on packing up his completely unused and unnecessary medical kit. "Alluding to the state of your panties? Yeah, if that's sympathy, I'm a regular Mother Theresa."

"No, seriously." Grady fitted his foot into the stirrup and vaulted into the saddle, easily controlling Voyager's sidling step. "For you, this counts as a good mood. Practically . . . what's that word that means bubbles?"

"Effervescent?" Ben supplied, amused.

"Yeah! That's you. Effervescent." Grady gave him a Grouch eyebrow wiggle. "I take it the wedding night was a success."

"A gentleman does not kiss and tell," Ben said, tossing his gear in the back of the truck. "But since I'm no gentleman, I'll say this. My wife is especially lovely by moonlight."

"Wow." Grady reined Voyager over until he was close enough to lean down and put his scarred right hand against Ben's forehead. "You don't feel feverish. But what else could account for this delirium, Doctor?"

"Shut it." Knocking his best friend's hand away, Ben put his hands on his hips and stared Grady down.

The teasing smirk faded from Grady's face, replaced by a hint of a frown. "Seriously, buddy, I'm glad. After what happened at the reception, well, we wondered if y'all would be able to get back into the wedding day spirit."

"Ah yes, the incredibly crass gate-crashing by my esteemed parents." Ben dug in his pocket for the truck keys. He'd successfully sustained a good mood through the daily debacle of trying to convince Alex that food belonged in his stomach and not splattered on the walls, an all-too-brief good-bye kiss from Merry before she rushed out the door to a meeting with a contractor at the barn, and a false-alarm phone call on his day off by *not* thinking about his parents.

But now that Grady brought it up . . . "I wish I knew what my father is planning."

"Other than to hang around and make your life miserable?" Grady shrugged. "That seems bad enough to me, man."

"You don't know my father," Ben said grimly. "Making my life miserable is his default setting, requiring no special effort from him at all. In retaliation for me having the unmitigated gall to get married without his permission, I think we can expect much worse."

True concern darkened Grady's eyes, shadowed under the brim of his dingy red and white Nats cap. "There's nothing he can do, though. You and Merry are both legal adults—you don't need anyone's permission to get hitched. You've got everything all sewed up."

"Not everything," Ben pointed out, feeling a deep, dark brood coming on at the thought of it. "The adoption papers are drawn up, but Merry won't sign until after we live together for a year."

"Makes sense." Grady gave a pragmatic shrug. "Still, it's her decision. Don't see what your dad could do to influence her one way or the other."

"I hope you're right." Ben climbed into the cab of the truck and stuck the keys in the ignition. "But if there's one thing I learned growing up in that house—other than how to tie a bow tie—it's this: never underestimate Tripp Fairfax."

"I tell you what. To make up for the false-alarm emergency call today, I'll spend the afternoon poking around, see if I can figure out what they might be up to. They've got to be staying at the Fireside Inn, that's the only decent hotel in Winter Harbor. I've got a friend on the reception desk there, I'll give her a call."

"If you want to waste your afternoon the way you wasted my morning, go right ahead," Ben said, slamming his door shut. He leaned out the open window to finish the conversation. "I'll bet you five bucks you don't find out anything worth knowing. My father is a cagey old bastard—he's not some stupid Bond villain who's going to spill his evil plans to the receptionist."

Grady lifted one hand in a salute. "Can't hurt to try. I'll call you."

Waving him away, Ben started the truck and pulled onto the rutted country road in a spray of loose pebbles. By the time he turned down Shoreline Drive and reached the first of his NO TRESPASSING gates, he'd forgotten about it.

But the buzz of his cell in his back pocket reminded

him, and he was conscious of a low-level current of curiosity zipping through his bloodstream when he saw Grady's name and number on the screen.

He lifted the phone to his ear. "Fairfax here," Ben said automatically.

"You owe me a fiver." Grady sounded far too pleased with himself.

"Hmm, judge's ruling? Nope, I don't owe you squat until I hear what you dug up and evaluate its worth for myself."

"Even Judge Barrow would side with me on this one." Grady paused for effect and Ben had a momentary vision of himself reaching through the phone to strangle the guy. "Your parents are not going to be an issue."

Ben snorted. "What makes you think that?"

"Because according to my friend, they checked out of the Fireside Inn this morning. They're gone, man. You won!"

Light-headed with a sickening mixture of relief and dread, Ben was glad he'd already pulled over to open the gate. Hopping down from the truck and heading for the latch, he tried to make himself believe it.

"Hello?" Grady asked, frustrated. "Did we get cut off? Because I expected to hear a few more promises of paying off your gentlemanly wagers."

"Sorry, I'm here." Ben gripped the freezing metal of the gate and held on tight. "And you'll get your five dollars—this is definitely information worth having."

"I must be missing something. Why don't you sound more stoked?"

The gate hinges shrieked a protest as he pushed it open; time to get out here with the WD-40. "You know that feeling you get when you spot a water moccasin out on the lake, and if you take your eyes off it for one second, it disappears?"

"So . . . you're saying just because they're gone doesn't mean they can't slither up and bite you."

Ben stared up at the bare branches overhead. "Exactly. I'm not sorry they're gone—but somehow, I felt safer when I knew where they were."

Chapter Twenty

Until the moment Taylor knocked on the open door of the barn office, she wasn't sure if she was going to, or if she'd wuss out. "Merry, can I talk to you about something?"

Eyes sparkling like sunshine glinting off the waves, Merry gave her a conspiratorial grin. "More boy troubles? I've been wondering how it's going at school between you and Matt."

Taylor swallowed what felt like a flock of butterflies into her stomach. "No, it's not about Matt, actually. I was wondering if you have any idea what's going on between my dad and your mom."

Gesturing Taylor into the office, Merry came around her desk to settle down on the cracked vinyl sofa against the wall, where they'd had their heart-to-heart the other day. She patted the cushion beside her, and Taylor settled down tentatively. "What do you mean?" Merry asked.

"Are they going to take the next step and get married, or what?" Taylor burst out, impatience getting the better of her.

"Maybe you should ask Jo or Harrison about that," Merry hedged, and Taylor sighed.

"I can't. Things are too weird between us right now. Ever since the night they came to get me from the sheriff's office." Taylor fought the urge to squirm, remembering the things she'd said and the hurt on Jo's face.

Monday's riding lesson had been especially sucktastic. Jo had tried to be normal, but it was just so obvious that they were both tiptoeing around what they really wanted to say.

Merry cast her a sidelong look. "Things seemed better at the lesson today."

"You were watching? Geez." Taylor ducked her head, wishing the couch would crack open and swallow her up. "I messed up the flying lead change so many times."

"That looked impossible to me!" Merry jostled her arm. "I was amazed when you got it right. I could hardly even tell the difference, but you and Jo both seemed to know what you were looking for."

"I guess that's true." Taylor sighed out a laugh. "At least I know enough to know when I'm screwing it up."

"Lots of things are like that," Merry said, kind of dreamy and thoughtful. "All you can see are your mistakes and failures, up to the moment when you finally get it right."

Taylor gave her a suspicious glance. "Is that a metaphor for how I should be patient with Dad and Jo for being so slow to get their act together?"

Merry's eyebrows shot upward and she grinned. "No! I was thinking about something else completely—but now that you mention it . . ."

"Ugh, come on." Taylor nudged her with her shoulder, like she was being playful, but part of her wanted to lean on Merry's shoulder. "Being patient is the worst.

I'm supposed to be patient about everything! Sometimes I wonder if it ever pays off—do you ever wake up one day and realize all the crap you've been patiently waiting for has actually arrived?"

"What a cool idea." Merry hooked an arm over Taylor's shoulders and tugged her in close, as if it were the easiest thing in the world. "But the need for patience is one of those things you never outgrow, unfortunately."

Taylor groaned, but she couldn't help smiling. It was sort of cool to have someone to talk to who was a little older, but not, like, parental old.

"So here's what I think about Jo and Harrison. Are you ready?"

Merry paused dramatically and Taylor gave the obligatory eyeroll and snotty "No," but she wasn't deterred.

"I think we should push them to get married."

"Wait." This time Taylor did pull away. "Seriously?"

"Dead serious." Merry did stern eyebrows for half a second, then ruined it with a smile. "They've been dating for years now. They're totally in love, their lives are already intertwined. It's very possible that Mom is overthinking this whole thing."

"According to Jo," Taylor said, in her most mature voice, "blending families is very complicated."

"That might be true, but it's not the kind of complicated you can solve without jumping in and working it out."

"See, that's what I think, too!" Taylor said excitedly. "We can figure it out as we go along, if we're all willing to try."

"I don't believe Jo's unwilling to try. But she's afraid of making another big mistake that will affect all of us."

"All of who?" Taylor cocked her head.

"All her kids. Ella, me, and you." Merry pinned her with a severe stare. "And do not say one word about you not being Jo's kid. I don't want to hear it. Of all of us, you're the one she's most scared of messing up."

A lump jumped into Taylor's throat, making it hard to talk. She swallowed around it as best she could. "Why do you say that?"

The corners of Merry's mouth turned down. "Because she's already made a ton of mistakes with Ella and me, and we've worked through them. Well, we're in the process. But with you, it's like she has a chance to finally be the mother she should've been to Ella and me. And speaking as someone who's staring down the barrel of motherhood and quaking in her brand-new paddock boots, trust me—Jo is scared to death that she'll screw it up. And this time she won't have alcoholism as an excuse for failure."

Merry sat back in her corner of the couch, but Taylor caught her hand and squeezed it.

It had cost Merry something to share all of that, Taylor could tell. And she could only repay Merry for treating her like a grown-up one way: with honesty. "That's a lot to think about. I'm not sure I can believe that's totally where Jo is coming from—it's easier, in a stupid way, to believe she just doesn't want me as one of her daughters. But I'll think it over, I promise."

"Try the idea on for size, see how it fits." Merry smiled faintly, her eyes bright in the slanting natural light pouring in the slot window near the office ceiling. "And even if you can't believe I'm right about Jo's fears and feelings, you can believe this. I'd be happy to have you as my little sister."

In some ways, that was even harder to swallow, after everything Taylor had done to try and break up Ella and Grady, and what a little snot she'd been to Merry—

but as she stared at Merry's open, honest face, Taylor's breath caught.

"You mean it," she whispered. "You really mean it."

"I told you," Merry said, smiling. "I could get used to this older-sister gig. It's more fun than I would've thought—and rewarding."

On pure impulse, Taylor pushed up on her knees and threw her arms around Merry, hugging her quickly before scrambling off the couch. Heat scorched up her neck and over the tips of her ears, but she managed not to stare down at the tips of her brown leather boots. Instead, she held Merry's gaze and said, "For the record, you're pretty good at the big-sister thing. And maybe you're a good mom, too."

"Thanks." Merry's voice was a little husky. "Also, for the record, you give good hugs."

Taylor glanced away, thoroughly embarrassed and pleased. Casting around for a way to break the taut, charged moment, she blurted, "Hey, did you know Ben's here?"

Merry stood up and went to the office door to peer down the barn hallway. Taylor could tell the moment she spotted her husband's medical kit outside Java's stall by the miniature thundercloud crackling with lightning over her head. "That man! I told him not to go into Java's stall on his own."

"See, you're a good wife, too," Taylor said encouragingly.

Merry's sudden hectic blush was visible even in the low light, and a rush of awkwardness swamped Taylor. "I mean because you worry about his safety, and like, nag him to take care of himself. That's all!"

"I know what you meant," Merry protested, voice gone high and breathless. She was still flushed, and Taylor wrinkled her nose.

"Yikes. TMI."

"Oh, but it's all okay when we're talking about *your* boy problems?" Merry sent her an amused smile.

"That's different. Matt and I aren't even friends, at the moment. We're not doing the nasty."

"Good, you better not be. But for your information, it's not nasty when you're married," Merry said primly.

"It is when it's your sister," Taylor said daringly, and she felt something in her chest expand like a balloon filling with helium when Merry only rolled her eyes and laughed in reply.

"Time for me to be a good wife," Merry said, smiling as she started down the hall toward Java's stall.

"Good luck," Taylor called, heart racing and full of the fun kind of nervousness. "Go give you husband hell for disobeying orders."

She raised her voice enough to carry down the hall and maybe give poor Dr. Ben a little warning. "Somebody's in troooooouble . . ."

After all, if she was going to be the bratty baby sister of the family, she had some lost time to make up for.

Chapter Twenty-One

Give your husband hell for disobeying orders.

"Oh, I intend to," Merry muttered as she marched up to Java's stall and peered inside. Her heart thumped erratically and her palms sprang damp and cold with fear at what she might see.

Ben crumpled and broken on the ground, blood like thick black ink trickling from his head, trampled under the rampaging stallion's unshod hooves.

But once her eyes adjusted to the gloom and the haze of remembered terror cleared, what she saw was Ben, whole and perfect, standing with his back to the stall door as he ran competent, sensitive hands over Java's quivering flanks.

The stallion's ears flicked nervously back and forth. He swished his tail as if brushing away a pesky fly, but otherwise he seemed calm.

All the air went out of Merry in a silent whoosh, and she closed her jaw on the relief that wanted to explode out of her as scolding and recriminations. Any outburst could startle Java out of his complacence and have him acting out against the nearest threat . . . which would be Ben.

She crossed her arms on the chest-high stall door, and watched quietly as Ben went through the rest of his exam. He spoke softly to the stallion as he worked, a low, murmuring undertone that sent shivers all through Merry.

The last time she'd heard that tone from her husband was in the darkness before the sun rose this morning. He'd been smoothing his palms over her skin, making her writhe restlessly and arch into his touch, and while he gentled her down, he'd kept up a tender whispered commentary on how she looked in his bed, how she felt in his arms.

By the time he finally reached the center of her body, Merry was nearly delirious with need.

No man she'd ever been with had spent as much time as Ben. He studied her sensitive spots, which things made her moan and or cry out, as if he were preparing for an exam that would determine the entire course of his future.

If Merry were grading him, he'd get an A-plus.

Ben circled around the stallion and caught sight of Merry outside the stall. He looked guilty at being caught with Java for about half a second, but then his eyes narrowed.

"I thought you'd be mad. What are you smiling about?"

Merry hastily wiped the cat-in-cream expression off her face and replaced it with a stern scowl. "I am mad," she whispered, so as not to spook Java. "This horse is still dangerous."

He opened his mouth to argue, but she held up a hand to forestall it. "And more importantly, you promised me, Ben."

"You're right." He sounded supremely annoyed about it, but Merry could read anger at himself in the tightness of his mouth. The horse beside him picked up a hoof and stomped a little, nervously, and Ben put an absent, calming hand on his withers. Exhaling slowly, Ben attempted a sheepish smile. "I guess I'm not used to having someone worry about me."

"Well, get used to it," was Merry's advice. "Alex and I kind of like you. We want to keep you around for a long time."

That turned up the volume on Ben's smile. "Where is the brat, anyway?"

"With Auntie Ella. She wanted to spend some time with him—which is good practice for when she has kids of her own."

Ben shook his head. "You are really pulling for Ella and Grady to tie the knot and settle down right away, aren't you?"

"What are they waiting for?" Merry threw up her hands. "Alex needs a cousin to play with! And how fun would it be to plan another wedding?"

The humor died out of Ben's expression. Busying himself with checking Java's hooves, his face was hidden when he said, "A real wedding, you mean? With more than two weeks to plan?"

"No," Merry said, more sharply than she intended, but good grief. This man. "That's not what I mean, at all. Our wedding was perfect—I wouldn't change a thing."

Ben straightened, a slight flush in his cheeks from being bent over. Or maybe from her answer. "Except maybe to stop me from making that call to my parents beforehand."

There was the familiar sardonic tone Ben used whenever he mentioned his parents—but running underneath it was something else, something Merry couldn't quite place. Hurt? Disappointment?

She puzzled over it as Ben gave the stallion a farewell pat to the haunches and unlatched the stall door. She stood back to let him swing it open enough to slip out of the stall, admiring the swift economy of his movements. She could picture him in a hospital, performing some precise, difficult surgery that would save someone's life. She didn't say it out loud, but part of her could understand where Ben's father was coming from in his inability to understand the choice Ben had made to leave the high-risk, high-reward life of a surgeon for the simpler existence of a country vet.

"Have you heard from them since the wedding?" she asked instead.

He shook his head over his medical kit. "It's been a week," he said tensely. "I would have thought my father would do something by now."

A week, Merry thought, with some amazement. It felt longer than seven days since she'd first crossed over the threshold of Isleaway Farm as Ben's wife.

Seven days of slowly learning what it felt like to be loved by Ben Fairfax. Seven days of playing with Alex at bathtime, all three of them ending up soaked and laughing; seven days of working side by side at the vet hospital, looking up from filing to catch Ben quirking that sweet half-smile across the office.

And seven nights filled with the kind of passion Merry had spent years searching for—and only found once she finally stopped looking.

She cleared her throat and refocused on the conversation. "Maybe your dad heard you, and he's trying to respect your wishes and leave us alone."

"Maybe." But Ben didn't sound convinced. Shaking

it off like a dog emerging from a dip in the lake, he
hefted the strap of his kit over his shoulder and said,
"Isn't this supposed to be your day off?"

"I came to talk to Mom about the fund-raiser, and
then Taylor wanted to talk to me."

Ben, who'd heard all about the trials and tribulations
of Merry's attempts to connect with Taylor, arched a
brow. "What did she want?"

"She wants Jo and Harrison to get their act together
and tie the knot, already. Really—I think she just wants
to know that she has family. She's not going it alone."

Ben cocked his head. "It's good not to be alone. You
know how glad I am to have you and Alex in my life—I
benefited hugely from the fact that you wanted a partner
in raising him. But I want you to know . . . I honestly
think you would've been fine without me. You're stronger than you give yourself credit for."

The words knocked all the breath out of Merry's
lungs. It was as if Ben had dug down to the bottom of
her soul where she hid her darkest fear, and dragged it
out into the brilliant afternoon light.

When she could speak again, she forced herself to
hold Ben's calm, steady gaze. "That means a lot to me.
More than you know. Maybe you're right and I would've
been fine. But . . ."

She swallowed, the feelings gripping her heart so
new, so big, she was afraid to give them a name. Ben
thought she was strong, though . . .

"But maybe I don't want to just be fine," she said
slowly, licking her suddenly dry lips. "Maybe fine isn't
good enough anymore. And with you, my life has a
shot at being so much better than fine."

Not quite a declaration of undying love, but Ben lit
up like a bonfire anyway. It was still new enough to

give Merry a thrill when Ben put his arm around her waist and matched his steps to hers as they walked out of the barn to his truck.

Someday, she promised herself, she'd figure out how to trust that this new life was hers to keep, that it wouldn't be snatched from her at a whim. And when that day came, she'd finally be as strong as Ben thought she was.

She'd finally open up her heart and let him read whatever was written there, word for word.

For now, though, she'd settle for a ride home. She could leave her little sedan parked at the barn overnight. Climbing into the cab of the truck on the passenger side, she said, "So . . . Ella's not dropping the baby off at our house until after dinner."

Ben's lips quirked into the delighted grin that made him look like a naughty little boy. "I thought you were trying to entice your sister into settling down and popping out a kid! Dinnertime with Alex probably isn't the best way to do that."

"Well, I don't want her going into it completely blind," Merry said generously. "She's my sister, and I owe her a lot."

"So you're letting her try to feed Alex as a warning?"

"A gentle reminder," Merry corrected him. "That there's more to babies than dressing them up like dolls and cuddling them."

"Specifically, more goop." Ben started the truck. "More bodily fluids, more screaming, and more mess of every kind."

A pang of fear struck her chest. They were teasing each other—this was only banter, the kind of back-and-forth that marked most of her conversations with Ben. He didn't mean anything bad by it.

Still, a little bit of defensiveness sparked in her belly.

It was one thing for Merry to acknowledge how challenging it could be, at times, to live with a newborn. But somehow, it felt very different coming out of Ben's well-shaped mouth.

She couldn't help searching Ben's perfect, stern profile, but she tried to keep her voice light and easy. "Is that what you've learned from three weeks of living with Alex?"

Ben nodded as he expertly maneuvered the truck and attached horse trailer up the driveway and out onto the main island road. "Yeah, that. And a few other things, too."

"Like what?" Merry braced herself for another joking complaint about how loudly Alex tended to screech first thing in the morning, or something similar.

Ben paused long enough that Merry took her eyes off the dashboard and cast a curious glance at him. He pressed his lips together, appearing lost in thought, until he noticed her staring.

With a wry grimace, he said, "I can't come up with a way to make this sound less like something you'd find in a stupid greeting card, but living with you and Alex . . . taught me how infinite the heart is, in its capacity to love." He cleared his throat. "My heart, specifically. I knew I loved Alex from the first moment I held him, but I never anticipated the way that love grows, every single day. It's almost frightening—if it's this big now, five months in, how big will it be by the time he's ten years old? Fifteen? Thirty?"

Heart swollen too big to allow her to catch a full breath, Merry smiled. "Don't be afraid. I hear the love shrinks a little in the teens. That should make it more manageable."

"Personally, I don't hold out much hope for that," Ben said grumpily, downshifting with a jerk of his wrist. "Alex has spit up, peed *and* pooped on me, and deliberately mashed boiled carrots in my hair, and I still love him. Hard to imagine him doing something worse than that at fifteen."

Merry let out a shaky breath. "But even if he does, we'll be there for him. And for each other."

Ben stilled. He kept his eyes front, but Merry saw the tight clench of his jaw before he relaxed enough to say, "I think that's the first time you've talked about a future for us, together."

"It's the first time, maybe in my whole life," Merry said haltingly, "that I can see a way forward. That I know what I want my future to be."

There went that muscle in his jaw again, but this time he clamped down on the question fighting to get out of his mouth. Merry breathed through the fragile moment, in and out.

She could be this brave, at least. Reaching out, she put her hand over his stiff, tense fingers curled around the gearshift.

"I want my future to be here on Sanctuary Island." She dragged the words up from the bottom of her heart. "With Alex, and my mother and our new family . . . and most of all, with you."

The truck took a curve that brought them out of the trees and onto the stretch of sparkling white beach that gave Shoreline Drive its name. Sunlight burst into the cab in a brilliant explosion of sparkling blue off the water.

Merry blinked, dazzled by the glare, and when it faded she saw that Ben had slowed the truck and pulled over to the side of the road. She turned to him to ask what was wrong, but the look on his face stole the breath for words right out of her lungs.

"I have to kiss you. Right now."

Ben was always intense, but the way he stared at her now, the force of his desire turning his gray eyes to molten silver, stopped Merry's heart.

He moved, reaching over the gear console for her, and Merry launched herself into his arms with a tiny cry.

The kiss was fierce, almost savage, as if all the passion and need Ben normally kept so tightly chained had broken free. Merry met him with biting, sucking kisses of her own, her arms wound tightly around his neck and the gearshift digging into her stomach.

Sunshine through the windshield warmed the side of her face and Merry let herself get dizzy on the cool water taste of Ben's mouth, the strength of his arms and the heavy beat of his heart against hers.

He hauled her that extra inch closer, and she caught her breath against the jab of the gearshift. It didn't matter, she could ignore it—but that small gasp of something other than passion was enough to make Ben pull back, concern darkening his eyes.

But Merry wasn't done with him yet. "There are blankets in the trailer, aren't there?" she asked, not even trying to hide the breathless want in her voice.

"I married a genius." Ben's eyes glittered and she had to steal one last kiss from his luscious mouth before scrambling out of her seat belt and wrenching the passenger door open.

"Last one into the trailer has to be on the bottom," she crowed around a mouthful of giddy laughter.

She heard Ben cursing as he wrestled with his door. Her booted feet hit the ground and she was off, running for the back of the truck. Putting out a hand to steady herself on the corner of the tall aluminum-sided trailer, Merry glanced out over the salt marsh stretching between the road and the narrow sliver of sand.

There they were. The wild horses she'd seen on her

first day, fresh off the ferry and completely entranced by Sanctuary Island.

A band of six mares, shadowed closely by their young colts and fillies, grazed along the edges of the marsh, less than a dozen feet away from where Merry stood. The horses, used to the comings and goings of Sanctuary's human residents, didn't take much notice of her—all but one.

The stallion, larger and rangier than his brood, lifted his shaggy head and met Merry's gaze. With two graceful steps, the big bay placed himself between the truck and the nearest dam and filly, a pair of bright golden palominos who kept right on placidly foraging for tender shoots of cordgrass among the fading autumn foliage.

Untamed wildness shone from the stallion's dark eyes, deep and still in the brisk salt spray breezing in off the ocean. Merry stared, transfixed, heart drumming in her ears.

The moment was broken only when Ben's large, warm hand landed on her shoulder, startling her into looking away from the horses. "Merry?"

He knelt in the open back of the trailer, a question dancing across his flushed face.

Merry gave him the smile singing in her blood and took one last deep draught of the cleanest, purest air she'd ever breathed, before climbing up into the trailer beside him.

"I won," he reminded her hoarsely as he lowered her gently onto a pile of thick wool blankets that smelled of hay and horse. "That means I get to be on top."

"Can I tell you a secret?" Merry gasped as Ben kissed down her chest, his heat and strength covering her and enfolding her. "This feels pretty much like a win for me, too."

    After that, there was no talking, other than the bro-
ken whisper of each other's names and the occasional
moan, masked by the wind in the bare tree branches
and the distant lap of waves over sand.

    It was much later, as the afternoon light began to
fade and dusk purpled the sky outside the trailer's windows, that Merry finally said, "That stallion reminds
me of you."

    "My work here is done." Smug satisfaction colored
Ben's voice as he crossed his bare arms beneath his
head.

    Merry turned her face to hide her grin against the
smooth, hot skin stretched over Ben's ribs. "You dork.
Not because of that."

    "What then?" His voice was sleepy, and beneath her
lips, his heartbeat had slowed from the frantic pace of
moments past.

    Merry rubbed her cheek against that comforting
heartbeat and murmured, "Because the horses live all
over the island—the mares go where he goes." One of
Ben's hands cradled her head, his fingers carding
through the tumble of her hair.

    "They know they're safe with him," Merry finished
softly, feeling the words reverberate through Ben's chest.
"He's their home."

Chapter Twenty-Two

There was nothing like the relaxation of well-used muscles, Ben reflected with bone-deep satisfaction as he pulled himself back up into the truck after closing the last driveway gate behind them.

Unless, maybe, it was the relaxation that would come with finally telling Merry he loved her. The words were always on the tip of his tongue, a tickle in the back of his throat, but something was holding him back.

Mostly likely, the sure and certain knowledge that it was too soon.

Merry smiled at him as he settled back behind the wheel, her curvy form curled in the middle of the bench seat so she could lean her temple against his shoulder while he drove slowly through the stand of trees that screened his property from the road. The trusting tilt of her head squeezed Ben's heart. He dropped a quick kiss on her dark hair and shifted the truck into gear.

Oh sure, Merry liked him fine. Enjoyed the way their bodies fit together. Cared about him, even, and was beginning to invest in the idea of a shared future together.

But love? Ben was under no delusions about that. It

would take longer than the six months or so that they'd known each other to turn Merry's initial dislike into the strong, true, abiding love Ben hoped for.

Hope. The last time he'd hoped for something, wished and prayed for it, been willing to do anything for it, he was hoping for a cure for Justine. And that had been a doomed wish right from the start, because there was no cure for a chromosomal abnormality.

Doomed or not, Ben had been unable to stop himself from hoping.

This time, however . . . Ben's hope didn't seem entirely pointless and self-punishing. There were signs, new indications every day, that Merry's feelings were growing, deepening.

And even though part of him wished he could speed that process up, like a time-lapse video of a rose budding into bloom, he knew if he waited and worked at it, eventually that flower was all his. He just needed time.

The truck crested the last rise before the house came into view, and Ben frowned down at the sight that greeted them. Automatically slowing to accommodate the flock of excited animals that rushed to greet the familiar truck, he stared at the sleek black Town Car parked in the circular drive in front of the house.

"Uh oh." Merry sat up straight, tugging nervously at the chest strap of her seat belt as if it were trying to strangle her. "They're back."

The Town Car's doors opened, and his father got out of the driver's side. No chauffeur this time, apparently. Ever the gentleman, he came around to open Mom's door for her. But Ben's glare narrowed on the door behind the driver's side, and the strange man who unfolded himself from the back seat to crack his neck and stretch his shoulders.

"And they brought a friend," Ben muttered, a bad feeling percolating in his midsection.

The bad feeling morphed into full-on dread when he glanced at Merry and found her sheet-white and shaking, her chest hitching with quick, shallow breaths.

"What's wrong?" Voice sharp with alarm, Ben threw the truck into park and focused on Merry.

"What. What is he doing here? Ben . . ."

There was a complex welter of emotion throbbing through her tone, and she hadn't taken her eyes off the stranger.

The guy wore a battered leather bomber jacket open over a white undershirt, and jeans tight enough to endanger his circulation. Ben was reminded in a flash of the rocker-chick style Merry had sported when she first hit town. Even thirty-five weeks pregnant, she'd favored shiny, pleather leggings and band T-shirts stretched over her rounded belly.

Rocker Boy was about Merry's age, too, Ben noticed, and he had the swoopy, spiky blond hair and self-consciously gym-toned body of a wannabe model or actor. Ben pretty much despised him on sight.

But it was nothing compared to the fiery hatred that consumed him when Merry closed her eyes and said, "That's Ivan Bushnell. Alex's father."

Merry moved through a soupy fog of numbness, only the dull roaring in her ears telling her she was still conscious.

The jarring collision of her ugly old life with her shiny, oh-so-fragile new one was enough to send anyone spinning, but Ivan's sudden appearance also brought back a flood of memories she'd done her level best to squash down into the deepest recesses of her brain.

Ivan's face, pale and freaked out, nearly in tears as

he shouted accusations and questions. *How did this happen? You're supposed to be on the pill. Is it even mine?*

That hadn't been the worst of it.

The truck jounced over a rut at the bottom of the drive, jolting Merry from her ugly memories. "This is crazy. I can't believe he's here."

"I can. I should've expected something like this." Ben glared grimly out the front windshield, his profile all sharp lines and angles. "My father would never simply retreat and accept defeat. He knew he couldn't do anything about the marriage itself, so he struck at the weakest point in our arrangement."

"The adoption," Merry realized, heart turning to lead.

"It's not finalized, and won't be for eleven months and ten days."

Merry blinked. But there was no time to say anything more, no time to formulate a plan or a defense or even to work out how she felt about it all, because they pulled up beside the Town Car and Ben slammed out of the truck. He stalked around the front of the car to confront his father.

Scrambling to undo her seat belt and follow him, Merry kept her eyes on Ben. She was half afraid he'd haul off and slug his father in the mouth—that was how pissed Ben looked. Even his mother took a swift, stumbling step back from the force of his anger.

"What are you trying to do here, remind me that I'm not Alex's biological father?" Ben's voice was low and icy, somehow all the more frightening because he wasn't yelling or snarling. "Believe me, I'm well aware of that."

"Don't blame me for the fact that you failed to spot the obvious flaw in your plan to acquire a family to replace the one you lost," his father replied, unruffled.

A pang burst through Merry's soul at that—it struck at the core of one of her deepest fears about Ben, that she and Alex were no more than a replacement family, a place holder in a heart still consumed with love for his first wife and dead daughter. But she shook it off. Her insecurities could wait.

Merry hurried to Ben's side and slipped a tentative hand around his strong, hair-roughened wrist. The sturdy bones flexed under her fingers as he tightened his fist, then abruptly relaxed. Ben glanced down at her, and for a heartbeat, she couldn't read the look in his stormy eyes. Then he said, "Merry, you have a visitor."

Unwillingly, she turned to stare into the face of a man she thought she'd never see again. "Ivan," she said. "What are you doing here?"

Ivan looked the same as he had when they dated. "Dated" wasn't really the right word, though, was it? Unless going to punk clubs every night and moving in together a week after meeting counted as dating. It had been a whirlwind relationship based almost entirely on sex and a similar taste in music, but Merry had truly thought she was in love with Ivan, at first.

At least, she'd wanted to be in love with him.

It struck her that her relationship with Ben was almost the exact opposite—they'd known each other for months before moving in together, they'd gotten married before sleeping together. And she'd never wanted to be in love with him.

Maybe that was why everything with Ben felt so different.

Ivan blinked his big brown eyes at her and nervously flipped the soft fall of blond hair off his forehead. "That's not real nice, Mare bear. I've been looking for you for a long time."

Against her will, part of Merry yearned toward those

words. The belief that when she left town, Ivan hadn't even noticed except to be relieved—that had stung deeply. And now here he was, all handsome boyband features and slim, muscled body, giving her his best appealing gaze.

She'd seen him turn that same expression on female bartenders to get a free drink, on bouncers to skip to the head of a line, on club managers to get backstage access. And now he was using it on her.

Merry narrowed her eyes. "Seriously, Ivan. What do you want?"

His gaze flickered, sliding sideways for a moment, as if this wasn't going down the way he'd expected.

Oh, Merry could easily picture what Ivan had expected. He thought he'd find her the same sobbing mess she was when he left her in their dingy disaster of an apartment, never to return.

Straightening her shoulders, Merry tried to imagine what Ivan saw when he looked at her now.

She'd mostly shed the baby weight, although there was a lingering softness to her hips and a fullness to her breasts that she kind of liked. Her hair was bouncier than ever, as if it enjoyed being its natural dark sable color.

Instead of her D.C. uniform of tight pants and T-shirts, she was wearing dark jeans liberally streaked with red clay dust and brown saddle-leather stains, and a thick gray and white plaid flannel button-down over a black thermal.

And when Ivan's glance dropped to her hand, Merry remembered the biggest change . . . her wedding rings.

To her surprise, a look of genuine sadness tightened Ivan's mouth for a moment. When he spoke, his voice was quiet with real regret. "I'm here to see you—I hated how we left things. And . . ."

Merry heard the click of him swallowing.

"And he wants to see his son," Tripp Fairfax finished firmly. "Which he has every right to do."

"Stay out of this," Ben growled. "You've done enough already, bringing him here."

Ivan flushed, his mouth going sulky at the corners. "Screw off, man. The old guy's right. I do want to see the kid. And I'm his dad, so, like, I do have rights."

"Where have you been for the last year, then?" Ben demanded, his lanky frame rigid as steel. "When Merry needed you, when Alex was born . . ."

Flinching back from the lash of Ben's scorn, Ivan burst out, "Hey, she left me! Skipped town without a word, left me holding the lease . . . I had to leave my apartment, sell some of my stuff."

"How awful for you." Ben's flat voice contained no sympathy whatsoever, and Ivan bristled. He never could stand it when reality intruded on his version of events.

"Now just a minute," Merry interrupted. Anger flooded her, replacing the shock and disbelief of the last surreal ten minutes with a cleansing tide of strength. "We weren't together long, but it was long enough for me to know you have a habit of rewriting history. And as I recall, you were the one who slammed out of the apartment and didn't come back. I waited for two days, Ivan. Crying my stupid eyes out and hoping you'd change your mind. But eventually I had to wake up and realize that you meant it when you said you never wanted to see me again."

The memory still had the power to hurt her, even after more than a year and a lot of growing up. She paused to keep her voice from wobbling, and was grateful for Ben's warm, supportive hand on her shoulder.

Into the brief silence, Ben's mother, Pamela, cleared

her throat delicately. "Ben, darling. I think we ought to let these two talk in private, don't you?"

"I'm not leaving *my wife* alone with this loser." Ben spat the words as if he hated the taste of them.

"Don't be paranoid." Tripp rolled his eyes. "This woman is the mother of his child, I'm sure she's perfectly safe with him. And they have lots to discuss, none of which concerns us. It's really a family matter, wouldn't you say?"

Merry's heart clenched at the expression on Ben's drawn face. Tripp had scored a direct hit with that one. She grabbed for his hand as it slipped off her shoulder, but he stepped away from her.

"Enough." Pamela's demure, ladylike voice could be sharp as a whip when she wanted it to be. "Regardless of anyone's feelings on the matter, the fact remains that Mr. Bushnell and Merry do have issues of a private, personal nature to discuss. Ben, I'm certain that Merry would prefer not to do so in front of your father and me. The only polite thing to do is to leave them to it—so please show us into your home and offer us a beverage. I raised you better than this."

"The nanny raised me," Ben muttered, but Pamela waved that away.

"Semantics," she said. "You know I'm right."

Much as Merry hated to admit it, she couldn't help but agree that the conversation she needed to have with Ivan was definitely not one she wanted to undertake with Tripp and Pamela Fairfax listening in. But she couldn't bear the slightly lost look at the back of Ben's eyes.

"Stay," Merry said, pasting on a smile. She reached for Ben's hand and twined their fingers together determinedly. "I mean it, it's fine. There's nothing I could say to Ivan that you all can't hear."

Ben returned the smile, but it was like a copy of a copy—faded and unconvincing. "No, she's right. My mother is always right about the polite thing to do."

Tugging to draw him a little bit away from the group, Merry muttered, "I don't care about politeness, I care about you. It *is* a family matter, and you're my family."

Heat flared between them, and Ben's smile deepened enough to pop the dimple in his cheek. He lifted their joined hands and pressed a kiss to the backs of Merry's knuckles. "That means more to me than you know. But I'm fine. Let me get my parents out of the way so you can find out what Ivan is really after."

"It's a plan." Merry felt better, knowing they were still in this together.

Ben nodded. "Call me if you need me. I'll be right inside."

Glancing over her shoulder to where Ivan stood, slightly apart from the Fairfaxes and shifting his weight from foot to foot like an anxious kindergartener, Merry said, "I'm pretty sure I'll be okay. Who knows? Maybe this is a good thing. A chance to clear the air, so we can all move forward."

"Yes, clearing the air." Darkness slid over Ben's shuttered face as he followed her gaze. "I'm sure that's exactly what my father had in mind when he tracked down Alex's birth father and brought him to Sanctuary Island."

Chapter Twenty-Three

With the tips of two fingers, Ben twitched the living room curtains aside and peered through the glass.

"Come away from that window," his mother said. "You look ridiculous, peeping at them like that."

"I'm checking on my wife. They've been out there a long time."

Ben clenched his jaw, hideously aware of how defensive he sounded, but for once neither of his parents called him on it. They were probably exchanging significant glances behind his back, communicating in the silent shorthand they'd developed over years of attending crowded benefits and society dinners together. He'd learned to ignore that a long time ago, and it was even easier now, with all of his attention lasered in on the other conversation he couldn't hear or be a part of.

This was one of those times when Ben wished he'd made more of a study of body language. But that was the sort of soft, fuzzy science he tended to avoid, so he refused to make too much of the fact that Merry had led her ex up onto the porch and sat beside him in the swing. They were close enough that their shoulders brushed occasionally when Merry kicked out a heel and pushed the swing into gentle motion.

The glass was cold, soothing, against Ben's forehead. He braced one arm above his head and watched as Ivan said something apparently funny. Merry laughed, tucking a wing of hair behind her ear, and even from a distance, Ben could tell her blue eyes were bright with tentative happiness.

"It sounds as if things are going well out there," Tripp observed neutrally.

Ben curled his lip at his own reflection and put his back to the window. "Depends what you're hoping for as an outcome."

Tripp spread his arms along the back of the couch, like a king lounging on his throne. "I'm hoping to reunite a father with the child who was ripped away from him by his emotional, impulsive lover."

Ben controlled his reaction to the word "lover." It had been a while since he'd been forced to call on his early training in the art of hiding emotion, but it turned out to be more muscle memory than anything else.

The trick was distance. If you pushed the emotion away, outside yourself, then your reaction to it wouldn't show on your face. "I don't concede your premise that Merry was the one at fault. If Ivan Bushnell wanted to be a father, he had ample opportunity to take his place by Merry's side. If you haven't noticed, we live in the digital age and getting in touch with her would've been as simple as sending her a Facebook message."

"No one is assigning blame," Pamela insisted, with a quelling glance at her husband. "I'm sure it was a very difficult time for both of them. And Mr. Bushnell admits he made mistakes. But he is so very young, Benjamin. Well. They both are."

"She's twenty-three, Mother. Hardly a teenager."

Pamela raised her ruthlessly plucked brows. "She's closer to her teens than she is to her thirties."

Ben swallowed. He'd never thought much about the age difference between himself and Merry. But seeing Merry and Ivan together, Ben was forced to concede that they sort of . . . matched. For lack of a better term.

He knew Merry had lived a life with its share of difficulties and problems—but somehow, there was still something pure and unsullied about her. Innocent. And as much as Ivan was no innocent, there was a youth and softness to him that Ben knew he himself had shed years ago. If he'd ever had it to begin with.

"Merry is old enough to know her own mind, and to take responsibility for her actions," Ben said hoarsely. "She decided to raise that baby on her own, without any help from its father."

"And that was very brave." Pamela widened her eyes. "But now that her baby's father wants to be a part of their lives, she won't have to be on her own any longer."

"Merry is not on her own. She hasn't been for a long time." But even as Ben said it, a shaft of doubt slid between his ribs. "She has her mother and sister, and all our friends on the island. She has me."

"Oh, Ben." Pamela sighed. But it was the pity lurking in the depths of his mother's eyes that set Ben's heart pounding as if he'd run a mile flat out.

His mother was an expert at reading people; she'd built a social empire out of that skill, crowned herself queen of the hospital benefit committee and the country club set. It was all too easy to believe she knew something he didn't.

He was saved from the foolishness of showing his vulnerable underbelly by demanding to know what she meant when the front door opened.

Merry and Ivan blew in on a cool blast of air, cheeks reddened and mouths smiling. Ben felt slightly better when Merry's gaze found him immediately.

She came straight to him and put one slim arm around his waist. Ben had to control himself carefully to keep from crushing her to him with a too-tight grip. No matter how tightly he held her, he was afraid he'd still feel her slipping away.

"Ivan's going to stick around for a few days, to spend some time with Alex," Merry announced. Her fingers flexed against Ben's side, but when he studied her face, he saw only calm purpose. "I've asked him to come back tomorrow morning to meet him."

One more night to pretend that nothing was changing. Ben closed his eyes briefly in thanks.

"Surely we can wait until the child is returned here," Tripp said impatiently. "Ben says you expect your sister to bring him back after dinner."

Ben stiffened against the urge to yell at his father to get the hell out and leave them in peace.

"I wanted to stay and see Alex tonight," Ivan interrupted. He looked excited after his conversation with Merry, like a kid being presented with a gift wrapped in shiny paper. "But Merry says he'll be tired, probably crying a lot and stuff. If we wait until tomorrow, he'll be in a better mood."

"Besides," Ben said, fixing his father with an inflexible stare. "There's only one evening ferry back to the mainland. You wouldn't want to miss it and get stuck out here on the island."

"They could stay with us, if they needed to." Merry's voice was uncertain, lilting up questioningly at the end as she looked to Ben for confirmation.

"We wouldn't want to impose," Pamela said smoothly,

rising from the armchair where she'd been perched. "Tomorrow will be quite soon enough. Ben, walk us out to the car."

"Gladly." Ben held the door open for his parents and Ivan, then hurried around to open the front passenger door of the Town Car for his mother.

As he'd suspected since she'd made her demand about being walked out, Pamela had something to tell him. The moment the car doors slammed behind Tripp and Ivan, she leaned up to speak into Ben's ear.

"I'm sorry about this, Benjamin. I truly am. She seems like a very sweet girl, but if you follow through with this plan of adopting her son, I'm terribly afraid you'll miss out on life's greatest joy—becoming a parent."

The thread of sincerity tightening his mother's voice hit Ben like a sucker punch. "I'll be Alex's father, in every way that matters. That's what I want."

"It's what you want now," Pamela said gently, wrapping her soft fingers around Ben's tense wrist as he reached for the door handle. "But what about when you finally move past what happened with Ashley? Eventually, you'll heal. You must see that all I'm trying to do here is to ensure that when that day comes, you'll have the opportunity to create the next Fairfax heir with a suitable partner."

"All I see is that you and Dad can't stand for me to be happy." His tongue felt thick in his mouth, his throat as tight as if he were going into anaphylactic shock. "I always knew you didn't love me, since I was a kid. But this is the first time I ever felt like you actually hate me."

She drew back as if he'd struck her across the face, eyes wide and shocked. "Benjamin! How can you say such things? We're trying to protect you from making the worst mistake of your life. Giving the Fairfax name to a child without a drop of Fairfax blood . . ."

Unutterably tired and sick at heart, Ben wrenched open the car door. "Just go. Please."

"It's for the best, Ben. A quick, clean break now will be so much better than something messy and drawn out. And you know that a break is inevitable; she won't stay with you. Water will always seek its own level."

Conviction rang clear as a bell in his mother's voice, every word the truest he'd ever heard from her. Apparently satisfied that she'd gotten the last word, she sank gracefully into the deep black leather seat and twitched her skirt away from the door.

Moving on autopilot, Ben slammed the door and watched the car drive away, scattering a curious goose, the three-legged goat, and a hissing one-eared cat as it went.

Water will always seek its own level.

One of his parents' favorite sayings, often used in conjunction with "Blood will tell." Ben had never thought about it seriously before. His mother meant it as something very snobbish and easy for him to dismiss—but she was actually talking about how people would automatically seek out those who were most like them . . . and Ben couldn't dismiss that notion quite so easily.

After all, wasn't that why he'd been alone for most of his life?

The days were growing shorter, the evenings much cooler once the sun slipped down behind the trees. A shiver worked through him as he trudged back toward the warmth of the house.

It was hard to imagine anyone less like him than vibrant, friendly, openhearted Merry.

Maybe his mother was right. Like the changing of the seasons, nothing lasted forever. Maybe it was time to start protecting himself.

To Merry's surprise and cautious delight, the first meeting between Ivan and Alex went well. In a display of sensitivity she could hardly believe, he'd opted to come to the island on his own, asking Tripp and Pamela Fairfax to stay at the hotel in Winter Harbor.

"He said he didn't want a big audience while he met Alex," Merry explained, leaning in the bathroom doorway while Ben ran the water into the baby tub, meticulously testing the temperature.

Ben had also made himself scarce for the big meeting, citing work commitments—but Merry was pretty sure he simply didn't want to be around Ivan and Alex together. Which she understood, but she had to talk about it with someone or she'd go nuts. "He told me he noticed how tense your parents' presence made everyone, so he thought it was for the best that they sit this one out. That was good, right?"

"What a prince," Ben muttered, eyes fixed on the flow from the antique brass faucet. "Let me know when they schedule the awards ceremony so I can see him get his medal."

Something twisted in Merry's chest. "Ben . . ."

He sighed and pushed to his feet, holding out his hands for Alex to start the evening ritual they'd devised to get the baby to sleep through the night. She'd noticed that if Alex had a warm bath with Ben followed by quiet time in the rocking chair with his mama, he'd drop off to sleep without much fuss. And, at nearly six months old, he'd sleep a good seven or eight hours straight.

Merry handed him over with a tinge of reluctance.

She dreaded the moment when Alex went to sleep and left her and Ben alone to have the talk they'd managed to avoid all day.

"Sorry." Ben's clipped tone didn't betray a lot of regret. He sounded angry, more than anything else, but Merry couldn't tell if he was ticked off at her or himself.

"I know this is . . . awkward. For all of us." Proud of herself for keeping her voice steady, Merry followed the slow, precise movements of Ben's bare hands and arms as he lowered Alex into the bath. The sleeves of Ben's dark gray chambray shirt were rolled to the elbow, exposing the strong, corded tendons of his forearms, the graceful jut of his wrist bones.

Momentarily distracted, Merry hauled herself back to the point. "Do you think it's easy for me, being around my ex? The last time I saw Ivan he yelled at me, accused me of sleeping around, and said . . ." She swallowed, looked down at her feet. "All kinds of terrible things. Just to avoid any possibility of taking part in my baby's life."

"Exactly. This man—I'm using the word 'man' loosely here—ran out on you and your kid and stayed away for more than a year. What I don't understand is how he can show up here after all that, and five minutes later, you're ready to play happy family with him."

"This isn't a game," Merry said tensely. She didn't want to lose her temper, but it was getting tough. "I'm not playing around, Ben. This is my son's future happiness, his entire concept of family and love—and Alex deserves the chance to know his biological father. I'm not trying to hurt anyone, especially not you. You've been so good to us. But I have to take this chance, for

Alex's sake. I don't want him growing up wondering what he did to make his own father abandon him."

Ben paused in the act of pouring a slow stream of warm water over Alex's dimpled back. Keeping his hands on Alex to steady him in the slippery tub, Ben twisted his torso to meet Merry's gaze.

Whatever he saw in her face made his hard-edged features blur into something gentler. Sadder. That was even worse; Merry preferred angry, pissy Ben to unhappy, resigned Ben.

"You grew up without your mom, knowing she'd chosen her addiction over you and your sister," he said quietly. "And when your father didn't show up for our wedding . . . you didn't seem surprised."

"After the divorce, Dad worked a lot. All the time, really. I'm not complaining—he had to support two kids on his own, he didn't have any family to turn to. But even when he was home . . ." She leaned her head on the doorjamb, suddenly too tired to hold it up on her own. "I think we reminded him too much of Mom, and everything that went wrong in his life. He never hit us or even raised his voice, even when I got in trouble at school or stayed out past curfew. Sometimes I wondered what it would take to make him look at me and really see me. You know?"

"There are lots of ways to be abandoned." Ben turned back to the bath, the slow, almost hypnotic motion of his soapy hands over Alex's little body. "Fatherhood is more than biology, Merry. Sharing genetic code doesn't guarantee a good relationship."

She swallowed, knowing he was thinking of his own father. "I know that. But if Ivan is serious about wanting a relationship, how can I deny them both that chance?"

From behind, she saw the way Ben's shoulders went rigid, as if he were braced for attack. But his voice stayed low and expressionless. "So I guess the real question is . . . what happens when a marriage of convenience becomes inconvenient?"

Chapter Twenty-Four

The heavy silence behind him rushed in Ben's ears like the roar of a jet engine, deafening white noise that blocked out everything but the sound of his own heart beating far too quickly.

"I'm not saying that I want to move back in with Ivan and pick up where we left off!" Merry finally croaked out, the words shredded and thin. "What do you—Ben, listen to me. This is not about me choosing him over you. It has nothing to do with our marriage!"

"Don't kid yourself. You are absolutely choosing between us." With great care, Ben lifted a sleepy Alex from the tub, water streaming down his forearms and dampening the cotton of his shirtsleeves. He pivoted, ready to hand Alex off to Merry, who was supposed to be waiting with Alex's soft terry-cloth towel.

But tonight, Merry stood frozen in the doorway, her fingers white-knuckled against the wood as if she was worried she'd fall over without the support.

Ben paused, hope flickering to life in his gut. "Unless I'm mistaken," he said slowly. "And you *do* intend to ask Ivan to sign away his paternal rights."

Merry jolted as if he'd touched her with a live wire, her face going tense with surprise before it settled back into unhappy lines. "Ben, I can't. Not now, when everything is so new and they've barely had any time together. I'm not saying that will never happen—but we have to be patient and see how things play out. I owe it to my son to try and make things work with Ivan. And waving some piece of paper in his face that relinquishes all rights to his kid isn't going to help anything."

"Right." Ben shook his head in disbelief as the feeble flicker of hope snuffed out. He snagged the terry cloth himself and wrapped it around Alex until he looked like a baby burrito. "It wouldn't help anything at all . . . except to make it possible for me to actually adopt Alex in a year, as discussed when we entered into this arrangement."

"Arrangement," Merry echoed faintly. "Yes. I remember what we discussed. And the adoption was never guaranteed. That's what the year-long grace period is for."

Her voice sounded weird, but when Ben frowned over at Merry, her eyes were trained on Alex. She held out her arms, and Ben passed him over, the move as smooth and habitual as a choreographed dance.

They were good together, the three of them. Ben fumed, frustrated beyond belief. Why couldn't Merry see that? Why didn't she want to protect that as much as Ben did? "But it ought to at least be a viable option," he argued. "At this point, with Ivan back in the picture, I might as well go ahead and give up on the adoption ever happening."

Merry shook her head. "All I'm saying is that I need time to see where this thing with Ivan is going—and you already agreed, in writing, to give me that time. Nothing has changed."

Her refusal to see what was going on here made Ben's temper flare. "Everything has changed. Don't you get it? My parents brought Ivan here for a reason. They didn't cross paths at an opera gala or run into each other at the club—my father tracked Ivan Bushnell down and deliberately brought him to Sanctuary Island to cause trouble. He's hoping Ivan will do exactly what he's doing—assert his paternal rights and prevent me from ever adopting Alex."

"Don't you use that tone with me," Merry hissed over the baby's head, her cheeks red with anger. "That superior, sarcastic, you're-a-moron tone. I'm not an idiot, Ben, I know what your parents are up to. They don't just want to stop the adoption—they want me gone, the marriage dissolved, all trace of me and my son removed from the Fairfax family register forever."

Alex fussed, aware of the deviation from his routine and the tension in the air. Arching his back, he tried to launch himself out of Merry's arms. With the ease of practice, Merry held on to her bundle of damp baby and went for the door.

Pausing in the hallway, she turned back to say, "And by the way, you're the one playing directly into their hands by letting Ivan come between us."

The knowledge that she was right did little to soothe Ben's ragged emotions. Running his wet hands through his hair, he squeezed his eyes shut and fought to control his breathing. "My parents know me pretty well, as it turns out. If they wanted to break us up, they hit on the perfect way."

He opened his eyes in time to see Merry suck in a breath as if she'd been slapped. Her eyes glittered with moisture even in the dim light of the hallway, but her face was still and calm, whiter than Alex's terry-cloth towel. "Your parents will only get what they want if you choose to give it to them."

She faded away into the darkness of the hall, leaving a vast, yawning emptiness behind her. Ben cocked his head to track the soft sound of her bare feet moving farther and farther away, and when he heard the quiet click of the guest room door closing behind her, he sank down on the edge of the tub and buried his face in his hands.

All Merry wanted was time, she said. But that precious commodity was slipping away from them both, moment by moment, like bath water running through their spread fingers.

He'd missed his chance to make Merry fall in love with him, to show her how good it could be to build a life together. The moment another option became available to her, she threw open the door to welcome it.

If Ivan wanted her back, what would she need Ben for? There was nothing to be gained by filling himself with false hope and illusions of potential. He'd risked everything, from his fiercely guarded privacy to his scarred heart—and he'd lost it all.

Inevitable, probably. The equation of Ben plus Merry had never really made sense. Someone like her was never meant for a man like Ben.

He wished he could promise himself he'd stop taking risks, but deep down, he was afraid if it came to a cage match between his sense of self-preservation and his innate stubbornness, stubbornness would deliver an epic beat-down every time. As long as there was even a remote possibility of getting everything he wanted, Ben would defy common sense to fight to the end.

But when the end came . . . when Merry and Alex

left him, he'd be alone again. And this time, he swore, he'd bury his stupid, idiotic heart so deep inside, no one would ever touch it again.

The next week was one of the worst times in Merry's life.

She and Ben were hardly speaking, and when they did, every conversation was stiffly polite and revolved around the baby—working out who would do what with Alex's care, sharing information on when he'd last been fed or changed. It was like living with a remote stranger who had zero interest in even casual get-to-know-you chit chat.

There were no more snide asides from Ben when Merry set up times for Ivan to come by and see Alex, no more fights about Ben's parents and the way they'd moved into a suite at the Fireside Inn across the water as if they wanted front-row seats for the breakup of their son's fledgling marriage.

But there was no laughing, either. No teasing, no hilariously sly accounts of the idiotic things his patients' owners did and said, and none of the shared joy in the everyday milestones of life with a fast-developing baby. The sudden cessation of all that togetherness made Merry realize just how much she and Ben talked—and how much she'd come to count on him.

Not as a source of security, and not even as parental backup to help with Alex . . . but as the person she shared everything with. Like the very best friend she'd ever had, but better . . . because when the lights went out and Ben's long, hard body lay next to hers in the dark, she felt things she'd never felt with a girlfriend.

Not that there'd been any of that in the last week, either. After spending months trying to convince herself she could live without sex and passion, it was amazing how cold and empty her body felt after having tasted bliss for a handful of days before it was snatched away again.

Merry held in a gloomy sigh and tried to psych herself up for a trip to the barn. These days, her favorite place to spend time had some drawbacks—mainly, that Jo could tell something was going on with her, but Merry had no intention of talking about her marriage problems with her mother. Not out of stubbornness—or, not completely—but because once she told her mother that she and Ben were in trouble, she knew what Jo would say. She'd immediately offer to let Merry move back into her old room at Windy Corner. And then Merry would have to consider that as a serious option, and this whole thing would become completely, irrevocably real.

She wasn't ready for that yet. No, Merry was still clinging to the belief that this thing with Ivan would smooth itself over, that they'd all get used to it and figure out how to work around it, and Alex would end up with two married parents who loved him *and* a healthy relationship with his biological father.

Was that so much to ask?

"Ba ba ba ba," Alex said emphatically from his car seat in the back. A glance in the rearview mirror showed him scowling in fierce concentration as he grasped the toe of his sock and worked it off his little foot. That was his new thing. No matter how cold it got outside, they couldn't keep him in socks for more than twenty minutes.

"Almost there, buddy," Merry said, making the turn-off for Windy Corner Stables. She'd started talking to Alex a lot more, she'd noticed, an endless stream of forced cheer and slightly desperate chatter to fill the silence left by Ben's retreat into himself. "We're going to have so much fun today! And guess who we're meeting at the stables?"

Ivan had expressed an interest in seeing where Merry worked, and since she wasn't about to take him down to Ben's vet hospital, she'd agreed to show him around the barn.

Ella had promised to be on her best behavior, disapproval thick in her voice. She'd never liked Ivan, even before he basically called her sister a cheating slut and dumped her for getting knocked up. And, as she was the person who'd dealt with the fallout of Merry's hormonally enhanced reaction to said dumping, Ella had earned the right to hate Ivan forever. But she was a good older sister to the end, and even though Merry could tell she really didn't get what Merry was trying to do by allowing Ivan access to Alex, she wasn't going to interfere.

"Da da da. *Da,*" Alex cried at the top of his lungs, kicking his bare feet excitedly.

Merry grinned, grateful for the way her amazing, hilarious boy could always take her mind off her problems. "No, not Dada," she said automatically, fondness warming her from the inside the way it always did when she thought of the look on Ben's face whenever Alex said "da da." "We're meeting—"

She stopped, disconcerted. Ivan was technically Alex's father. But what would Alex call him? Not that it mattered yet, but it soon would. By the time Alex was a year old, he'd be ready to start naming the things and people around him, imitating the words he heard from the adults in his life. So what would they call Ivan?

Stop overthinking everything, Merry told herself to quell the strange panic bubbling in her chest. *Who knows where we'll all be in six months! By then, probably none of this will even be an issue.*

Because probably, if Ivan stuck around and Merry never got him to sign away his rights, then Ben wouldn't be able to adopt Alex as his son. And if Ben couldn't adopt Alex . . . would he even want to stay married?

He might not have truly married her to provide an heir to make his parents happy—but after what had happened with Ben's first marriage and the tragic death of his daughter, Merry knew how important Alex was to Ben. Maybe it wasn't so simple as Ben looking for a replacement family, but she couldn't fool herself that Ben would've been as eager to marry her in the first place if he'd known there was no chance he could adopt her child as his own.

That was the thought that had tortured Merry over the last few days. Their last fight in the bathroom, with Alex splashing in the tub nearby, had thrown the reality of the situation under the harsh glare of the spotlight. Ever since, Merry couldn't stop remembering the frustrated anger on Ben's face when he'd told her everything had changed.

Everything—including the declaration of love she'd heard over the baby monitors?

It's not as if he ever came out and told you he loved you right to your face, Merry reminded herself. If he really meant it, really felt it—wouldn't he say it right out loud?

Sure. The way you do, you mean?

Merry flipped down the sun visor and made a face at herself in the tiny mirror on the back. In the corner of the mirror, she caught a glimpse of Alex squirming in his car seat.

"Everything is just a little confusing right now, baby," she murmured as they pulled up to the barn. "But don't you worry. Mama's going to figure it out."

Everyone was parking out back to leave room out front for the trucks dropping off construction supplies to be able to turn around. Merry slowly navigated the pitted, pocked drive around the side of the green barn.

The car lurched to a stop as Merry's foot jerked off the gas pedal. She stared, heart thumping with a combustible mix of dread and joy.

That was Ben's ancient, battered pickup truck with the shiny horse trailer hitched to the back.

He was here. On the one hand, the timing wasn't wonderful, with Ivan on his way out to the barn for a tour and a playdate with Alex. But on the other hand, Merry felt as if she hadn't seen her husband in a week.

He left for work as soon as Alex was fed, and calls seemed to keep him out of the vet office all day and well into the evening. And at night, although Ben was as tender and sweet with Alex as ever, going through the motions of bathtime and tucking him in, once Alex was asleep it was as if he shut down completely.

They hadn't touched for longer than it took to transfer Alex from one pair of arms to the other in days.

Knowing she was being stupid, Merry still nervously scrabbled through her purse for a tube of lipstick and applied the pink lacquer with a shaky hand. Her hair was kind of a wreck, but that's what happened when you carried around a six-month-old baby who was still figuring out his fine motor skills. Lots of hair pulling.

Well, that was the best she could do. Ben probably wouldn't notice, anyway. Which wasn't as comforting a thought as she could have wished for.

By the time she'd wrestled Alex and his bulging diaper bag out of the backseat, she was sweating through her long-sleeved shirt a little, even in the cool autumn morning. It was early enough that the sun hadn't turned the overnight frost into dew, and the rolling green hills surrounding the barn glittered as if they'd been sprinkled with diamond dust.

Every time the lush natural beauty of Sanctuary Island caught in her chest and stole her breath, Merry felt that little internal "click" that told her she'd made the right decision when she moved here.

What if Ben divorced her, though? she wondered with a sudden chill that had nothing to do with the breeze through the pines. Would she be able to handle living in such a small, close-knit community with the man who'd once shared his life with her and Alex . . . but who didn't love them enough to keep them?

She didn't have time to answer that awful question, even in the privacy of her own mind, because the moment she stepped into the warm, earthy darkness of the barn, she saw Ben.

He was standing at the other end of the long, wide corridor lined with horse stalls. The front barn doors were thrown open to let in the fresh air, and his tall, lanky form was outlined against the brightening morning light.

Head bent over one of the folders Merry had made for him when she took over the filing, Ben was absorbed in reading through the pages of medical history she'd printed out and ordered according to where the horses' stalls were in the barn, to make it as easy as possible for him to flip to the correct section.

Pride and satisfaction made for a nice change to the unsettled mood she'd fought for days. There was nothing quite like knowing she'd done a good job. She really had contributed to the smooth running of the vet office. The knowledge gave her the guts to smile and wave to get Ben's attention.

"Hi! We didn't expect to see you here today. Windy Corner wasn't on the schedule."

Ben's head reared back like one of the wild horses startled by the presence of a human. He recovered quickly while he shuffled the papers back into the color-coded folder. "Yes. Well, Jo called. She got word that Sam may have found a foster home for Java, so she asked me to do a check to see if he's good to travel."

Despite the dangers the abused stallion represented, and the fact that he'd actually injured Ben, Merry felt a pang of sorrow at the thought of Java leaving the barn. "Is he okay? He was in such bad shape when he got here, and it's only been a few weeks. Maybe he needs more time."

Right arm aching, Merry switched the removable car seat baby carrier to the left. Alex started up a steady stream of babble and cooing. He loved being in the barn.

Ben crouched down to put himself closer to Alex's level. Reaching out, he snagged the baby's bare, kicking left foot. "I see we've already ditched the socks today."

Merry groaned and set the carrier down to dig through the diaper bag for one of the spare pairs she'd started carrying around everywhere they went. "Lord. I put them back on after the car ride, but he must have shaken them off between the car and here. He's like magic."

"The Houdini of socks." Ben smirked up at her, silver eyes alight with the shared joke, and Merry's heart stuttered.

"It's been too long since I saw that smile." The words were out before she could stop them, but when Ben stood up without dropping either the grin or his gaze, she couldn't regret it.

His lips twisted a bit. "I could say I've been trying to give you the space you asked for, but that's not completely true. Maybe I was the one who needed a break from all the . . . you know, feelings."

Merry laughed, watching him from underneath her lashes. "I'd ask if you're *feeling* better now, but . . ."

"Back off, woman," Ben mock-snarled, that sexy smile still playing at the corners of his lips.

"Just to be clear," Merry said, determinedly keeping it light, "I never asked for space. Only time. Semantics maybe, but Ben, I don't need space away from you. In fact, I miss being . . . close."

Fire sparked in the depths of his eyes. "Is that right," he purred, stepping even closer. His gaze dropped to her mouth and Merry's blood started a giddy dance through her veins.

"Yes," she breathed through parted lips.

"You look pretty today." Ben's voice was as gentle as the hand he slid into her hair to caress the tender nape of her neck.

Merry clenched her thighs against the sudden shiver of low, heated yearning. "I didn't think you'd notice," she gasped.

"Merry, Merry," Ben murmured against her mouth. "I notice everything about you."

Their lips brushed and clung, the moment of shared breath and desire spinning out into an endless horizon of possibility.

"Am I in the right place? Whoa, it's dark in here. Hello? Mare?"

Ivan's loud tenor rang through the barn like the clanging of an alarm bell. Jolting backward, Ben stared over Merry's head, his face turning to stone while she watched.

Clutching at Ben's sleeve when he dropped his hand as if she'd burned him, Merry said urgently, "Ben, wait."

"No wonder you're all dolled up," Ben said in a cold, dead voice. "Sorry if I smudged your lipstick. You should've waited for Ivan to get here instead of wasting it on me."

As if completely oblivious to the moment he'd interrupted, Ivan continued to talk as he walked farther into the barn. "Wow, this place is bigger than I thought. Mare bear, is that you down there? I think I see . . . yeah, there's my little man. Hey Alex, boy, how you doing?"

Ben curled his lip for an instant, and Merry read the contempt in his face as if he'd come right out and said, "Alex isn't a golden retriever puppy, you moron."

This could get ugly in a hurry. Talking quickly, she faced Ivan with a wide, fake smile. He'd never know the difference. "Ivan, you made it! That's great. Would you mind taking Alex for a second and waiting for me in the office? It's right through there, and I'll be along shortly to give you the tour around the barn."

"No need to delay the fun on my account," Ben said blandly, already backing away. His foot nudged Alex's baby carrier, causing an indignant squawk.

"Hey, don't kick my baby!" Ivan shook his head. "Not cool, man."

Merry tensed all over, but Ben crouched down to touch Alex's waving toes again. "Sorry, Alex," he said seriously. "But I've got to go. Things to do, horses to check, travel papers to sign off on."

"Uh, I don't think he understands you." Ivan laughed, the slightly mean chortle he used when he felt threatened.

Ben stood in a burst of controlled power that reminded Merry, all at once, that he had at least four inches and several years on Ivan, who, for all his gym-toned muscles, wasn't all that tough.

"Ivan," she said sharply. "Please wait for me in the office. I'll be along in a minute."

"Fine." Digging his hands into the minuscule front pockets of his too-tight jeans, Ivan sauntered across the corridor to the office, pointedly not taking Alex with him.

Familiar with Ivan's little acts of defiance in the face of being told what to do, Merry pressed a hand to the headache brewing behind her eyes. "Now. Ben, seriously, this isn't what you think . . ."

But when she looked back at him, he was already walking away.

"Hey," she called, feeling as if he'd tethered himself to her heart somehow, and every step pulled the link between them tighter and thinner. "I'm not finished with you yet."

"Yeah, well. I'm finished," Ben said without turning around. "There's only so long a man is willing to wait for a woman to make up her mind if she wants him or someone else. Take your time, Merry. But don't expect me to always be there for you, waiting until you figure out what you want."

He disappeared into Java's stall, leaving Merry lost and alone in the middle of the hallway, unable to come up with a single argument to make Ben stay.

His final words sliced through Merry's brain while she moved on autopilot to pick up Alex's carrier and walk into the office where Ivan was waiting.

Don't expect me to always be there for you.

Chapter Twenty-Five

The condition of Java's hooves had improved, and he'd gained enough mass to take him out of the seriously malnourished zone and into being merely underweight. The stallion still had a tendency to startle badly at sudden noises, but he was at his most secure in his stall, which had clearly come to represent a safe space for him.

According to Ben's notes, it was when Java left the stall that they ran into trouble with him, but since most of the travel time would involve the stallion being enclosed in a small trailer, he should be fine. Ben made a note that he advised extreme caution when loading and unloading Java from the trailer, and that he recommended gelding Java as soon as the horse was stable enough after transportation. In Ben's experience, leaving a stallion with Java's issues uncut was only going to add to the horse's problems with a lot of hormones and urges he'd have trouble controlling.

Ben flipped Java's folder closed and hooked it to the back of his stall with a sigh. The horse himself was down in the paddock going through one last round of exercises with Jo Ellen before Sam picked him up the next day.

Wandering out of the barn and down the slight slope to the outdoor ring, Ben told himself he was only doing the responsible thing, performing a visual check of the animal's movement in the ring before he signed off on all the paperwork. But at the back of his mind, Ben knew there was one reason and one reason only that he was still hanging around the barn. Okay, two reasons.

Merry and Alex.

He'd caught glimpses of them as she walked Ivan through the barn, introducing him to the horses and explaining the changes they were making to the structure as they prepared to shift their focus from regular horse boarding and training to a facility that supported equine-assisted therapy.

Ben liked the way her voice lilted with enthusiasm when she told Ivan about the ways people could work with horses to assist their recovery from all sorts of trauma, including post-traumatic stress disorder. She'd swapped the handheld baby carrier for the little front-wearing backpack that allowed Alex to gaze out at the world around him with big, blue, interested eyes. His chubby arms and legs poked through the pack's openings like a starfish, and even Ben couldn't help but smile at the fact that the kid was wearing two mismatched socks.

As if he'd developed some sort of radar system to keep track of his wife, Ben was aware of Merry and Alex's location at all times. No matter how fiercely he pushed himself to concentrate on writing his notes for Java's next medical caregiver, he knew Merry had led Ivan down to the paddock to watch her mother put Java through his paces.

And Ben was drawn to follow her as if he'd been magnetized to her.

But at the bottom of the hill, Ben ran into Ivan.

"Oh hey, what's up?" Ivan didn't sound any happier to see Ben than Ben was to see him. "I'm looking for the bathroom."

"The door at the back of the office," Ben grunted, prepared to push past the punk with no other conversation.

But Ivan held his ground, the picture of pointless defiance in his ripped jeans and leather jacket with safety pins hanging from the zipper. He probably paid extra for the holes in those jeans.

"Look, man." Ivan stared at the ground, then flipped his hair out of his eyes in a practiced, boyish gesture that made Ben feel like yelling something extra old and cranky, like "Get off my lawn!"

"I know you're freaked that I keep coming around," Ivan said awkwardly. "I get that. But you gotta understand it from my side. Like, I messed up when Merry told me about the baby. Right? I know that. I shoulda been more supportive and stuff. But like, I'm between gigs right now, and even when I've got a job, let's just say it's not the kind of thing that pays, like, benefits and all that. All I could think when she came at me with the news was that I'm too young to be a dad. There's all kinds of stuff I want to do."

"You're the same age as Merry," Ben pointed out. He didn't want to listen to any of this, but there was a part of him that was curious about Ivan's reasons for being here.

Ivan waved that away. "I know, but she's a chick. She's, like, hardwired to want kids. But you remember what it was like to be a young guy, right? It's different for us."

"I have a vague memory of being young," Ben said,

with a dry twist that flew right over Ivan's spiked blond hair. "But it's not fair to pretend this has all been easy for Merry. She's worked hard to take care of Alex, to learn how to be a mother. Natural instincts only go so far."

Ivan flushed as if Ben had accused him of something. "Everyone acts like she's so perfect, the perfect mom. I could tell you stuff that would make you think twice about treating Merry Preston like some kind of saint."

The frustration of a narcissist who felt he was being denied the admiration he'd come to expect from life. Pure contempt curdled Ben's voice. "Nothing you could tell me would make me see Merry differently."

"Oh yeah?" Ivan put his hands on his lean hips over the precariously low waistband of his jeans. "How about this: when I told her I wanted her to get an abortion, and I even promised to pay for it—she said she'd do it. So who's the perfect mom now? No perfect mom would ever consider giving up her kid, right? I don't think so."

The past rearranged itself in Ben's head. Things Merry had said, the way she acted like she didn't have a right to happiness, her insecurities as a parent—all of it made more sense now. "She didn't go through with it, though," Ben said slowly. "She couldn't. And that's when you walked out."

When Ben didn't gasp in shock and horror, fury sparked in Ivan's eyes. It was the thwarted anger of a child who hadn't gotten his way. Flags of red burned high over his sharp cheekbones, blotching all down his neck. Overdeveloped pecs heaving, he shouted, "Yeah, well, I'm walking back in now. And nothing's going to get me to leave again, even if you offered me double!"

Ben had a bare instant to wonder *Double what?* before a terrifying equine scream sounded from the paddock.

The entire world slowed down, time melting into a

collection of seconds that ticked horribly, relentlessly by. Ben looked over Ivan's shoulder, his vision sharpening as if he were peering through a telescoping lens, and saw Java rear up on his hind legs.

Face white, jaw clenched, Jo kept a firm grip on the longe line—but when Java lashed out with his front legs, he tangled one hoof in the line on the way down, yanking the leather from Jo's hands. Jo cried out and fell to the paddock floor, cradling her arm to her midsection—it probably felt like it had been pulled out of the socket.

In the blink of an eye, Java pivoted and thundered away from the center of the ring, eyes rolling white with fear, long ears flattened nearly to his skull, hooves pounding hard enough to kick up clouds of sawdust as he raced for the gate into the paddock . . . exactly where Merry was heading, with Alex cradled in the backpack snugged to her chest.

"What's happening?" Ivan said, panicky and loud, but Ben was already pushing past him, hurtling down the path to the paddock.

Time sped up again as he ran, legs pumping, lungs bursting. His entire focus narrowed to the infinitesimal window of time he had to reach Merry and Alex before the stallion did.

Merry, eyes only on Jo as she fumbled with the gate to get to her fallen mother, called out, "Mom? Are you okay?"

Even from this distance, Ben could see the exact moment when Jo looked up and realized Merry's danger. She put out her good hand as if she could stop what was about to happen, terror spasming over her face. "Look out!"

Slow to react, Merry only had time to stumble back and turn her body, curling around Alex and shielding him with her torso and enfolding arms, before Java was upon them.

The big stallion cleared the gate, knocking his right hind leg hard against the top rail. His front hooves came down three feet from where Merry huddled around Alex. One more step would have the fear-maddened horse plowing directly into them.

Mind blank of everything except the words "get to her, get to her, get to her," Ben threw himself between his family and the runaway stallion, arms spread wide in an effort to block Java.

Ridiculous, Ben noted absently. As if one human male with his arms out could stop a thousand pounds of raw muscle and aggression. But he had to try.

Braced for the pain of slashing hooves, Merry held her breath against a moment of impact that never came.

Disoriented, she kept to her crouch with her arms locked around her baby, but turned her head enough to see Ben appear about of nowhere.

"Ho," he said, loudly enough for Java to hear him over the labored bellows of his own breathing, but in that firm, no-nonsense tone that animals of all shapes and sizes found so soothing. His arms were out to the sides, not waving or flailing, and Merry's heart clenched at the knowledge that he was empty-handed.

Unarmed, facing down a traumatized stallion with nothing more than the force of his will.

She took all that in with a single glance, in the space of a heartbeat. In the next breath, Java screamed again, that same chillingly human shriek, and reared up.

The horse's front hooves flew out, sharp and deadly and inches from Ben's face, but Ben didn't back down. "Ho, boy. Easy," he said again, pitching his voice so deep, Merry felt it in the pit of her churning stomach.

Snorting, Java dropped all four hooves to the ground and hung his head, sides heaving with every breath.

Slowly, with infinite care, Ben lowered his arms and picked up the trailing leather lead still attached to Java's halter. The horse followed every movement, his prey response going full tilt. His ears flicked forward to pick up any sound that might give him a clue as to which direction the danger would approach from.

But for the moment, the danger seemed to have passed.

Limp and shaky as the adrenaline washed out of her system on a tide of relief, Merry stayed down on her knees. Perfect opportunity to say a little prayer of gratitude, she thought, sending up an incoherent babble of thanksgiving that her outraged son was alive and whole to sob in her arms. The sound of his indignation at being jerked around and crushed against her chest had never been so sweet and welcome.

"Merry, my God, are you okay?" Mom, at least, knew enough to keep her voice low as she approached. It wouldn't take much to startle Java again.

"I'm fine. We both are," Merry said, the words thick and clumsy on her tongue. "Because of Ben."

"Here, let me take the horse," Jo said, reaching out for the lead line with her left hand.

"How's your arm?" Ben wanted to know, keeping hold of Java's halter.

"Just strained," Jo assured them with a grimace. "He's got a hell of a pull when he's spooked. Hasn't happened in a while. I wonder what got him riled up this time. Come on, big boy, let's get you settled back in your stall."

As her mother led Java up to the barn, Merry got her knees under her and tried to stand up. It was always a little tricky to get up from a sitting position with eighteen pounds of wriggling baby strapped to her chest.

Right now, with her knees still wobbly and her balance shot, Merry didn't stand a chance.

She plopped down onto her rear end right in the grass to wait for the moment when her legs would decide to hold her again.

"Need a lift?" Ben asked, putting his hands down for her to grasp.

Merry shook her head but grabbed on to his big hands anyway. "Come down here with us. Help me get Alex to quit freaking out."

In fact, Alex's infuriated cries were already tapering off into sniffles, but Merry couldn't let go of Ben. He didn't seem to mind, if the way he sank into the grass beside her was any indication.

"You're really all right?" His voice was tense again, now that Java was out of earshot. "Maybe we should catch the ferry to Harbor General, have you and Alex checked out."

"Ben." Merry jiggled the baby carrier with one hand under Alex's little butt, and leaned into Ben's side to feel him warm and breathing and alive. "There's not a scratch on us. Because you jumped in front of a runaway horse to save us, you complete whack job. Oh my gosh, you could have been killed! That horse has already given you one concussion, this time it could've been so much worse. What were you thinking?"

"Wasn't really thinking." She felt him shrug under her cheek. "Just moving on instinct, I guess."

"It's weird," Merry observed, her mouth pressed to his shoulder. "Part of me wants to yell at you for putting yourself in danger. But the rest of me just wants to thank you."

"Go with the rest of you," Ben suggested. "No yelling. That's what got us into this in the first place."

"What do you mean?" Merry struggled to sit up and get a clear view of Ben's face.

"Nothing." His mouth went flat and expressionless. "Put your head back on my shoulder, that was nice."

Merry obeyed easily, since it was what she wanted to do anyway. "In case I wasn't clear before, thank you. For saving my life and keeping Alex safe. Again."

"Again?" She heard the frown in his voice and hid a smile in his shirt. So like Ben, not to keep track of the ways he'd been heroic—but maybe he didn't think of it as heroism.

Just instinct.

"The night Alex was born," Merry reminded him. "You rushed through a storm to help me through hours of labor in less than ideal conditions. And you got us both through it in one piece—just like today. So thank you, Ben Fairfax. That's two I owe you."

"You don't owe me anything. I didn't do it, any of it, to make you feel indebted."

"I know that." Reacting to the seriousness of Ben's voice, Merry sat up and scooted around to look him in the eye. "Ben. I do know that. I'm sorry, it was only a figure of speech."

The lines bracketing his mouth smoothed out a bit, although the shadows remained in his eyes as they searched her face and scanned over her body and Alex's as if double-checking for injuries, stealth blood spurts or secret broken bones. "When I saw that horse coming for you—"

He broke off, his throat clicking with the movement of his Adam's apple as he looked away.

Merry's heart picked up speed. "We're fine," she said again, palming Alex's downy head and shuffling closer to Ben. "But feel free to examine us for yourself."

Ben didn't move, so Merry did. Knee-walking between his spread legs, Merry matter-of-factly picked up Ben's heavy arms, one at a time, and draped them around her. The moment she was in his embrace, Ben's arms tightened, pulling her gently, carefully against him, ever watchful of the lump of Alex snuggled in between their chests.

Letting out a long sigh, Merry fit her head into that perfect curve between Ben's neck and his shoulder. "This is nice. I've missed this."

"So have I." Ben whispered it, like a secret confession, and Merry let the words wash through her.

Perfectly content for the first time in days, she murmured, "It sucks that it took poor Java having a fit out of nowhere for us to get here."

Pressed as tightly together as they were, Merry couldn't miss it when Ben went rigid.

"What?" she asked.

Ben didn't answer, but another voice did. "He doesn't want to say."

"Ivan!" She'd completely forgotten about him. He went to the bathroom so long ago, and she'd been a little distracted by nearly getting trampled. But still, guilt tugged at her until she sat up to stare at him. "Did you see what happened?"

"Oh, I saw it." All his habitual cocky charm was gone, subsumed into a depression she'd only seen on him once or twice in the year they'd lived together. Self-loathing curled his upper lip and firmed his jaw. "What your husband is too stand-up a guy to tell you is that it was all my fault."

Chapter Twenty-Six

"Your fault!" Merry pulled out of Ben's arms, leaving them feeling cold and a little useless. He dropped them to rest on his knees as she moved away. "How could it be your fault?"

"It wasn't," Ben interrupted firmly. "Or if it was Ivan's fault, then it was equally mine. We were talking, and it got a little . . . heated."

"I yelled." Ivan crossed his arms over his chest, his hunched posture making him look smaller. "Even though you told me about that horse, you warned me not to make loud noises or sudden movements, but when I got mad, I just forgot all of that and I yelled, and you and the kid almost got crushed to death."

This opening brought back memories. Ivan was in full confessional mode. In a minute, he'd admit to every tiny wrongdoing he'd been feeling guilty about, offloading the whole lot in a giant dump with a sigh of relief and the happy expectation of imminent forgiveness.

When they were together, it had worked on Merry pretty much every time—all the self-blame and brutal honesty was attractive, and it felt good to be able to pet

Ivan and forgive him. Making him feel better about himself had made Merry feel good, too.

Looking at him now, Merry had to hold in a sigh. She was about to let him off the hook again . . . but this time, it was because she wanted him to go away and let her get back to whatever was happening with Ben.

"Ivan, it's fine. We're okay, no one was hurt. You made a mistake, but honestly, you couldn't even have shouted all that loudly—Mom and I didn't hear it. It's only that Java was abused, we think, by a male owner, so he's sort of attuned to masculine voices raised in anger."

But there was no stopping Ivan in confessional mode. He was determined to get through this part to the petting and forgiveness. "I should never have even come here—I've done nothing but cause trouble."

Merry bit her lip and cast a sideways glance at Ben. That much was absolutely true, and she wouldn't contradict it. But to her surprise, her rational, reserved husband's eyes burned with outrage. Anger pulled every muscle of his body taut, jerking him to his feet like a marionette.

Hopping back a step, Ivan's face went ashy. "Hold on, man! I'm trying to come clean and apologize."

Wait. What else did Ivan need to confess?

"Just shut up," Ben snarled, with a quick glance down at Merry, still sitting on the ground.

She was starting to feel at a disadvantage down here, at eye level with everyone's knees. "Ben, help me up. Come on, heave."

He grasped her wrists and pulled her off the ground, steadying her until he knew her knees would lock into place. "Maybe you should take Alex up to the office and put him in his playpen, see if he'll nap. He's had a lot of excitement this morning already."

Pulling away to stand on her own, Merry looked back and forth between her husband and her ex. Something was going on here. "No. I want to hear what Ivan has to say."

Even though, for some reason, Ben didn't want her to hear it.

Something flashed through his gaze, too fast for her to catch, but he ignored her stiffness and put his arm around her shoulders, standing with her as they faced Ivan together.

"Okay." Ivan sniffled, digging the toe of his Doc Martens boot into the grass. "The truth is, life's been kind of crazy, you know—I lost my job, I was running out of money—and then these rich people showed up."

Merry went cold all over, as if someone were cycling out her blood and replacing it with ice water. "Ben's parents," she said through numb lips.

Ivan nodded, shamefaced. "And they offered me money—like, a lot of money, enough to cover rent for a year—to come here and see my kid. And I was curious anyway! It's not like I really never wanted to see you again, and I had plans to look you up as soon as things turned around for me, so when they said they'd write me a check if I came and asserted my rights . . . it was like, perfect."

Perfect. Merry had almost wrecked her marriage fighting for her son's relationship with a man who thought it was "perfect" that he'd had to be bribed into seeing him.

"You are unbelievable." She barely recognized her own voice, it was so shaky and enraged. "Get out of my sight, Ivan, I can't even look at you right now."

Ivan's big brown cow eyes went round with surprise. "But . . . I'm sorry! I want a chance to make it up to you!"

"This time, that's not enough," Merry told him, clenching her jaw. "And honestly, I don't care what you want. I have to think about my family first."

And find out exactly how Ben knew what you were about to say.

Understanding settled slowly over Ivan's even features as he glanced from the inflexible look on Merry's face up to Ben. "Oh. Right. Um, I'll just . . . is there a place in town I could get some food? I'm kind of starving, and the next ferry isn't for a while yet . . ."

"The Firefly Café," Ben said briskly. "Corner of Main Street and Wildflower Bend, right across from the library. Tell Penny we sent you, she'll take care of you."

"Okay, I guess I'll just . . ." Ivan gestured behind him, all his usual smooth charm evaporating like the morning frost melting off the grass.

Merry turned her back on him, barely aware of the halting sound of his boots retreating up the path to the barn. All her attention was for Ben, now. Ben, who stared down at her with shadowed eyes.

"You knew," she said, cupping her arms reflexively around Alex. "Since when?"

He sighed. "About five seconds before Java got loose. Something Ivan said when we were arguing—that I'd have to offer him twice as much to get him to leave."

"Oh." Merry felt sick all over again.

"But I didn't put it together until he was standing there spilling his guts. I'm sorry, Merry."

"You!" She shook her head. "What are you apologizing for?"

His mouth twisted wryly. "For being born to Tripp and Pamela Fairfax? I want to say I can't believe they'd do something like this, but the truth is, I can. So maybe I'm apologizing for not figuring it out sooner and stopping them."

Ben tucked a lock of Merry's hair behind her ear, the brush of his fingers sending shivers skating down her neck. "Or it could be that I'm sorry for the way this is hurting you."

Merry turned her head to press a kiss into the palm of Ben's hand. "I wasn't the only one who got hurt. I know you felt pushed aside when I let Ivan in. I regret that, so much. But there was more going on than I was ready to deal with." She paused, unsure she'd even be able to get the words out.

"I felt guilty," she admitted, her voice a thread of sound. Ben tilted his head down until their foreheads were almost touching. "Because I've been so angry at Ivan for leaving me, for refusing to take responsibility—but I was almost as bad. When I found out I was pregnant, I wasn't happy. I was terrified. I didn't know anything about being a mother—I barely even remembered my mom from when I was a kid—and my whole life was about to change. I thought really seriously about ending the pregnancy."

"Shh," Ben said softly, pain pulling his mouth into a frown. "Sweetheart, you don't have to—"

"I do, though." Merry sucked back the tears that wanted to overflow. "I need you to understand. I honestly thought there was no way I'd be able to care for a child, that any kid of mine would have a disaster of a mom who ruined everything. But when it came right down to it, something stopped me. I just couldn't go through with it—even though, rationally, it was nuts for me to have a baby on my own, no job, no way of supporting myself. But it was the right choice for me. And when I think about it now, it stops my heart every time, how close I came to never having Alex at all."

"I know."

Merry jerked back, shattered. "You know?"

"Ivan told me." Ben tipped her chin up with his fingers and forced her to meet his gaze when it was the last thing she wanted to do. "In the middle of our fight. Ivan threw it at me like a punch, as if he expected it to change anything about what I feel for you."

Breathing hard, Merry said, "And? Did it?"

"Don't take this the wrong way." Ben cupped her jaw and gazed lovingly into her upturned face. "But you're an idiot."

That was it. Merry laughed and sobbed at the same time, emotion welling out of her in an uncontrollable fountain. She threw her arms around Ben and hung on for dear life.

"I just wanted," she said, her words muffled by his chest. "I wanted so badly for Ivan to be exactly what he said he was: regretful, eager to have a relationship with his son. I thought, what could be wrong about Alex having three parents who love him?"

"I get that." Ben's voice was so tender, it made Merry's heart ache. "I do. And I wish I hadn't been such an ass about it. You're right—the more love in Alex's life, the better off he'll be."

But that wasn't enough. From the beginning, Ben was the one making all the concessions, putting aside what he wanted and letting Merry dictate the terms. This time, she was going to make damn sure he got everything he wanted and deserved—and that included her and Alex.

"Take me to the Firefly," Merry said, scrubbing her face dry, determination giving her new energy. "I want to catch Ivan before he leaves the island."

Resignation and acceptance settled over Ben like a worn, comfortable jacket. "Okay. Might as well put the dumb kid out of his misery and tell him he's forgiven."

"Oh, I will," Merry said as they started up the hill to

Ben's truck. "Ivan *is* a kid, an immature child who's been spoiled by all the people in his life catering to his every whim and indulging his moods—but he didn't mean to endanger us with his tantrum. The bribery, though."

She paused, still a little gutted by the fact that she'd so misread the situation.

"My parents can be very persuasive," Ben said grimly.

"I'm sure it didn't take much. You heard him—he was offered money to do what he already had a half-formed desire to do anyway. In Ivan's world, that's a win-win, no downside. In his mind, I'm sure he wasn't even lying about his motives for being here. But I don't think I can forgive him for what he almost did to our marriage—at least, not yet."

"Then why are we going to the café? So you can tell him off again? Not that I'm arguing." Ben opened the passenger side door and helped Merry transfer Alex to the baby seat in the back.

"No." Determination flooded Merry in a strengthening tide as she climbed onto the bench seat and waited for Ben to go around to the driver side. "You and I made an agreement, and I should never have endangered that. No matter what you say, you are the one who's always there for Alex when he needs you. Screw genetics—you're his father. I'm going to tell Ivan I want him to sign away his paternal rights, so you can officially adopt Alex as your son."

It was exactly what Ben thought he wanted, handed to him across the bench seat of his old pickup truck. Merry was watching him with bright eyes, her hair still a mess and grass stains on her knees from hitting the dirt to protect her baby.

Ben's chest was in lockdown, his ribs cranked too tight for breath, but all he knew was that as much as he wanted Alex as his son, he wanted everything out on the table with Merry even more.

"Can we forget about our agreement for a minute?" His mouth was so dry, dust scouring his lungs and turning his voice into a heavy croak.

Fear speared through Merry's gaze. She curled her hands around the hem of her sweatshirt and nodded.

"I'm sorry," she babbled. "I know it's too little, too late—and I don't want to be like Ivan, always apologizing as if that makes up for the fact that he does whatever the hell he wants the rest of the time, regardless of anyone else's feelings. But I am sorry, Ben. This marriage is important to me."

She swallowed. With amazement, Ben realized he could actually see the flutter of her rapid pulse in the hollow of her throat. "I don't want anything to come between us . . . because I'm in love with you."

Ben felt the smile start in the pit of his stomach and travel up through his chest, loosening the constriction there, before it ever hit his mouth. She loved him. Merry loved him, after all.

"As apologies go, that was a pretty good one," he said, hauling himself up into the cab of the truck to get closer to her. "Come here."

Merry leaned eagerly over the drive shaft and Ben met her halfway, thrusting his hands into her hair to hold her head for a kiss.

"I love you, too," he whispered against her mouth, the words escaping like a prayer or a vow. "And I love Alex. You're right, I'll be there for him no matter what . . . even if there's no piece of paper out there that legally binds us together as father and son."

"But . . ." Merry drew back to search his eyes. "You are the last Fairfax heir. Do you really not care about passing it on?"

Ben considered the caldron of anger still seething in his belly at the stunt his parents pulled with Ivan. "Right now? I'm thinking it would be a good thing for the Fairfax name to die with me. That much attachment to a legacy isn't healthy or rational."

"You might feel differently as we get older," Merry pointed out. "When your parents pass on, and you're the only one left."

Ben smiled and nudged kisses against her cheek, her temple, her nose, the fragile skin of her closed eyelid—whatever he could reach. "I won't be alone. I'll have you. And as long as I have you and Alex in my life, for good, he can call me whatever he wants. Stepdad, Daddy, Pops, Uncle Ben . . . okay, maybe not Uncle Ben. I don't like rice."

Merry laughed, and in the backseat, Alex clapped and laughed, too, already starting to mimic the emotions of those around him. That's why it was so important to keep his mother happy, Ben reflected with satisfaction as Merry pushed her face up for another kiss.

"The point is," Ben finished, a few long, heated moments later. "I've loved you for a long time. And if you want to stay married to me and be a family, not because of an arrangement but because you love me—I'm happy. That's all I wanted from life."

Merry pulled away and kicked open her door, rushing around to the back to pull Alex, barefoot and giggling, from his car seat.

"What are you doing?" Ben asked, heart clenching.

"Ivan can wait—we'll figure out what to do about him later. Right now, I'm taking our son up to the barn and telling his grandmother she's on babysitting duty," Merry said, wrestling with the diaper bag. "And then I'm taking you home and kissing the daylights out of you."

Joy went off like a firecracker in Ben's chest, a spinning pinwheel of sparks and love. "Are you sure?" he said gravely. "I know how much you hate asking for your mom's help."

He was mostly teasing, so he was a little dismayed when Merry stilled and stared at him thoughtfully. "You know," she said, "I think I'm over that. If I've learned anything, it's that no parent is perfect—we all make mistakes. All you can do is work hard to do better."

Ben jumped down and went to help her with the diaper bag, which was wedged under the driver's side seat. "Everyone can use a second chance, sometimes."

"Or a third or fourth," Merry said, laughing, as Ben hefted the bag onto his shoulder. Side by side, holding hands, they walked up to the barn. "Besides, being with you—I feel stronger. More confident. Like, what am I trying to prove by cutting my mother out of Alex's childhood?"

"All you'd be doing is depriving us of a free babysitter," Ben agreed.

At the door of the barn, Merry stopped and turned around. They looked out over the sloping coastal farmland and the red-gold glory of fall on Sanctuary Island.

"It's amazing," Merry said. "I moved here to get to know my mother and try to put our family back together. And now that family has grown and expanded to include Grady, Harrison, Taylor, everyone on the island . . . it's more love than I ever dreamed I'd have in my life. But the best, most surprising part is that not only did I find the family I always wanted on Sanctuary Island, I found you. The man I didn't even know enough to dream about."

Ben reveled in the fact that he could put his arms around Merry and Alex now, the way he couldn't all those weeks and months ago. She rested her head on his chest with a happy sigh, and Alex clutched at the chest pocket on Ben's shirt with his strong little fist.

Standing there with his whole, perfect world in his arms, Ben's rational side told him there was no such thing as perfection. "I love the fall," he said. "But winter always comes after. It will be that way for us, too. There are storms ahead, problems to face and arguments to negotiate. There will be tears and laughter, joy and heartache, trouble and strife."

"Mmm," Merry hummed, content as a cat sprawled in the sun. "And you'll be there for all of it."

"I will," Ben said, and that was his vow. Right there, standing in the spot where he'd first decided to propose. He would be there for everything—really there. "No more hiding behind a wall of sarcasm and cynicism to keep people out."

"Fair warning: this family is going to knock down all your walls and leave you nowhere to hide. We'll burrow so deep into your heart, you'll never get us out again."

Ben buried a kiss in his wife's hair, breathing in sweet hay and apples. "I'm good with that."

Being part of a family like Merry's would never be simple or easy—but it would always, always be worth it.

The beloved Billionaire Brothers novella trilogy
comes to print in…

HOMECOMING:
The Billionaire Brothers

Coming in Summer 2014 from St. Martin's Paperbacks